THE COTTAGE
AT
HOPE COVE

HANNAH ELLIS

To Dave, Mark and Pete
With love

Chapter 1

The first time Elizabeth Beaumont had doubts about her wedding, she was shopping for a bridesmaid's dress. If she wasn't getting married, then she wouldn't be enduring the torment of shopping with her sister. They were only shopping for a dress and shoes, for goodness' sake. How difficult could it be? At the rate they were going they'd need another shopping trip – and she wasn't sure she could handle that.

"Do you hate me?" Josie asked, pulling up the legs of her scruffy jeans to look down at the elegant beige heels she wore.

"Of course I don't hate you," Elizabeth said, her fingers clenching into fists. Taking a deep breath, she unclenched her hands. "But it's my wedding and you're my bridesmaid. Will you please wear them? They're only shoes."

"Shoes that might maim me," Josie said. "I've told you a million times: I've got odd-shaped feet. I can't wear shoes like this. It's agony. I'll end up barefoot and bleeding."

Elizabeth squeezed the bridge of her nose. "But you're a bridesmaid – you can't wear a pair of scruffy old Converse."

"Maybe I shouldn't be your bridesmaid then," Josie muttered, then winced as though she expected the comment to lead to World War Three.

Actually, Elizabeth agreed. The only reason she hadn't suggested that herself was because she didn't want a family argument. For once, she and Josie were on the same wavelength.

She was about to say something to that effect when her mother looked up from the bridal magazine she was studying. Susan Beaumont had been keeping out of the petty bickering until that point.

"Of course you'll be a bridesmaid," she said, glaring at Josie and clicking her tongue. "You're sisters." She paused. "And of course you can't wear your tatty old trainers."

"I know that!" Josie snapped. "I'll get a *new* pair." She looked seriously at Elizabeth. "You can choose whichever Converse you want me to wear. There are some limited edition white ones with just a smattering of glitter—"

"Oh my God!" Elizabeth screeched, pacing the shop. "I can't believe you're serious. You're being ridiculous."

"Because I don't want my feet to bleed?" Josie said. "I don't understand what your problem is. It's your wedding day. Surely you'll have better things to think about than my footwear?"

Elizabeth dropped onto the couch. "Please wear the shoes. It's one day. Just wear the shoes!"

"I don't even know why I had to come today. My opinion means nothing to you. You should have picked the dress and shoes for me."

The dress had been the first issue of the day; that had been difficult enough to find. It hadn't occurred to Elizabeth that choosing shoes could be even more problematic.

"That would probably have been better," she agreed, glaring at her mother, who'd organised the shopping trip for the three of them.

"Oh, come on, girls," Susan said. "I thought we'd have a fun morning together."

"You're just having a mid-life crisis anyway," Josie mumbled.

Elizabeth sat up straighter. "What did you say?"

Perching on a stool, Josie massaged her feet, looking sheepish. "You and Phil have been together forever," she said. "And you decide to get married after all this time? It seems like you're having a mid-life crisis." She avoided eye contact with Elizabeth and concentrated on putting her socks and shoes back on.

"People don't get married because they're having a mid-life crisis," Elizabeth spat. Josie always knew how to get under her skin. By now, she should have learned to ignore her. Unfortunately she hadn't. "They buy a sports car or have an affair. They don't get married! Besides, I'm not even middle-aged, so how can I have a mid-life crisis?"

Josie grinned mischievously. "You're thirty-four!"

"Exactly. That's not middle-aged."

"You can't think you're still a youth?" Josie asked, amused.

"Of course not."

"Then you've got two choices: middle-aged or old. Take your pick!"

Elizabeth closed her eyes briefly. "Will you please tell her I'm not middle-aged?" she said quietly to her mum.

Her mum's silence unnerved her. She turned and glared at her. "I am not middle-aged!" she said, a little louder than she had intended. A passing shop assistant stopped in her tracks. After a moment, she flashed a professional smile and continued on her way.

"You also never had an engagement party," Josie said. "You didn't even announce your engagement. It's hard to take it seriously."

"Announce my engagement?" Elizabeth said. "Nobody does that any more. You really expected me to put an advert in the newspaper?"

Josie stared in disbelief. "I meant on Facebook! Of course not in a newspaper!"

"Why should I put it on Facebook? I never go on Facebook. I wouldn't even know how to announce something on there."

"Give me your phone," Josie said, standing in front of her.

"No!"

"Oh, come on. At least let me change your relationship status. It's like poor Phil doesn't exist if anyone looks at your page."

"Fine," Elizabeth said after a pause. She handed her phone over. "But can you please choose some shoes so I can go home."

Josie ignored her and tapped on the phone. It made Elizabeth nervous.

"Give me that back," Elizabeth finally said.

"Congratulations on your engagement!" Josie said sarcastically as she tossed the phone into Elizabeth's lap.

Susan sighed heavily. "Why do you have to

bicker all the time? All I wanted was a relaxed morning with my girls."

"Well, it's been lovely," Josie said, rolling her eyes as she dragged her fingers through her light brown hair, pulling it back into a ponytail. "But would anyone care if I left now?"

"What about the shoes?" Elizabeth asked.

"I don't care," Josie said. "Buy the awful things. Or don't. Whatever. It's, like, a year until the wedding anyway."

"Nine months, actually," Elizabeth said as Josie turned to leave.

"How are you going to get home?" Susan called after her.

Josie waved over her shoulder. "I'll figure it out."

"It would be good if you two could make more effort to get along," Susan said once she and Elizabeth were alone.

"We get along fine," Elizabeth said, moving slowly through the shop. "When you don't force us to spend time together."

"If I didn't get you together, I'm not sure you'd ever speak to each other."

"Oh, don't worry, she's not shy about calling me when she wants something. You know I ended up giving her friend an internship at the magazine just so Josie would stop calling me about it?" Elizabeth was the managing editor at *MyStyle* magazine. It was a high-powered position, overseeing all aspects of the publication. Josie's friend, Emily, had been looking for some work experience. Elizabeth was sure she'd regret it, but she'd caved in just to put an end to Josie's persistent phone calls.

"I heard," Susan said, pulling her sunglasses from the top of her head as they stepped into the sunny Oxford street. "She *should* call you when she wants something. She's your sister."

"But that's the only time she calls me."

"You do realise it's you who doesn't have time for her, not the other way around?"

Elizabeth ignored the comment and focused on finding a coffee shop. She was in desperate need of caffeine.

"You work too much," Susan went on. "It's not healthy. You need balance in your life. You should make more time for friends and family."

"Mum!" Elizabeth snapped. "I thought you wanted a fun morning? Stop nagging."

"Sorry."

"Anyway, I'm going on holiday next week. A complete break from work."

"Oh yes, your trip to Devon. When do you leave?"

"Friday."

"Good. It's about time you took a break."

Elizabeth nodded. It had been ages since she'd taken any time off work, and the cottage she'd booked in Devon looked stunning. It was right on the coast in a little village near Salcombe. A bit of sun, sea and sand would surely do her and Phil the world of good. So would actually spending some time together. That would be a welcome change. Their demanding jobs meant that quality time together was limited, and in recent weeks work had been particularly hectic.

Yes, some time with Phil and a change of scene was exactly what she needed. She couldn't wait.

Chapter 2

When she got home Phil was in the kitchen, hunched over his laptop. He muttered a hello, but didn't look up. When she kissed his cheek, he made a vague attempt to drag his attention away from his work but only managed a tilt of his head in her direction. His focus never left the computer screen.

"How was shopping?" he asked as she slipped into the chair opposite him.

"About as good as a shopping trip with my sister could be."

He acknowledged her with a vague grunt. Elizabeth pushed gently at the lid of the laptop until it began to close. Phil reached over to stop her. They exchanged a smirk and he kept his eyes on her as she went on.

"Josie had the cheek to call me middle-aged."

"How dare she?" he said, his lips twitching in amusement. "You have to admire her bravery. I'd never dare say such a thing!"

"So you think I'm middle-aged too?"

"We're not exactly spring chickens any more," he said.

"Speak for yourself!"

Phil was approaching forty, and definitely had a whiff of middle age about him. But Elizabeth was only thirty-four and had never considered herself middle-aged. Surely it hadn't crept up on her without her noticing? It was a depressing thought.

"I don't know why you let her get to you," he said.

"She also thinks we're only getting married because I'm having a mid-life crisis."

Phil looked amused. "She really does know how to push your buttons." His gaze drifted back to the computer and Elizabeth tried another tactic: she walked over and sat on his lap.

"But what a ridiculous thing to say."

"And yet you're still thinking about it?"

Elizabeth frowned. "She thinks it's weird that we've been together so long and are only just getting married."

"It's what people do, isn't it?"

She raised her eyebrows. "How very romantic of you!"

"You know what I mean," he said, as she got up and walked over to the fridge. "It's what people who are in love do…"

"I guess so." She poured a glass of orange juice. "I'll leave you to your first love, shall I?" she said, nodding at the laptop. "Feels like I interrupted something."

"Sorry." He took her hand, pulling her back as she began to walk away. "Dennis broke his leg. He had an operation yesterday to have pins put in it. He's out of action for a while so I need to pick up the slack. It means next week will be hectic, so I thought I'd get on with some stuff."

Dennis was Phil's boss at Taylor & West, a

financial services consultancy firm. With him out of the picture, she knew Phil would have to take over. "That's not good."

"Nope."

"It won't be a problem for the holiday, will it?"

"I don't think so," he said. "I'll have to keep in touch with the office while we're away, but it should be fine."

"Good. I really need a break."

"Yeah, right," he said. "You expect me to believe you won't do any work while we're away?"

A smile spread slowly over her face. "I might check my emails once or twice…"

"And the rest!"

"It's the change of scenery I'm excited about."

"We're only going down the road. Remind me again why we're going to Devon and not somewhere exotic?"

"Because I have fond memories of Devon and it's years since I've been there."

"I know," he said. "I'm only teasing. I can't wait." He gave her hand a squeeze before releasing it. She took that as her cue to leave.

She headed upstairs to the study and got her own laptop out. It was a safe bet that she wouldn't get much attention from Phil for the rest of the weekend. Not that she minded too much – she also had work to get on with. As always. There was nothing that couldn't wait until Monday, but she wasn't the sort of person to put things off. If something needed doing, she got on and did it. The trouble was, that meant she rarely had a break.

Another week, then she could switch off. It would

definitely be good for her and Phil to have some time together. Maybe they'd even rekindle some passion. There hadn't been much of that in their relationship recently. But surely that was normal after ten years together?

For a moment, Josie's words niggled at her again. Ten years together and then they'd decided to get married. Elizabeth wasn't even sure why they'd decided to do it now. There'd been no big romantic proposal. They'd been at a work do, and a couple of Phil's colleagues had joked about him making an honest woman of her. In the taxi home, merry from too much wine, he'd vaguely suggested that maybe they should get married. *Maybe they should?* That had been the extent of his proposal.

She'd agreed that maybe they should – and things had snowballed from there.

Chapter 3

As expected, the weekend passed in an uneventful blur. Phil barely looked up from his laptop and they moved around the house hardly registering each other, except for short conversations about meals. It was Monday morning before Elizabeth knew it.

The train into London from Oxford was always awful, but Monday mornings seemed to be the worst, and the summer months were horrific: all those sweaty bodies in a confined space. Occasionally, she'd drive, but it was a stressful journey, so she didn't do it often. The train was a marginally better option.

She checked her reflection in the mirror when she stepped into the lift in the *MyStyle* offices. As always, her rich brown hair was held neatly in place at the back of her head with a clip. She pushed a stray strand off her face and ran her fingers under her eyes, checking her mascara hadn't smudged. Quickly, she applied another coat of ruby blush lipstick and pressed her lips together just before the doors opened.

The room was a hive of activity. Elizabeth felt the energy as she exited the lift. Even so early, phones were ringing and fingers tapped on keyboards. Elizabeth had always enjoyed the buzz of the place, and greeted people cheerfully as she walked through the main hub.

When she reached her office, she found her boss waiting for her. Karen was an intimidating woman, and today her features were set in a look that said she meant business. As editor-in-chief, she ran the show, and did so fiercely. She was a fair and reasonable boss but not the sort of person that anyone wanted to cross.

When the office door clicked shut behind Elizabeth, Karen's face relaxed and her shoulders slouched. She transformed from the Boss to the Best Friend in under a second.

"How was your weekend?" she asked.

Elizabeth took a seat in her swivel chair. "I survived."

"Did you find a dress for Josie?"

"Dress, yes. Shoes, no!"

"Did she behave herself?"

"It's Josie. If there was no drama I'd be worried about her. She called me middle-aged and wants to wear trainers to the wedding."

"I love her," Karen said, wrinkling her nose. "She's so adorably cocky."

"She thinks I'm being unreasonable asking her to wear elegant footwear. She hates anything vaguely feminine."

"You've gotta love her. She's such a little hippy. But she's right – why wear something you're not comfortable in?"

"She could make an exception for my wedding."

"Just think yourself lucky she's the only bridesmaid. I did you a favour refusing the maid of honour gig. If you were choosing my outfit too, we'd have a real problem."

"You can still change your mind," Elizabeth said hopefully.

"You know how I feel about the institution of marriage. I'll come and watch. I'll drink a lot. And I fully intend to take advantage of any eligible bachelors. But that's all you can ask of me."

"Fine," Elizabeth said, chuckling.

They were interrupted by the door opening. Karen shot back into boss mode, correcting her posture and setting her features back to stern. "Get Darcy on the phone," she said loudly. "Find out what he thinks…" Abruptly, she stopped talking and snapped her head round to the young woman in the doorway.

"Oh, sorry," the newcomer said weakly, looking at Elizabeth in a panic. "I didn't know you were in a meeting. I brought your coffee."

"Thanks," Elizabeth said, reaching for the mug.

The woman glanced nervously at Karen. "Can I get you anything?"

Karen shook her head dismissively.

The woman flushed bright red and backed quickly out of the room.

"That's your new intern?" Karen asked, relaxing again as soon as she'd gone.

Elizabeth nodded. "Emily."

"She looks terrified. What are you doing to her? Get your own bloody coffee, you lazy cow."

"You sat there with your scary face on!"

"I'm the boss. I need to maintain an air of superiority. What would this place be like if people knew what I was really like? Do you think I'd get any respect?" She raised her eyebrows. "Do *you* respect me?"

"Not at all," Elizabeth said lightly.

"There's my point! So how did you end up with a mouse of an intern?"

"Josie nagged me to give her a go."

"She's friends with Josie? That seems unlikely."

"They met at drama class," Elizabeth said, with a shake of her head. A drama class would be her idea of hell. "She wants to be a journalist and needed some work experience."

"Well, look after the poor kid. Don't make her your coffee slave. We live in a time of feminism. If you want someone to bring you coffee, get yourself a male intern."

"I'm going to teach her about budgeting this morning," Elizabeth said. "She'll soon wish all she had to do was bring me coffee." Elizabeth had originally wanted to be an editor to make use of her obsession with grammar. She'd never expected to end up a magazine editor and spend most of her time dealing with staffing and budgeting, schedules and deadlines. She often thought it would be lovely to actually read or write something.

"She might be geeky enough to enjoy budgeting," Karen said.

"I'll find out if you ever leave me alone to get some work done."

"I need to show you my new top first," Karen said, standing and unbuttoning her blazer. "What do you think?"

Elizabeth smirked as she took in the tight T-shirt, and specifically the wording slashed across the bust: *Do or do not. There is no try.*

"Are you wearing that to annoy me?" Elizabeth

asked.

"I did notice it combines your two favourite things."

Actually, it was a combination of Elizabeth's two pet peeves: inspirational quotes and writing on clothing. "It's ridiculous," she said. "Whoever had the crazy idea that clothes should have writing on? Who wants to be read? You read a book, or a magazine, or whatever. You don't read clothes."

"So you like it?" Karen said, rebuttoning her blazer.

Elizabeth shook her head. "Who's the quote from?"

Karen rolled her eyes. "The Master, of course."

"The Master?" Elizabeth said, wrinkling her forehead in confusion before she caught on. "You have a quote from Yoda on your T-shirt? It's a wonder you get any respect from anyone. It's not very business-like."

"What bloody year is it?" Karen said. "We can wear what we want for the office. How many times do I have to tell you to put some personality in your clothing?"

"Someone has to dress appropriately round here!"

"You can be very boring," Karen said. "Anyway, I've got wine in my desk. I think we should reinstate Monday night drinks."

"When did we stop going to bars?"

"When we got old."

"Don't you start. I get enough 'old' comments from Josie."

Karen smiled briefly but it vanished the moment she opened the door. Elizabeth was amused by how she could change so quickly back to the fierce editor-in-chief persona.

She hoped to be editor-in-chief herself one day. That was her goal. Karen was in her mid-fifties and planning an early retirement. It was no secret that Elizabeth had her sights set on her job. She wondered if she'd be a fierce boss like Karen, or find a more relaxed way to get the job done. Karen joked that Elizabeth would do all the work herself instead of delegating, so it wouldn't matter what sort of a boss she was.

At the office doorway, she scanned the busy room until she caught sight of Emily and beckoned to her. She sighed at the task ahead. When she was the boss she would definitely delegate the budgeting to someone else.

Chapter 4

Elizabeth barely saw Phil that week. Working late wasn't anything unusual for him, but it wasn't normally every night. It was after 10pm on Thursday when he came in and sank on the couch next to Elizabeth. He lay with his head in her lap.

"I might have a small problem," he said as she ran her fingers through his hair.

"What?"

"Claire's been signed off work with pregnancy complications."

"Is she okay?" Elizabeth asked.

"Think so, but she's on bed rest for the remainder…"

"Poor Claire."

"Yeah." He paused. "She was supposed to be doing a big presentation next week to the managers at Carlton and Croft, so I need to figure out what to do about that."

"Can't you rearrange it?"

"I've tried, but they weren't happy about it, and it's in the contract so I'm a bit stuck."

"Well, *you* can't do it!" she said, nudging him off her as she realised where the conversation was heading. "We're away all next week."

"I know," he said wearily. "I've been trying to

think of a way around it, but there's only me left in the office who knows the account." He squeezed the bridge of his nose. "It's our biggest client."

"I know. But what about our holiday?"

"We might need to postpone…"

"No," she said, the idea sitting like lead in her stomach. "It's tomorrow! I need a break. I've been looking forward to it. And I can't rearrange my time off at such short notice. Please don't do this to me."

"It's not exactly filling me with joy either," he said. "I didn't ask for this."

"I know," she said, softening. "But is there really no one else who could do it?"

"No," he said, annoyance in his voice. "Don't you think I've considered every option? I would like a holiday too, you know."

"Well, when's the presentation? Maybe we can go for half the week?"

"I was thinking that too," he said. "It's on Wednesday."

"So we could go tomorrow as planned and stay until Tuesday?"

"Except I have a load of preparation to do. It would be better if we go on Wednesday afternoon, after the presentation."

"But we only have the cottage until Friday. That means one full day there! It's not much of a break. We'd almost spend more time driving there and back than we'd spend there."

"I know. I don't know what to say."

"You're saying we can't go?"

He sighed dramatically, as though she was making things harder for him. It probably wasn't a hard decision for him – holiday or work. He'd be a hero in the office if he cancelled his holiday to step in and take over. Surely it would have taken more backbone for him to stand up and say he was going away as planned and they'd have to figure things out without him. But what if Karen had asked Elizabeth to cancel a trip to help her out? She supposed she'd do the same as Phil, so it was difficult to be too angry. Even so, she hated the thought of cancelling their trip.

She glared at him. "We won't get the money back if we cancel at such short notice." She knew he wouldn't care about that. He'd never been one to worry about money; he'd never needed to. But to her it seemed such a waste.

"You could always go without me," Phil said. "I could come and join you on Wednesday after the presentation."

"What am I going to do on my own?" she asked tersely.

"Work, probably," he said, raising an eyebrow. "You said you wanted a change of scenery."

"I'd also like to spend some quality time with my fiancé. We don't seem to spend any time together any more."

"Oh, come on. Don't be like that. It's only this week that work's been so hectic."

"No, it's not," she said firmly. "We may sit in the same room together in the evenings, but we both have our heads in our laptops."

"But that's the way we've always been. It's why we're so compatible."

She frowned. Their romance really was dead.

"Don't look at me like that." He pulled her close

and planted a kiss on the side of her head. "I love you."

"I know," she said with a sigh. "We really have to cancel?"

"Let's say we're postponing it. We'll reschedule and you'll have longer to look forward to it!"

"Great," she said, trying to match his lightness. There wasn't much point in being angry. It couldn't be helped. "What am I going to do with my week off?"

"I told you – go alone. The sea air will do you good. Or stay here and get on with some of the wedding planning. That would be useful, wouldn't it?"

"Wedding planning isn't exactly a holiday."

"You're going to make me feel very guilty about this, aren't you?"

"No," she said, managing a smile. "I'm sure I'll find something to do."

Chapter 5

Elizabeth was staring blankly at her computer screen when Karen came into her office the following morning. She'd already finished everything she wanted to get done before her week off, and was just killing time. There were extra things she could be doing, but her mind wouldn't focus.

"What are you doing here?" Karen asked.

"I only took a half day today. I'm leaving at lunchtime."

"I know that, but I told you not to bother coming in this morning. Why be friends with the boss if you don't get any perks? You could've at least worked from home and saved yourself the train trip."

That had been her original plan, but when she got up she'd felt like getting out of the house. It wasn't a good omen for her week off. Lazing around at home had never really been her thing. She needed to pull herself together. Wallowing about the holiday was pathetic. It wasn't the end of the world.

"What's wrong?" Karen asked.

"We're not going to Devon. The trip's cancelled."

"What?" Karen moved across the room and took a seat. "Why?"

"Phil has to work."

Karen's eyes flashed with anger. "I might've

known it would be the weasel's fault."

Here we go again. Karen's recent divorce had made her very bitter. Apparently she thought all men were weasels and were not to be trusted. Elizabeth knew it was all bravado, really, but it was starting to grate on her nerves.

"Please don't call him a weasel. It's not helpful. He has to work. It's not his fault."

"Why can't he bring his laptop and work from Devon?"

"He's got a big presentation he has to do next week."

"Oh, come on. Surely someone else could do it?"

"It's not his fault," Elizabeth said again, unsure why she felt she had to defend him. "His boss is in hospital, and there are other staff off too."

"Oh, whatever," Karen snapped. "Don't make excuses for him. If he acts like a selfish prick before you're even married, there's no hope for you."

"You're not making me feel any better. And if it was the other way round and I had to work, he'd understand."

"You'd never ask him to cancel a holiday for your job."

Elizabeth raised an eyebrow. "If you were in hospital … Oh, never mind, it's irrelevant. Besides, he didn't ask me to cancel. He thought I should go alone."

"Hmm." Karen looked thoughtful for a moment. "A little getaway on your own? That doesn't sound too bad."

"I'm not going alone."

"Why not? No one around to annoy you. You can

do whatever you want. Sounds like bliss to me."

"It's weird. What will I do on my own in Devon?"

"Probably work, knowing you! But you can also lie in the sun and walk on the beach. I don't know. Just relax."

"I think I'd rather stay at home for the week."

"No!" Karen said adamantly. "Don't let that weasel steal your holiday time."

"Phil's not a weasel!"

"Of course he is. But at least he had the decency to tell you to go alone. You should go."

"I'm not the sort of person to go away alone. I like to eat out. That's no fun on my own."

Karen curled her lip. "It's a shame one of us has to be here or I would've come with you."

"I'll be fine. I'm going to have a relaxing week at home. It's not the worst thing in the world."

"I suppose," Karen said, walking to the door. "I'm gonna be bored without you around. Come and say bye before you leave." She turned, her hand on the door. "For what it's worth, I think you should still go."

"I'll think about it," Elizabeth promised.

And she did think about it. The idea niggled at her all morning and on the journey home. She hadn't cancelled the cottage, so it was still an option. It felt odd, however. Wouldn't she be lonely rattling around a strange house on her own? Plus, despite Phil claiming they were only going down the road, it was about a four-hour drive, and that was quite a way to go alone. What if she got lost? Or broke down?

Gosh, when had she become such a wimp? Josie would laugh at her. Her sister was always so adventurous and would go anywhere alone. In fact, she'd once told Elizabeth that she preferred doing stuff alone because it felt like more of an adventure.

At home, Elizabeth made herself a cup of coffee and a sandwich. She'd unpacked her suitcase the previous evening in a sulk, so if she did go she'd have to repack. No, it was a crazy idea; she wasn't going on her own. Why was she even contemplating it?

Her phone pinged. She opened it to find an email from Karen. *Hoping I get an out-of-office reply to this! I dare you not to check your work email for a whole week...*

Laughing to herself, Elizabeth set up an out-of-office reply on her email account and wondered why having a complete break from work was such a ridiculous concept. Surely she could manage a week away from it without falling apart?

Without thinking any more about it, she decided she would do it: no work emails; no calling Karen and talking about work; nothing. A complete break would be good for her.

She managed a couple of hours: she cleaned the kitchen and sorted through a drawer full of junk in the hallway that she'd been meaning to do for a while. She flicked idly through the TV channels, knowing she wouldn't find anything to hold her interest on a Friday afternoon. When she reached for a magazine she hesitated, wondering if that technically counted as work.

Back in the kitchen, she opened her laptop and hovered her cursor over a folder containing potential magazine articles from journalists – stuff she'd intended to go over when she got back from Devon, but had thought she might do while she was away.

She snapped the laptop shut and sighed. How could she manage a whole week when she was already twitchy after a couple of hours? A new email popped up on her phone. It was her personal email so she opened it happily. It was from the owners of the cottage she'd booked in the little village of Hope Cove in Devon. They wished her a wonderful holiday and told her not to hesitate to get in touch if she had any queries.

Maybe she *should* go alone. It was all paid for, after all. Being at home on her own for a week wouldn't be much fun. And what was the worst that could happen? She could always come home if she hated it. For a few moments, she sat at the kitchen table, drumming her nails on the lid of her laptop which seemed to be taunting her, begging her to open it up and do a bit of work. She was pathetic.

Before she could change her mind, she hurried upstairs and grabbed her suitcase, flinging it open on the bed. She repacked quickly and lugged the case down the stairs. Then she sent a quick message to Phil: *Going to Devon. Talk later x*

Hannah Ellis

Chapter 6

For a while, she was caught up in a surge of adrenalin. She couldn't believe she was actually going alone. Drumming her fingers on the steering wheel, she hummed along to songs on the radio. It definitely felt like an adventure and she grinned from ear to ear as excitement pulsed through her.

When traffic slowed to a stop on the M5 it became less exciting. On the radio, she heard too late about the tailback caused by an accident. After ten minutes, the traffic began to crawl and an hour later she passed the flashing lights of emergency vehicles and a wrecked transit van. She picked up speed and the journey continued at a decent pace. Then the rain began and everything slowed again. When she stopped at a service station three hours after her journey had started, she was only halfway there. Sipping a coffee in the café, she got out her phone to call Phil.

"You made it?" he asked.

"No. Traffic's been awful."

"Driving down on a Friday afternoon was probably a bad idea," he said.

Bloody know-it-all. "There was an accident," she said defensively. "And now it's pouring. I've just stopped for diesel and a coffee."

"Good idea. I'm glad you decided to go anyway. I don't need to feel so guilty now!"

"You should still feel guilty," she said. "So far I'm having a terrible time."

"You'll be fine when you get there. You'll enjoy it."

"Maybe. Anyway, how are you getting on?"

"I'm snowed under," he said. "Everything's in a bit of a mess."

She should probably have been more sympathetic, but it was difficult. The ridiculously long drive would have been much easier if she weren't alone. The decision to go by herself already seemed like a bad one, but she was trying her best to stay positive. Phil was right: when she got to the cottage she'd feel much better. She'd be able to relax then.

"I'm sure you'll sort it all out," she said. "I'll leave you to get on."

"Send me a message when you get there."

"Will do," she said, then ended the call feeling unreasonably angry with him. Maybe it wasn't unreasonable. Maybe he was a weasel like Karen said. She sighed. She knew she shouldn't listen to Karen when it came to men. Besides, she wasn't angry with Phil; she was angry that her excitement at her trip had only lasted half an hour and then fizzled into frustration at a terrible journey. Hopefully her journey wasn't indicative of the week to come.

Getting back in the car was unappealing, so she ambled round the little shop in the service station while she psyched herself up. It was only when she started the engine that hunger niggled at her. She should have eaten while she'd stopped, but there were limited options in the service station. She'd go a bit further and stop again, she decided.

Her eyes grew heavier the closer to Hope Cove she got, and her body was stiff and aching from sitting for too long. By the time she passed Exeter, it was dark. The unfamiliar roads were hard to navigate. The expected four-hour drive had taken over seven.

She didn't find anywhere to stop for food, but her mood lifted when she finally reached Hope Cove. She was exhausted and hungry, but the dimly lit village had a charm about it that made her feel hopeful. Hope Cove, indeed.

The village streets were narrow and dotted with bright white cottages with neatly thatched roofs. When she reached the bay she stopped the car and gazed out. A full moon hung over the water, and the sea sparkled beautifully in its reflected glow. It was quite a sight. She couldn't wait to see it in daylight.

Setting off again, she soon found the little road she was looking for. She crawled along, searching for the cottage. Streetlights were few and far between. When she finally spotted her accommodation for the week it was eerie and foreboding: a cottage standing alone in the darkness. Arriving so late at night wasn't ideal.

The owner had told her the place would be unlocked and the key on the kitchen table. She'd thought it quaint and romantic at the time but she hadn't expected to arrive alone at night, and it suddenly felt dangerous and irresponsible. Anyone could be lying in wait for her.

Ignoring the niggling worries, she marched confidently up to the front door. It was locked. Panic seeped slowly through her. She was tired and irritable and this had been an awful idea. She could be at home now in her lovely warm bed, having eaten a delicious meal.

Finally, she switched on the torch on her mobile and ventured round the back of the house. Thankfully, the back door was open and the key on the table as expected. She must have misunderstood the owner's instructions.

Poking her head into the living room, she saw that everything seemed to be in order. It was nicer than she'd expected, actually. There was a fireplace and the room was furnished with classic oak furniture. She couldn't believe her luck when she found a few supplies in the fridge. While she sat at the kitchen table and devoured the pre-packaged chicken sandwich, she made a mental note to email the owners and thank them for their attention to detail. It's the little things that make a big difference, she thought. With some food inside her, she felt much more positive.

After sending a quick message to Phil to say she'd arrived safely, she went up to bed, exhausted after the gruelling journey. She was just dropping off when something startled her. A noise somewhere. She wasn't sure what it was but listened intently, waiting for it to come again.

Old houses always made noises, she told herself, trying to stop her imagination running away from her. It unsettled her, however, and it took her a while to fall asleep.

Chapter 7

When she woke, she was vaguely aware of the sound of running water. Her sleep-fogged brain told her she must have left a tap on the previous evening. The bed was wonderfully big and comfy, and she didn't want to leave its warmth, but eventually the sound of the water roused her enough to get up.

Weirdly, the bathroom was all steamed up, and the shower was running. She couldn't have left the shower on, she thought; she hadn't been near it. When she pulled the shower curtain back, she gasped at the sight of a naked man. Her eyes went wide and for a moment she stood staring at him.

"What's going on?" he shouted, whipping the shower curtain back into place. Elizabeth retreated, unable to find appropriate words. Why was there a man in the house? A naked man. Very naked.

The water stopped and his toned forearm reached for a towel. He glared at her as he stepped out of the shower. "Why are you in my house? Who are you?"

"I'm—" She stopped. He was still fumbling with the towel, which didn't quite cover him. "Sorry," she said, her gaze darting to the safety of the ceiling. "I rented the cottage for a week. I arrived last night. Who are you?"

"I'm Max," he said. "The cottage isn't for rent.

35

Have you been here all night?"

"Yes." She squinted until she'd checked his towel was safely in place. "Sorry about that," she said, pointing vaguely at his towel area and then blushing. "I've got an email confirming that I've rented the cottage."

"I don't think so," he said, his voice calm but adamant.

"I have. I'll show you." She rushed to the bedroom to get her phone and opened the email. "See," she said, holding the phone out. He reached for it and scanned the email. Slowly, his features relaxed. There was laughter in his icy blue eyes when he looked at her. "Well, Elizabeth Beaumont, it seems like you booked into Seaview Cottage for a week."

"That's what I told you," she said, snatching the phone back. "And I know I got the dates right."

"You've got the wrong place."

"No! I can't have."

"This is Sea*side* Cottage."

She covered her mouth with her hand. "Oh my goodness."

"Sea*view* Cottage is next door."

"But it was unlocked," she said quickly. "The key was on the table like it was supposed to be."

"That's just where I threw it," he said. "And Hope Cove isn't the sort of place where people worry too much about locking doors. Although I might have to rethink that!"

"I am so sorry." The realisation of what she'd done suddenly hit her with full force. "I'm so embarrassed. I can't believe I slept here and I walked in on you in the shower." She blushed again. "I'm mortified."

"No harm done." His eyes crinkled as he stifled a laugh. "I might put some clothes on now…"

"Yes, of course." Backing away, she bumped heavily into the wall. Just when she thought she'd reached her limit for embarrassment. "I'll get my things together."

She scurried around the bedroom, getting dressed and throwing things back into her suitcase then hurriedly making the bed. On the landing she met Max appearing from another bedroom in a pair of jeans and a T-shirt. He rubbed his dark blond hair with a towel and then ruffled it into place.

"I'm so sorry," she said again, feeling as if she might burst into tears through sheer humiliation.

"Really, don't worry about it." He took the case from her and carried it downstairs.

Elizabeth followed him. "This probably happens all the time?" she asked hopefully.

"I think it's a first." His eyes sparkled with amusement. "Seaview Cottage is set back from the road so it is harder to find."

"Whose clever idea was it to give them such similar names?" Elizabeth said.

He looked at her for just a moment too long. It made her uncomfortable.

"Come with me," he said, beckoning for her to follow him.

Hesitantly, she followed him through the kitchen and out into the back garden. It was slightly overgrown but a good size and bordered with a high hedge.

"Where are we going?"

"You'll see."

She followed him to the end of the garden. There was a door in the hedge which she only noticed when they drew near it. It was green and blended right in. Max opened it and stood aside to let her through.

They were on the coastal path. Her shoes crunched on the mix of sand and gravel underfoot. Straight ahead, a few stone steps and an uneven path led the way to a small sandy cove. Beyond, the sea stretched in an almighty and breath-taking display.

"Wow," she whispered. "That's..." It wasn't often that Elizabeth was lost for words, but the sight was so fantastic it was hard to find words to do it justice. "It's..." She scanned the shore, then inhaled the glorious scent of salt and seaweed that floated on the breeze. Wild flowers grew beside the path, and their gentle beauty seemed at odds with the fierceness of the sea and the rocks bordering the sandy cove.

Her mouth hung open until she felt Max watching her. "Wow," she said again, smiling as she gave up on finding anything more meaningful to say.

"Not a bad view, is it?" Max said, his low voice startling her. He was close beside her.

The view had her captivated. "It's stunning."

"This path leads into the village," he said. "There are a few houses along the way, but it's pretty quiet."

The salty air filled her lungs and the sound of waves breaking gently on the shore drifted like music. "I feel like I've just stepped through to Narnia. It's magical."

"It's the best view in the world," Max said. "In my opinion." He moved past her towards the beach and then looked back to the house. "There's your place," he said, pointing to a cottage off to the right, partly hidden by trees. "You can see how they got their names."

"Seaview and Seaside. I suppose they are quite aptly named." Automatically, she slipped off her shoes and wandered onto the beach. "It's like something from a fairy tale." She turned in a circle, taking it all in. It was a beautiful place for a holiday.

They stood in silence for a moment, then Max's features scrunched into silent laughter. "Should we get you moved, Goldilocks?"

She couldn't help but laugh.

Hannah Ellis

Chapter 8

They were walking back through the kitchen when the front door burst open and a young man barrelled in. He had the same striking blue eyes as Max and looked about twenty, if that.

"Hi," he said, grinning at Max. Then his gaze landed on Elizabeth and he frowned in confusion. His eyes darted to the suitcase in the hallway. "Oh, God. I'm so sorry. I didn't know you had someone here with you. Gran told me to come and help you out for the weekend. This is awkward."

"It's not like that," Max said, smiling.

"No, no," Elizabeth chimed in, embarrassed. "I'm not someone. I mean, I am *someone,* of course. Just not…" She waved a finger between herself and Max, then felt like a complete fool. When had she become such a babbling idiot?

"This is Elizabeth," Max said confidently. "Elizabeth, this is my nephew, Conor."

She reached out and shook Conor's hand, but he still seemed confused.

"Elizabeth's staying next door," Max explained. "She got the wrong place."

"Oh!" Conor said, relieved. "That's good."

"Thank you, though," Max said, slapping Conor lightly on the shoulder, "for assuming I'm cheating on

Jessica. Good to know how highly you think of me."

"Sorry," Conor said, looking sheepish and raising his eyebrows at Elizabeth.

"I'd better get out of your way," she said, picking up her suitcase.

"Do you need help?" Max asked as she struggled out with the case.

"No, I'm fine, thanks." She glanced up and down the road, trying to get her bearings.

Max pointed. "The driveway is just a bit further down."

"Thanks," she said. "And I'm sorry again."

"Don't worry about it." He closed the door slowly. "Enjoy your stay."

The suitcase juddered as she dragged it down the uneven road. She soon found the driveway, clearly marked with a sign for Seaview Cottage. How had she missed that?

She felt disappointed when she got in and had a nose around. There was nothing in particular to complain about. The place was clean and functional, but it lacked the charm of the neighbouring cottage.

After she'd lugged her suitcase upstairs and unpacked a little, she got out her phone and called Phil.

"How's the cottage?" he asked.

"It's lovely," she said, choosing not to bother mentioning the little mix-up. She was embarrassed enough without Phil teasing her. Actually, he probably wouldn't tease her at all; instead he'd give her a lecture about safety. She didn't need that either.

"I was thinking," he said, slowly. "Why don't I drive down tomorrow for the day?"

"Really?" she asked, surprised. He'd been so consumed by work the last couple of weeks. If he could manage to take a day off, she'd have thought the last thing he'd want to do would be drive to Devon.

"I feel bad that you're there all alone," he said. "And I know I've not been paying you much attention recently."

"It's fine," she said. "I understand." And deep down she did understand. Her own job could also be very demanding. That didn't mean she couldn't also be annoyed at the situation.

"So shall I drive down for the day?"

"You know it's about a four-hour drive, if there's no traffic?"

"You know I love you enough to do it…"

She chuckled. "I know how stressed you get driving!"

There was a pause, and she realised he was only offering to lessen his guilt about working. He expected her to let him off the hook and, honestly, she didn't want him to make such a trip. "I know what will happen: you'll arrive in a bad mood, then you'll be stressed about work and checking your phone every two minutes. And after about an hour you'll start panicking about how long it'll take you to get home. And after another hour you'll leave…"

"But I would do that for you!"

"You're offering me two hours with a grumpy fiancé?"

"It's up for grabs."

"I'll pass," she said. "You should stay home and relax."

"I love you!" he said cheekily.

"Love you too," she said. "I'm going to go out and explore. I'll talk to you later."

She hung up and wandered around the cottage again. It was basic, but the view from the upstairs windows was magical. She could happily sit in the window and watch the sea all day. She did, in fact, lose track of time gazing out for a while, until her stomach started to growl with hunger.

In the kitchen, she opened the fridge. Of course it was empty, but she was reminded of the sandwich she'd eaten at Seaside Cottage the previous evening – Max's sandwich.

She grinned and picked up her phone again.

"You'll never guess what happened," she said after she'd filled Karen in on her decision to go away without Phil. "I walked in on a naked man in the shower this morning."

"What? What kind of holiday is this? Where are you staying?"

"You won't believe it," Elizabeth said. "I got the wrong cottage. I slept in the wrong bloody house all night and then walked in on a very surprised man in the shower this morning!"

"Oh my God."

"I know. What a start to my week." Josie was right about it being more of an adventure on your own. That would never have happened if she'd had Phil with her.

"What kind of sight are we talking here? Wrinkly old man or hunky hottie?"

"It wasn't a terrible sight," Elizabeth said, flushing at the memory.

"Nice!" Karen said. "I told you you'd have a great time alone. Did you make sweet love and decide to stay with him for a hot holiday fling?"

"No," Elizabeth said. "Don't be filthy! I packed my things and left quickly. It was mortifying. I've never been so embarrassed."

"Well, you were the one wondering what you'd do for a week on your own," Karen said flippantly. "An affair would keep you occupied."

Elizabeth was used to Karen's particular brand of humour. "I was thinking of something that wasn't completely immoral!"

"Fine," Karen said. "Go back to your original plan of working while you're away. I think it's pathetic, but—"

"I'm not going to do any work," Elizabeth interrupted. "That's why I ended up here. I got your email and decided I would actually have a complete break from work. But I wasn't doing well at home so I thought I'd distract myself with the trip to Devon."

"You still won't manage it," Karen said. "As soon as you hang up, you'll be getting your laptop out."

"I didn't bring my laptop," Elizabeth said smugly.

"Bloody hell! Well, your phone then. There's no way you won't do any work all week. You're a workaholic, you know."

"Maybe. Which is why I'm going cold turkey."

"I'll give you a day," Karen said.

"I'll manage a week. You'll see."

Hannah Ellis

Chapter 9

The walk to Hope Cove was beautiful. Elizabeth took the coastal path and was in a constant state of awe at the view. After ten minutes of climbing steadily, she reached the highest point and stood for a moment looking out to sea.

The village was visible from her vantage point. There was a short strip of golden sand, and numerous small boats were anchored out in the bay. Elizabeth remembered reading about the history of smuggling in the area, and could just imagine it in the perfectly secluded cove.

The wind blew wildly, whipping at Elizabeth and forcing her to continue on the path. Seagulls squawked, and the waves hitting the rocks created a constant purr in the air. When she reached the beach, she couldn't resist slipping her shoes off and walking to the shoreline. The cool water was bliss as it swept around her feet.

A couple of fishermen stood on some rocks, far to her left, but she felt very much alone. Her stomach groaned once again and she remembered her task of finding food. As she walked up to the village she wondered how she'd felt so alone on the beach – cars rolled through the narrow streets and there were a number of people around. The waves and the seagulls must have drowned everything else out.

There was a café with a couple of tables outside, and she headed straight for it. A young guy stood in the doorway chatting to an older woman in an apron. He was wearing a navy polo shirt with the RNLI logo on it. Elizabeth was fascinated by lifeboats and the people who volunteered on them. She made a mental note to visit the lifeboat station and leave a donation.

They smiled at her as she took a seat, and she spent a moment trying to decipher their conversation. They had thick Devon accents and she could only just make out the words as they spoke about the weather and the expected number of tourists. After a couple of minutes the man left and the woman came over to Elizabeth.

"Sorry about that," she said, her accent suddenly not quite so strong. "When someone gets me chatting it's hard to stop. Did you have a look at the menu?"

"Yes." Elizabeth smiled. "I was wondering if it would be wrong to have scones for breakfast!"

"Scones are fine at any time," the woman said happily. "With a bit of jam and clotted cream you'll be set for the day."

"It sounds divine, but I think I'll save it for afternoon tea one day. I'll be good and stick to toast and coffee for now."

"That sounds like a great plan too. Coming right up!"

Elizabeth cheerfully watched the world go by as she waited. Pretty much everyone who passed gave her some sort of greeting – from a simple nod of the head to a chirpy "good morning".

"On your holidays, are you?" the waitress asked

when she delivered Elizabeth's breakfast.

Elizabeth nodded. "I'm staying in Seaview Cottage for a week."

"What do you think of our little village so far?"

"It's gorgeous. I could sit here all week looking at the view."

"You're very welcome to do that," the woman said with a chuckle. "And if you want to take the view home with you, there's a shop round the corner that sells some wonderful pictures. All by local artists."

"Really?"

"Hope Cove Gallery," she said proudly. "Follow this road to the top of the slipway. You can't miss it."

So that was the next stop on Elizabeth's little morning exploration. As soon as she'd eaten she set off eagerly in search of the gallery. It was easy to find, just past a row of brightly coloured cottages.

Elizabeth loved it as soon as she walked in, and she felt decidedly childlike as she tried to take everything in with wide eyes.

The smiley man at the counter gave her a brief nod. "Shout if you need any help."

"Thank you," she replied, stepping forward to inspect a wall full of stunning pictures. They were all local scenes, some of which Elizabeth already recognised. She was immediately drawn to a watercolour depicting the view she'd stared at over breakfast. She could imagine the boats in the painting bobbing just as they did in real life.

The shop was only small but was packed full of treasures, from simple painted pebbles to mirrors created from driftwood. There was something for everyone. Elizabeth was adamant she wanted a picture to take home, but spent a long time wondering where she would hang it. Her and Phil were minimalists when it came to decor, and she just couldn't imagine any of the pictures in their home.

Never mind – she would figure out where to put it later. Her eyes kept returning to the stunning watercolour and she knew she had to have it. She generally wasn't one for impulse buys, but she felt incredibly happy as she handed over her credit card. The framed painting was too large to carry, so she arranged to collect it later with the car.

There was a spring in her step as she left Hope Cove Gallery and walked back the way she'd come. The local post office doubled as a small shop, so she stopped off to buy a few groceries. The beach had filled up with people taking advantage of the beautiful summer's day and the air was filled with laughter and chatter when she walked past, heading back to the coastal path.

Her hair was windswept when she arrived back at the cottage and she ran a brush through it and tied it up again before unpacking her shopping. A smile flickered on her face as she pulled a chicken sandwich out of the shopping bag. She needed to apologise to Max for eating his food as well as sleeping in his cottage.

In the back garden there was a gap in the hedge which led through to the next garden. She heard Max and Conor chatting outside and followed their voices. It was only when she was about to say hello that she realised they were arguing. Or bickering, at least. Something about windows. She was about to back away when Conor caught sight of her.

"What do *you* think?" he said.

Was he talking to her? Instinctively she glanced around. "What?"

"Sorry," he said, "I thought you must have overheard. We could do with another opinion."

"Leave her alone," Max said. "She's on holiday. Sorry!" he said, leaning into view.

"It's fine," she replied. "Actually, I was just coming to replace your sandwich." She held it aloft, feeling like an idiot.

"You really didn't have to," Max said.

"I'll take it," Conor said, grabbing it. Then he beckoned for Elizabeth to join them in the garden. "Come here a minute and help us settle this."

She squeezed through the gap in the hedge to stand with them.

"I'm sorry about Conor," Max said. He sat in a patio chair, looking vaguely irritated by his nephew.

"What do you think about the windows, Lizzie?" Conor asked.

"It's Elizabeth."

"Really? You seem like a Lizzie. Anyway, the windows."

She looked at the cottage, slightly confused. "Erm…"

"Imagine you're a potential buyer," Conor said. "What would you say about the windows? Be honest."

"Are you selling?" she asked, glancing at Max.

"It's not my house," he said. "It's my mum's. She's selling. We're supposed to spruce the place up a bit before it goes on the market."

"Oh, I see."

"So what do you think about the windows?" Max asked again.

"Well," she said, walking over to the kitchen window and wondering how honest she should be, "the paint's peeling, obviously." Without thinking, she put a finger under a piece of cracked white paint and it flipped easily away from the wood. "Sorry," she said quickly.

"Exactly!" Conor said.

"But would that put you off buying the place?" Max asked.

"No, I don't think so. It seems like it would be easy enough to fix."

"It is," Conor said excitedly. "Really easy!"

"It's absolutely not a one-day job," Max said, looking sternly at Conor. "I'm not about to start painting windows."

"But I bought all the stuff. Gran said—"

"I know what she said! She tried to talk me into it as well. I told her it's not happening. And, as Lizzie has pointed out, a bit of flaking paint isn't going to put anyone off buying the place. They'll paint it themselves."

"It's Elizabeth," she said.

"Sorry." He didn't seem sorry; he seemed amused.

She held his gaze for a moment and then took a few steps back to inspect the windows. "The new owners might paint them purple," she said slowly.

Max stared at her. "What?"

"The white's lovely," she said. "What if someone comes along and decides that since the windows need painting, they might as well do them in their favourite colour … and they end up purple?" Even Conor looked confused.

"Do you have something against purple?" Max asked.

"No," she said, lips twitching. "I just think white suits the place. I meant any colour, really … they could end up any colour. It'd be a shame if the place ended up with purple window frames."

"Or green," Conor said, getting on board. "They could end up green! If they're all freshly painted, no one will even consider changing the colour."

Max moved to the window, picking at another piece of paint. He shook his head. "It's not just slapping fresh paint on," he said. "We'd have to sand down the wood first. And if we do the windows, we'll have to do the doors too. And they'll need at least two coats of paint."

"But they wouldn't be purple," Elizabeth said.

Max caught her smirking. "Okay," he said, shooing her away, "get back through the hedge. You're not helping matters. Go on, *Lizzie*! Off you go!"

"It's Elizabeth," she said, but she was chuckling as she slipped back into the next garden. When she turned back, Max was watching her. He mouthed a sarcastic "Thank you" as Conor continued to make his argument.

There was a table and chairs in the garden at Seaview Cottage, along with a plastic sun lounger. Elizabeth gave it a quick dust-off before taking a seat and enjoying the sun on her face and the gentle breeze. For a while, Max and Conor's voices drifted through and then it went quiet. The urge to reach for her mobile and check her emails came out of nowhere and was hard to resist.

She was determined not to, and instead changed into her swimsuit and headed down to the beach for a swim. When she returned an hour later, she heard voices through the hedge. Peeking through, she saw Max and Conor working on the windows, and felt slightly guilty. It was obviously a bigger job than Conor had realised, and she'd only involved herself in the discussion because she'd found it amusing to side with Conor when he was clearly in the wrong.

To be fair, it would be a shame if the windows ended up something other than white. It was a gorgeous little cottage and the white window frames were a lovely feature. She'd probably done the right thing, she decided.

Chapter 10

After a day of exploring and swimming, Elizabeth was worn out. Her skin tingled from too much sun when she curled up with a book in the evening. When her eyes grew heavy she gave up and went to bed.

Not used to going to bed quite so early, she woke up far too early the next day. It wasn't even daylight, so she nearly rolled over and went back to sleep. But a thought occurred to her.

She pulled on a pair of jeans and a jumper and went down to the kitchen to make a mug of coffee. Then she headed outside with the drink in her hand.

She was on the beach just as the sun began to rise. She sat on the sand to watch. Only a few minutes after she arrived, the silence was interrupted.

"Morning."

The voice was soft but made her jump nonetheless.

"Sorry," Max said. "I didn't mean to creep up on you."

"It's fine," Elizabeth said, a hand over her heart. "You took about ten years off my life, but never mind!"

He hovered over her. "You stole my sunrise spot."

"Did I really?" she said with a grin. "Well, I'll

share my coffee if you share your spot…"

"Go on then." He sat beside her on the sand. "Coffee was a great idea."

"It's still warm," she said, holding it out and only then thinking it was an odd thing to do. She wouldn't usually offer to share her drink with someone she barely knew.

"Can I ask you a personal question?" she said when he took the mug.

He looked amused. "I think you might have an issue with boundaries."

"I'm sorry! I think you might be right. It's a new thing. I'm normally very proper."

"You do seem like someone with airs and graces," he agreed. "But then you sneak into houses at night and involve yourself in other people's discussions." He handed the mug back. "And share your coffee. It's all very confusing."

"Hey! Conor asked my opinion." She looked at the changing colours in the morning sky. "But maybe you're right. Maybe I should just…" She made a zipping motion across her lips and went quiet.

"You may as well ask your personal question now. Otherwise I'll forever wonder what it was."

"I was wondering why your mum's selling the place. It's so beautiful. I can't imagine ever wanting to sell somewhere like that."

"I don't think she particularly wants to," Max said. "It was our holiday home when I was growing up. Mum's been renting it out for years but it's too much for her to look after these days. She moved into a nursing home."

"Sorry…"

"Oh no, it's not like that. Not sad, I mean." A smile flashed over his face as he watched the waves roll onto the shore. "Henley House is pretty luxurious. That's also why she's selling. She needs the money to pay for the nursing home."

"Henley House? It sounds very grand."

"It is," he said. "She was lonely and nervous about living alone after she had a fall. One of her friends had moved to Henley House and was raving about it. I think Mum was a bit jealous. Anyway, she's made loads of friends there and is having a whale of a time!"

"She sounds like a character."

"She is."

They sat in silence for a few minutes, enjoying the stunning sunrise. It was such a gorgeous spot. If she were Max, she'd buy the cottage herself.

"Why don't you buy it?" she asked without thinking. "You're obviously attached to it." She lowered her gaze then, embarrassed. Why had she assumed he'd be in a position to buy the cottage? In her head, an image of Josie appeared, telling her she was a snob.

When she glanced at Max, he was miles away, looking lost in thought.

"I shouldn't have asked," she said quickly. "It's none of my business. It probably costs a small fortune…"

"It's not that," he said. "I did think about buying it. I'm just surprised you think I'm attached to it. I didn't realise it was that obvious."

"Who wouldn't love it?" she said gently. "And if you weren't attached to it, you wouldn't be so bothered by the colour of the window frames."

"I'm not that bothered by the windows," he said. "But I decided it might be fun to do with Conor. And it was a good excuse to drag my stay out a little longer."

He sounded gloomy, and she felt responsible. "Sorry. I didn't mean to pry."

"It's okay. I'll be sad to see the place sold, that's all."

"You'll still be able to come back. Maybe the new owners will rent it out…"

"I know. But it won't be the same."

Instinctively, Elizabeth reached out a hand and laid it over his. Her heart rate rose immediately and she gave a brief squeeze before letting go. Her issues with boundaries seemed to be escalating.

"I should probably get on with the windows," he said, standing. "I've a lot to do today, thanks to you!"

She winced. "Sorry."

"You know how easy it was to flick a piece of paint off with your finger?" he asked.

She nodded.

"That was deceptive. Most of it doesn't come off anything like as easily."

"If you're trying to make me feel bad, you've succeeded!"

"I wasn't." He smiled as he walked away. "I promise."

Chapter 11

After watching the sunrise, Elizabeth had a shower and breakfast, then headed out for a walk along the coastal path, away from the village. It was still early, and everything was peaceful. The only people she met were a couple of dog walkers and a group of hikers. It was exhilarating to do more exploring and she was reminded again of Josie's theory that everything felt more like an adventure when you were alone. It was true.

She'd brought her towel and swimsuit, having gathered from internet research that there were good beaches nearby. The beaches turned out to be much busier than the coastal path, and after spending a couple of hours lying in the sun at South Milton Sands she began to feel claustrophobic due to the number of people who closed in around her.

It was a gorgeous long stretch of sandy beach and the large car park with amenities ensured that it was a popular destination. There was also a little shop renting out equipment for water sports. A number of people were having fun with kayaks, surfboards and paddle boards on the water.

It was fun to watch the bustle for a while but soon Elizabeth felt drawn back to the peace and quiet of her cottage. She left the beach at lunchtime, after grabbing a drink and sandwich at the popular Beachside Café. The café was busy so she opted to take her food away, and ate sitting on the first bench she found, which looked out over the bay.

Back at the cottage, she made herself comfortable on the sun lounger and for a while she heard the low hum of Max and Conor chatting, but then they went quiet.

"Pssst!"

She jumped when Conor appeared at the gap in the hedge.

"I'll let you in on a secret…" He spoke in a stage whisper while looking around dramatically. "I don't reckon the windows are going to get finished today." He grimaced comically and she couldn't help but chuckle.

"No way!" she replied with an equal amount of drama. She walked over and peered past him at the house. The window frames were stripped to the wood, but the door still had the old paint on. "Where's Max?"

"Working on the front," he said, then paused. "Any chance you can throw?"

She screwed her nose up. "What?"

"There's a cricket set in the shed," he said, heading in that direction. He didn't wait for an answer but returned a minute later with a bat and ball. "Throw a couple for me?"

"What about the windows?"

He gave her a cheeky grin. "I'll aim in the other direction."

"That's not what I meant!"

Conor waved a hand. "It's fine. Come on. Max

won't even notice I've gone."

"All right," she said, following him down the garden.

Once again she was taken aback by the view as they stepped through the doorway in the hedge. There was something so magical about it. She wondered how long it would be before it no longer took her breath away.

It was breezy on the beach, and seagulls circled high overhead, squawking occasionally. Elizabeth kicked off her shoes and took up position opposite Conor, who waited for her throw. The bat and ball connected with a crack. The ball flew past Elizabeth and she chased it along the beach. She returned a moment later, breathless, her cheeks pink from the exertion and the whip of the wind. She felt exhilarated.

"Come on," Conor prompted cheerfully, waiting to take another swing at the ball. This time he chased it himself.

Max arrived at the beach half an hour later. Elizabeth was paddling in the sea. Instinctively she turned to find him watching her from the top of the beach. He broke into a smile and walked towards her. She wondered how long he'd been there. Conor lay on the sand, his hands behind his head and his face tilted up to the dazzling sunshine.

"Conor found a cricket set," Elizabeth confessed when Max reached her. The wind caught her hair, blowing strands onto her cheeks, and she pushed them back.

"I should've known you were trouble when I

found you trespassing in my house. Now you're leading my nephew astray!"

"Cricket was his idea," she insisted.

"Sure it was! How's the water?"

"Beautiful. I might grab my swimsuit and have a dip later."

"I forgot my swimming shorts," he said. "But it's very tempting."

"If you feel like skinny dipping, don't let me stop you," she said. "I've already seen you naked, after all!"

Woah! Where had that come from? Seriously, Elizabeth, boundaries!

His mouth twitched. He glanced at the water and then back at Elizabeth before pulling his T-shirt off and throwing it at her.

"I was joking," she said, panicking that he was about to strip off.

He undid his jeans and stepped out of them. Standing in his boxer shorts, he looked squarely at Elizabeth. "That's as much of me as you're going to see today. I know how you like to ogle."

"I never ogled!" she insisted, embarrassed.

"You ogled." He smirked as he walked into the water "I saw you."

As he dived under the water, Elizabeth sank onto the sand, a silly grin on her face. Without thinking, she raised Max's T-shirt to her face. The scent of him filled her senses and made her insides flutter. Feeling foolish, she laid the T-shirt beside her on the sand and watched Max's strong, graceful strokes cut a path through the water.

She resisted the temptation to join him.

62

Chapter 12

Conor was sitting beside Elizabeth when Max returned. He stood over them, dripping wet, and glared at Conor. "Painting almost done, is it?" he asked.

"I think you'll easily get it finished tomorrow," Conor said with a boyish grin.

Max raised an eyebrow. "I think I recall you saying you'd ring in sick if we didn't get it finished today."

Conor looked horrified. "I can't do that. Dad would kill me. You know what it's like ... you can't ring in sick to a place where illness isn't an acceptable excuse for not being at work. I'd at least need to be missing a limb, then I might be able to take a day!"

"Where do you work?" Elizabeth asked.

"I've been working at the law firm where my dad works for the summer. It's the place fun goes to die. Seriously, one day I lost some important document. It was like the end of the world. I thought Dad was going to disown me."

"What happened?" Max asked as he sat beside Conor.

"I'd left it on the photocopier! Crisis averted. It was a major drama, though. They'll probably be talking about it for years to come."

"If it's so bad, why are you so worried about ringing in sick?" Max asked.

"I've only got a few weeks left," Conor said, pointedly avoiding eye contact with Max.

"Exactly. What are they going to do? Fire you? It's only a summer job."

"That's mature advice, *Uncle* Max. Aren't you supposed to set an example? Teach me about responsibility and reliability and all that?"

Max kept quiet, searching Conor's face.

"Fine!" Conor said. "If I work the whole summer I get a small gift from Dad." He put air quotes around the word 'gift'.

Max smiled knowingly. "He's buying you a new car, isn't he?"

"Yes," Conor said sheepishly. He looked from Max to Elizabeth. "Don't judge me. I've earned it!"

"I guess I'll be painting alone then," Max said.

"How long are you here for?" Elizabeth asked.

He shrugged. "Until the windows are finished." He pulled a face at Conor before turning back to Elizabeth. "I don't need to be in work this week so I'm pretty flexible."

"What do you do?" she asked.

"He used to be a hot-shot lawyer," Conor answered for Max, a teasing glint in his eyes. "But he gave it all up to work on a make-up counter! And apparently no one notices whether he turns up for work or not."

Max laughed. He seemed to be used to this kind of teasing. "That's not true. I work for a cosmetics company and everyone thinks it's a big joke."

"But you used to be a lawyer?" Elizabeth asked,

trying to keep up.

"Yes," Conor said. "He and Dad worked together at the same firm. Two hot-shot lawyers taking over the world! Then one day Max walked out and went to work on a make-up counter—"

"I'm still a lawyer!" Max said. "I just work for a cosmetics company."

"Whatever. Stop ruining my story," Conor said, waving him away and leaning closer to Elizabeth. "He brought shame on the family. He's such an embarrassment. It's hard for me to even acknowledge him as my uncle." He grinned mischievously at Max. "If you weren't marrying money, we'd have to disown you completely."

"I'm not marrying money!"

"She drives a Porsche," Conor said, winking at Elizabeth.

"Which she worked hard for," Max argued.

"Yeah, right. It's all Daddy's money!"

"Don't you need to go and sand some window frames or something?"

Conor stood and squeezed Max's shoulder. "You know I like you better as a make-up artist, don't you?" He took off up the beach at a run.

Max chuckled. "I'm not a make-up artist."

"Shame," Elizabeth said. "I thought you might give me a makeover!"

"You really wouldn't want that." He shook his head in amusement. "I need to get back to work. Have a good afternoon."

"Thanks," she called after him. The silence felt strange for a moment after they'd left. Max and Conor were good company, and Elizabeth enjoyed the easy banter between them. Feeling restless, she made her way back to the house. She called Phil and was disappointed when he didn't answer.

Out in the back garden, laughter drifted from Seaside Cottage and she peered through the hedge. She couldn't see Max and Conor; they must be working on the front of the house. Picking up her phone again, she stared at the screen and then wondered why she'd picked the thing up. Checking her work email was an automatic reaction. She grumbled to herself and set it aside again.

Without thinking any more about it, she walked purposefully through the gap in the hedge to Seaside Cottage and then around to the front of the house.

"Hi," she said, suddenly feeling awkward.

Conor and Max stopped mid-conversation.

"Hi," Max said.

"Sorry to interrupt," she said. "I'm probably going to sound a bit weird … but I wondered if I might help you."

Max gave her a puzzled smile. "You don't need to do that – you're on holiday."

"Yeah," she said, wondering what she could say to sound like less of a weirdo. What was she doing? She'd felt the sudden need for company and was now offering her services for painting and decorating. Had she completely lost her mind?

Conor shoved a wad of sandpaper at her. "Most of the paint comes off easily," he said. "But you get some stubborn little flecks that just don't want to budge. And the door has panels with little grooves that are really awkward." He pointed, and gave her a playful shove in that direction.

Max intercepted her, taking back the sandpaper. "You really don't need to help us. I was only joking about not getting it done. I'm here all week. It's fine."

"I know," she said, feeling suddenly emotional. "I was supposed to be here with my fiancé, but he had to work. And now I'm not sure what to do with myself." It wasn't exactly true; so far she'd been surprised by how easy it was being alone – and how enjoyable. It was more that she felt like company, and Conor and Max were very easy to be around.

There was an uncomfortable silence before Conor spoke. "What an idiot."

"I had a few choice words to say about it myself," she said. "But what could I do? I either came alone or not at all."

"Well, I'm glad you came," Conor said.

"Me too," Max said, handing back the sandpaper. "We need all the help we can get."

"Thank you," she whispered, and got to work.

She soon found that Conor was right: the majority of the paint came away easily, but it was a tough job removing the tiny flecks.

"I'll be honest," Conor said, holding the ladder for Max, who was doing the upstairs windows. "I thought it'd be easier."

"I did try to tell you," Max shouted down.

"I'm sure we'll get it all done," Conor replied, but pulled a face at Elizabeth, shaking his head.

A couple of hours later, Elizabeth was tired and aching and wondering why on earth she was spending the afternoon stripping paint and sanding down window frames. It was turning out to be a very strange holiday. When all the window frames were

67

stripped and sanded, they stood together, admiring their handiwork. Despite the aches and blisters, Elizabeth felt a real sense of achievement.

"I'm in desperate need of a shower," she said, smiling at the men and moving in the direction of her cottage. "Thanks for keeping me entertained."

"We're having a barbecue on the beach before I head off," Conor said. "You should join us."

"I've intruded enough. But thanks for the offer."

"You're not intruding," Max said. "There's plenty of food, and we owe you for helping out."

She began to protest again, but Conor jumped in. "Stop arguing! Go and have a shower, then meet us on the beach."

"Okay," she said, giving Conor a quick salute before hurrying away.

Chapter 13

Elizabeth's phone was ringing when she got out of the shower. She answered it to hear Phil's voice.

"How's it going?" he asked.

"Er… It's all okay. I can't complain." She'd had some vague ideas about making him feel guilty about ditching her for a little longer, but it suddenly seemed petty. "The sun's shining, the beach is fab. You're missing out."

"I'd like to be there," he said defensively. "I'm not happy about having to work either."

"I know, sorry. I didn't mean it like that."

"I'm sorry," he said. "I'm stressed. I could really do with a break."

"We'll be on our honeymoon before we know it," she said brightly. They were going to Italy for ten days and had planned a mix of lazy beach days and sightseeing.

"I can't wait," he replied. "What have you been doing today?"

"Not a lot, really," she said hesitantly. It was difficult to explain that she'd spent the afternoon stripping paint with Max and Conor. What would Phil think? "I've been lazing in the garden and on the beach."

"It's good that you're relaxing and getting a

proper break."

"I haven't checked my work emails once," she said proudly.

"It's still the weekend," he reminded her. "Let's talk again tomorrow and see if you've still been able to resist."

"I'm taking a complete break from work."

"There's no way you can manage the whole week without checking in."

"I can," she said. "I'm not sure why everyone thinks it's an impossible task. Karen didn't believe I could do it either."

"We'll see," he said lightly.

"I'm going to have dinner," she said. "I'm starving. Call me tomorrow?"

"Will do," he said, and told her he loved her before ending the call.

She felt a pang of guilt for not telling him about her dinner plans. He'd think it odd that she'd made friends with the neighbours and was going to have a barbecue with them. Of course, she would have told him if she was having dinner with two women. Phil definitely wouldn't like it if he knew she'd made friends with two men. It was only dinner, she reasoned, and if Phil hadn't cancelled on her, she'd wouldn't have had to make friends with the neighbours, so basically it was all his fault.

She got dressed quickly and clipped her hair up. When she sat down to put on make-up, she paused, wondering why she was bothering. The sun had given her a healthy glow and she was only going to be sitting on the beach. She'd give it a miss, she decided, and felt good about it.

By the time she made her way down to the beach, it was early evening. Conor was standing over a disposable barbecue. Max handed Elizabeth a beer when she sat down on the sand beside him.

"Do you need any help?" Max asked Conor.

"Nope."

"You sure? I don't want food poisoning."

Conor shot Max a weary look. "I can manage to light a barbecue, thanks."

"Just checking!"

Conor's phone rang then, and he frowned when he pulled it from his pocket. "It's Dad," he said, glancing at Max. "He'll be checking up on me, wanting to know when I'll be home and reminding me I have to work tomorrow – as if I could forget!"

"Answer it," Max said. "He'll only call me otherwise."

Conor moved away from them to take the call. All they could hear was the odd muffled word.

"I take it your brother's quite a bit older than you?" Elizabeth asked.

Max nodded. "James is twelve years older than me."

"And you don't get on?"

"No. But not because of the age difference." His voice went from serious to amused. "Because he's a stuck-up prick!"

She smiled back at him. "Conor seems like a good kid."

"He's great. His dad's too hard on him. Conor won't want anything to do with him soon."

"That's a shame."

"It is. My big brother has a tendency to see the

worst in people." He paused. "Sorry. Family issues."

"All families have issues," she said. "I have a little sister – she's eight years younger than me – and we don't get on either. She's definitely not stuck-up, though. Josie is wild and crazy. She drives me mad."

"She sounds fun," Max said. His gaze lingered on her a fraction too long.

Elizabeth laughed. "I always think of her as my polar opposite so I don't know what that says about me!"

"You seem pretty easy-going yourself," Max said. "You make friends easily enough…"

"I'm just overly polite," she said. "Whenever I accidentally break into someone's house I try to be nice to them. Stops me getting in too much trouble."

"So this is a regular occurrence, is it?" he said. "Are you some sort of high-end squatter?"

"My secret's out," she said, chuckling.

Conor returned then, with a face like thunder. "He's so annoying," he grumbled, putting burgers on the barbecue. "He gave me a lecture about being punctual. I don't know why. I haven't been late to work once. I can't wait until I'm finished there. Just a few more weeks, and then I get my freedom back."

"So you're not going to pursue a career in law?" Elizabeth asked.

"God, no," Conor said. "I've got a bar job lined up and I'll figure out what I do after that. I want to do something fun."

He carried on chatting as he cooked, complaining about his dad and regaling them with stories about work at the law firm.

"James and I aren't at all alike," Max told

Elizabeth when Conor passed them a burger each.

"Not at all," Conor agreed quickly. "They're complete opposites. Dad's the most boring guy on the planet."

Max's face lit up. "There's a compliment! That must make me the coolest guy on the planet?"

Conor groaned. "No one says cool these days. It's very uncool!"

"Don't start making out I'm ancient," Max said.

"You are!" Conor said cheekily.

"Don't listen to him," Max said quietly to Elizabeth. "I'm thirty-three. That's not old, is it?"

"Not at all," Elizabeth said. Her mind flicked to Josie calling her middle-aged. Max definitely wasn't middle-aged, and she was only a year older than him so surely she wasn't either. But why was she even thinking about that? She shifted her attention to her burger instead.

Max and Conor settled into an easy silence as they ate, and Elizabeth was glad they'd insisted she join them. It was much better than eating alone.

"I should probably hit the road," Conor said drearily when they'd finished eating.

Elizabeth stood to say goodbye. She felt strangely fond of him, considering she'd only known him for a couple of days. "Thanks for dinner," she said.

It was a surprise when he embraced her warmly. "You're welcome. Thanks for helping with the windows." He kept his gaze on her when he released her. "And I'm glad your boyfriend had to work! It was great having you around."

"Thank you," she said shyly, then sat down and picked up her beer, watching as he hugged Max.

"Drive safely," Max said. "And let me know when you're home."

Conor slapped him on the back. "Yes, boss!"

"Thanks for your help," Max shouted after him as he set off up the beach.

"You're quite protective of him, aren't you?" Elizabeth said when he sat beside her. "Wanting to know when he's home safely."

Max took a swig of his beer. "He's my baby nephew. I still can't believe he's allowed to drive. How did that happen?"

"Maybe you're getting old?" she suggested.

"Definitely not!"

They fell into a comfortable silence and watched the waves for a while. As the sun began to set, the air turned chilly.

"Are you cold?" Max asked when she hugged her knees.

"I'm okay."

"Will you stay for another drink if I build a fire?"

She hesitated. Should she spend time alone with Max? It would be a shame to miss the sunset on the beach, and if Max was there too, that was hardly her fault. She wasn't sure why she felt the need to make excuses for herself. It wasn't as if she was doing anything wrong. It was just a drink with a new friend. In the most beautiful setting… with a romantic bonfire. Gosh, she liked to overthink things.

"That sounds good," she said. "I could also just get a jumper—"

But Max had already gone, seemingly intent on the idea of building a fire. It didn't take him long to collect firewood, and by the time the sun had

74

disappeared below the horizon the fire was kicking out a good amount of heat.

She wasn't sure why, but the atmosphere between them had changed. Maybe it was not having Conor there, or maybe it was the romantic setting, but she increasingly felt that she shouldn't be sitting there with Max. It felt too intimate. The trouble was, she was enjoying herself too much to move.

Idly, Max poked a stick at the fire as they chatted, then used the stick to write *Lizzie* in the sand between them.

She frowned. "I told you, it's Elizabeth."

"I bet your sister doesn't call you Elizabeth."

"No," she said, surprised by his accuracy. "She calls me Liz." Heat hit her cheeks as she went on. "She once said I'm too stuffy to be a Lizzie, but thinks I can pull off Liz or Beth."

"Beth's too gentle," Max said, underlining the letters in the sand. "Lizzie suits you perfectly."

"I guess I'm lucky," she mused. "There's not much you can do with Max, is there?"

He smirked at her choice of words. "Not much at all."

She turned away from his teasing eyes and surveyed the tranquil surroundings. The silvery moonlight bounced onto the water, making it sparkle. She lay back on the sand to gaze at the stars.

"I never do this," she said. "Just sit under the stars and enjoy the moment."

"It's pretty special here."

"I should do this more often," she murmured.

She lay watching the stars for a while and then reluctantly decided she should probably get to bed.

Hannah Ellis

Once Max had covered the fire with sand, they were plunged into darkness. The light from the moon was not enough to see by, and Elizabeth stumbled walking up the beach.

"Here," Max said, moving closer and offering his arm.

With him guiding her, they reached her cottage quickly.

"Thank you," she said, switching the kitchen light on and lingering at the back door.

"No problem," he replied. "I wanted to make sure you got the right house."

She couldn't help but chuckle.

"What do you think of this place?" Max asked, glancing over her shoulder into the house.

"It's fine."

"You sound unimpressed."

She frowned. "Your place is nicer, that's all."

"I might lock the doors tonight. I'm worried you'll creep back in!"

"I promise not to," she said. She was about to say goodnight when she caught a strange look in Max's eyes. "What?" she asked.

"Nothing," he said, but seemed embarrassed, as if he'd been caught out. "I keep thinking that we've met before."

Her eyebrows dipped. "I don't think so."

"No, we haven't. I meant like déjà vu or something." He paused. "Do I sound really creepy?"

"A little," she said lightly.

"Sorry!" He backed away. "I'll blame it on the beer. Thanks for helping today."

"You're welcome."

She watched him slip through the hedge and disappear from sight. For a moment, she stood, thinking about what he'd said.

It wasn't quite déjà vu, but she did feel a strange connection to him.

Hannah Ellis

Chapter 14

Elizabeth was still in bed when Karen called her on Monday morning.

"Do me a massive favour," Karen said, sounding fraught. "I've forwarded you an email from Heidi. Open it quickly and tell me what you think. I'm having a meltdown here."

"No!" Elizabeth said. "I'm not falling for that. I told you I'm not working this holiday."

"I can't believe you're actually doing it."

"It's only Monday morning – it's not a massive achievement yet."

"I know, but you can't usually manage to go a weekend without working so it's quite surprising. Should I be worried?"

"No. I'm fine."

"Good. Anyway, I really do have an issue with Heidi. She sent the horoscopes on Friday. You should see them – they get worse every month."

"Don't talk shop to me," Elizabeth said. "I told you I'm not working."

"Fine," Karen said. "But, as a friend, can you listen while I vent?"

"Go on, then…"

"She sent me three words for Gemini. Three words! *Don't look back.* That's creepy, isn't it? Then for Pisces she's written a huge essay about the sun being in Venus and Mars being on Jupiter or God knows what. It's garbage! And she genuinely believes all this stuff. I'm going to talk to her today."

"Don't," Elizabeth said, staring at the ceiling. "I'll deal with her when I get back. You sometimes forget to be tactful with Heidi."

"That's true. I'll wait for you; you're definitely better with people. That's why I hired you. For your tact and diplomacy."

"Along with my many other skills and qualifications, I'm sure."

"Possibly, but mainly because you seemed like someone who'd drink wine with me in my office."

"An often overlooked topic in job interviews!"

They laughed together. Karen was the main reason she enjoyed her job so much. She could be scarily serious when she wanted to be – especially approaching publication deadlines – but she was also lots of fun.

"So how's the holiday?"

"It's okay," Elizabeth said. "It's been a bit weird, actually."

"Have you been checking out more naked men in showers?"

"No. But I do keep seeing the naked shower guy. Fully dressed, but we keep bumping into each other."

"Are you grinning?" Karen asked suspiciously.

"No!" It was a lie. How did Karen know? Could she hear it in her voice? And why was she grinning?

"Are you hanging out with the hottie to get back at Phil for ditching you?"

"No," Elizabeth said quickly. "And he's not hot."

She paused. That was another lie. "I'm not trying to get back at Phil. I'm not angry with Phil any more."

"No, you wouldn't be, would you?"

"What's that supposed to mean?"

"Oh, calm down. I'm only teasing. Little Goody Two-Shoes wouldn't do anything inappropriate."

"I'm not a goody two-shoes."

"You are, actually, but whatever. I've got work to do. Have fun. And let your hair down for once."

"What?"

"How long have I known you? Ten years? I've literally never seen you with your hair down!"

"I thought you were saying I was uptight."

"That too! Maybe the two things are connected."

Elizabeth always wore her hair neatly tied up. It was how she liked it. She was half tempted to mention that she'd gone out the previous evening without make-up, but as her mind whirred back to the evening on the beach with Max she realised it wasn't a conversation she wanted to get into with Karen.

"Leave me alone," she said. "I'm going back to sleep."

"Talk soon," Karen said, ending the call.

But Elizabeth couldn't get back to sleep, and after a quick breakfast of coffee and toast she set off for a walk. She stopped a few times to sit and admire the view. After an hour or so, she came to a golf course. It had a great location, with the clubhouse sitting high up on the cliffs. A waiter was setting up the terrace, pinning neat white tablecloths onto the tables.

This was why she didn't like being alone. It was such a lovely place, but there was no way she'd go out for a meal at a fancy restaurant on her own. She considered it for a moment: she could take a book and enjoy the surroundings and good food. It might be fun. She could chat with the waiters and pretend that she ate alone all the time. It was the sort of thing Josie would do – if she could afford to eat at nice places. Elizabeth couldn't do it; she knew she'd feel awkward and rush through her meal.

Arriving back at the cottage at lunchtime, she grabbed a quick sandwich and pondered what to do for the rest of the day. She was about to put her bikini on when she caught sight of Max. Feeling a sudden need for company, she walked to the hedge and was about to step through when she stopped herself. What was she doing? The poor guy probably wanted some peace, and she kept arriving in his garden. What was wrong with her that she couldn't spend a day alone? She took a few steps back the way she'd come and then stopped again, dithering. She could say a quick hello. There was nothing wrong with that.

"Hi!" she called. He turned, with a paintbrush in his hand.

"Hi!" he said. "How are you?"

"Fine, thanks. Looks like you're hard at work again."

"No rest for the wicked," he said. "What have you been up to?"

"I went for a walk. Up to the golf course and back."

"It's beautiful up there. They do good food too."

She nodded vaguely, her mouth inexplicably dry. Her gaze moved to the paintbrush. "I could give you a hand if you want?"

"No," he said quickly, "you're on holiday."

She winkled her nose. "I enjoyed helping yesterday."

"You might be crazy, you know?"

"I know," she said. "It has occurred to me."

They stood in silence, gazing intensely at each other. Biting her lip, Elizabeth took a step back. "Sorry," she said. "I'm going to stop wandering into your garden, I promise. I was going to go for a swim anyway … I just thought … I don't know." Why was she so awkward? She almost fell over her own feet as she moved away from him. "See you!"

"Lizzie!" he called when she was almost inside. She stopped in her tracks. "Sorry. Elizabeth."

"Hmm?"

"I could probably do with someone to hold the ladder… If you really don't mind?"

"I *really* don't mind," she said. "I'll get changed and come over."

In her bedroom, she realised she wasn't sure what she'd planned to change into. Apparently she'd neglected to pack painting clothes.

Hannah Ellis

Chapter 15

She ended up in a pair of knee-length tailored shorts and a plain V-necked T-shirt. Not exactly painting clothes, but the things she was least worried about ruining.

When she joined him, Max gave her a paintbrush. "No stripping today, you'll be pleased to hear."

"Is that a promise?" she said, cheekily.

They got to work painting the downstairs windows at the front of the house first, then Elizabeth held the ladder while Max made a start on the upstairs. When she got bored of holding the ladder they swapped places.

"Careful," Max said when she leaned precariously off the ladder to reach the furthest part of the window.

"I am."

"No, really," he said.

She glanced down. "I'm *really* being careful."

"Let's swap again."

"I'm fine," she insisted, reaching out to paint the last corner.

"But I can reach further than you."

"It's all done!" She stretched her arm out and leaned back from the ladder. "Ta-da!"

"Please hold on properly."

Slowly, she made her way down, stopping

halfway and shaking the ladder.

"It's not funny," he said. "You're not going up the ladder again."

"Oh, I see. You used to be a lawyer, didn't you? You're worried I'll break my leg and sue you!"

"No." He held out his hand to her when she neared the bottom. "I'm just worried you'll break a leg."

She caught the concern on his face, and felt bad for teasing him. "What next, then?" she asked. "The back windows?"

He nodded. "Let's stay on the ground for a while."

The sun beat down on them as they worked on the windows at the back of the house, and the atmosphere was relaxed. Elizabeth hummed along to the radio that played in the kitchen. If someone had told her a week ago that she'd end up painting a neighbour's house while she was on holiday, she'd have been horrified, but she was having a great time. The afternoon was punctuated by light chatter and amiable silences, and time flew by.

Max wore a look of concentration as he painted the final window frame. Elizabeth had just finished the window next to him. She surveyed Max. His faded jeans were dotted with paint and smeared with dust. His dark T-shirt clung to his toned body, and his arm muscles flexed as he worked.

"You okay?" he asked.

She averted her gaze. "I was thinking it might be time for a beer." Setting down the paintbrush, she wiped her hands on her shorts. "I'll nip to the shop."

The walk along the winding path into the village

was exhilarating. The sea breeze caught her hair, pulling strands from her clip and whipping them all around. Her arms ached from the painting but she felt a wonderful sense of achievement.

At the seawall in Hope Cove, she gazed out over the bay. A couple of children kicked a ball on the sand. Seagulls squawked, boats bobbed, waves lapped, fluffy clouds floated in the bright blue sky. It was picture perfect and Elizabeth was mesmerised. It reminded her she still needed to collect her painting from the gallery.

A voice caught her attention when she was about to enter the shop and she saw the middle-aged waitress in the apron outside the café.

"When are you coming for that cream tea?" she called happily.

"Tomorrow!" Elizabeth replied. "Definitely tomorrow."

The village really was charming and she felt perfectly content as she did her shopping.

"Doing a spot of decorating?" the cashier asked when she paid for her items.

Elizabeth had been lost in a daydream and snapped her head up, confused.

"My other job's a detective," the woman said brightly, nodding towards Elizabeth's clothes. Elizabeth noticed her shorts were flecked with white paint. "Oh," she said, embarrassed, "yes, we're doing a bit of decorating."

"At Seaside Cottage?"

"Yes!" she said. "How did you know?"

"Lucky guess! It's a beautiful place. How are you getting on?"

"Fine," Elizabeth said. "Just giving the window frames a lick of paint … and me, apparently."

"How's Charlotte these days? I haven't seen her in so long."

"Charlotte?" Elizabeth said.

The cashier gave her a puzzled look. "The owner."

"Oh, right. That Charlotte! I only know her son, Max. Actually, I'm just—" She stopped. It was too complicated. "Never mind. I think Max said Charlotte's fine."

"Glad to hear it." The cashier glanced at the customer waiting behind Elizabeth. "All the best with the decorating."

She picked up her shopping bag. "Thank you."

Outside, she peered at her reflection in the shop window. It wasn't just her clothes that were splattered with paint, but her face and hair too. She frowned for a moment, then her features relaxed and she set off back along the path.

"You could've told me," she said accusingly as she approached Max.

"Told you what?"

"That I was covered in paint!"

He smiled and reached to wipe a thumb across her cheek bone. The paint didn't budge but he tried to wipe another splash of white at her hairline nonetheless.

When their eyes locked, he dropped his hand. "You might need a shower," he said, taking a couple of steps away from her.

"I can't believe I went to the shop like this," she

said.

"It's only paint."

"I know, but I'm a mess. My sister would be proud of me!" There was a pause. "What?" she asked in response to Max's smirk.

"Nothing," he said. "It just seems like you have issues with your sister."

"I have! Josie would dress like this on an average day."

"And that annoys you?"

"No." Elizabeth shook her head, not sure how to explain her sister. "There isn't *one* thing that annoys me about her. It's *everything*."

Max nodded slowly.

"I got beer," Elizabeth said, in an attempt to change the subject. "And dinner too."

"You're cooking for me?"

"Well, I've got a pre-cooked chicken and a pre-prepared salad," she said, passing him a beer and sitting at the worn patio table. "If you call that cooking."

"For a minute there I thought you were going to whip me up some gourmet cuisine."

"I'm on holiday; I don't want to cook." To be honest, she rarely cooked. It had never been her thing. "You didn't have anything else planned for dinner, did you? I can—"

"No," he said, cutting her off. "Chicken is great." He watched her pick at the label on the beer bottle.

"What?" she said.

"Do you usually drink beer?"

She mulled it over, as though it was a difficult question.

"You seem like more of a wine drinker, that's all…"

He was right; she rarely drank beer at home. Phil was a wine connoisseur, with a decent collection of what he deemed to be excellent wines. She'd always been happy to drink wine with him.

"The beer's refreshing," she said, skirting the question. "I like it."

He nodded and didn't comment further.

Dinner was relaxed and enjoyable. Max told stories about the mischief he'd got up to when he spent summers at Seaside Cottage as a child, and Elizabeth told him about her own childhood holidays, with her parents and her sister in France.

She beamed as she recalled locking Josie in an old wardrobe in a farmhouse they were staying in one year. The memory made her laugh so much that she struggled to finish the story. "I got into so much trouble," she said. "But it was worth it for that half hour of peace!"

Max sat opposite her, his legs stretched out, watching her. It made her self-conscious, and she looked away.

Time had run away from her again. She found herself gazing up at the beautiful starlit sky, wondering how the sun had set and the evening drawn in without her noticing.

"I'd better turn in," she said. "You've worn me out with all the painting."

"You volunteered! Don't go blaming me."

She smiled as she stood and wished him goodnight.

Chapter 16

Generally, Elizabeth slept fitfully. She would toss and turn, and always rose early. There was always so much on her mind that she found it hard to turn off and go to sleep. At Hope Cove, however, sleep came easily and was deep and peaceful. It seemed the more sleep she got, the more she wanted. The bed was comfy, and it was hard to drag herself out of it the next morning.

She called Phil and put her phone on speaker as she dressed.

"All okay?" he asked.

"You didn't call yesterday," she said. Not that it had bothered her. She'd only realised when she was getting up.

"Sorry. Work's crazy."

"Don't worry. You sound busy – shall we talk later?"

"Do you mind? I'm just in the middle of something."

"No, it's fine." She actually didn't mind at all. It meant she could be out enjoying the sunshine quicker.

"I'll call you tonight," he said distractedly. "Promise!"

She hung up and cheerfully made her way outside. Max was sipping a coffee on the patio. He seemed refreshed and relaxed as he waved to her through the hedge.

"I thought you'd be hard at work already," Elizabeth said, wandering over to him.

"I've only just woken up."

"Me too. I feel like I could sleep for a week. I'm usually up at the crack of dawn. I don't know what it is about this place."

"It's the sea air," he said. "But I'm glad you slept well. You're on ladder-holding duty today."

"Oh, really?" she said. "I'm on holiday, you know!"

"I know. I kept trying to tell you that. But you seem to like to work so I figure I'm doing you a favour."

Was she cheating if she just substituted one kind of work for another? Painting was far too much fun to be considered work, though. Helping Max had definitely taken her mind off work, and she was proud she'd managed to avoid checking her emails. She was more than happy to help with the painting again. Her plan for the morning had been to drive to the gallery to collect her painting, and indulge in a scone while she was in the village, but that could wait.

"Okay," she agreed. "I'll get breakfast and then come and help."

"Thank you!" he called as she walked back to the kitchen.

***

"Could you maybe take the ladder-holding business a bit more seriously?" Max asked later, from the top of the ladder. She rested one hand casually on a rung as she stared at the garden in a daydream.

"I've got it," she said, standing straighter and putting two hands on the ladder.

"You don't make me feel very safe."

"I should have warned you – I'm not very strong, so if the ladder starts to fall, there's probably not much I can do about it."

He chuckled. "You're filling me with confidence! But you realise you're supposed to hold the ladder so it doesn't start to fall?"

"Oh, right."

The ladder juddered as he climbed back down. He moved it to the next window. "Maybe you should paint. I don't feel safe with you holding the ladder."

"You had nothing to worry about. If you fell, I'd be there to call an ambulance. I'd even hold your hand until it arrived."

"I feel much better knowing that," he said dryly. "You want to paint?"

She hesitated and then took the tin of paint from him. It was a fresh tin and she almost dropped it as her muscles complained at its weight. The real reason she'd been relaxed about holding the ladder was because her arms ached so much that she couldn't lift them higher than her waist. The previous day's painting had left her in agony. She wasn't used to so much physical work. But she didn't like to complain, worried that Max would shoo her away if she said anything.

It was painful carrying the paint up the ladder and she was glad when she carefully hooked the handle over the prong which stuck out from one side of the ladder. If it weren't for that clever little device she'd never manage the painting. Her muscles screamed with every stroke of the paintbrush, but she pushed through and managed to get it done.

"Now look who's only got one hand on the ladder," she remarked, glancing down at Max.

"You've got nothing to worry about," he called up to her. "Well, the ladder's not going to fall. But you might if you try your Catwoman moves again!"

"You'd catch me, wouldn't you?"

"I doubt it," he said playfully. "I'd get out of the way quick."

"Thanks!"

"Don't worry; I'd hold your hand until the paramedics arrived."

She started down the ladder. "I think that's the main job of the ladder-holder." Back on the ground, she massaged her right bicep. "Are we done yet?" she asked hopefully.

"Not quite," he said. "But if you've had enough…"

"It's fine," she said. "I was kidding. I'm going to hold the ladder for a while, though: my painting arm aches a bit." It was possibly the greatest understatement of all time. Every tiny movement sent a searing pain through her arm. But she didn't want to leave Max.

Max painted the remainder of the upstairs windows while she made some pretence of ensuring ladder safety. When he stepped off the ladder for the final time, sweat had soaked through his T-shirt. He rolled his shoulders and stretched his neck.

"Okay," he said, flopping into a chair and leaning back. "I'm done in. I think I'll go for a quick swim.

Do you want to join me?"

"No, I'm okay," she said. "I'll get started on the downstairs." Truthfully, a swim sounded great but she was feeling guilty again about all the time she was spending with Max. Helping him paint was one thing, but hanging out with him in her bikini was something else. She wondered how she'd feel if she thought Phil were off frolicking in the sea with another woman. Not that she'd be frolicking, obviously. But still.

She picked up a paintbrush and got started on the downstairs windows, trying to paint left-handed to give her right arm a rest. When Max returned, his T-shirt was slung over his shoulder, and seawater dripped down his toned torso. He grabbed a paintbrush and started to work on the window next to Elizabeth.

She enjoyed the painting, despite her painful muscles. It felt therapeutic. She smiled at Max and then looked away, not daring to linger too long on the sight of his bare chest.

They made good progress, stopping for a quick lunch of chicken sandwiches made from the leftovers from the previous evening's dinner. It was late afternoon when they finally downed tools.

"All done," Max said. "And I think it looks good."

Elizabeth wiped her hands on her shorts and pushed a strand of hair behind her ear. "I just hope the new owners like white." She felt an odd sadness at having finished the job. It had been very enjoyable and she could've happily spent another day at it. Although, come to think of it, she'd probably struggle to lift her arms for the next day or two, never mind paint anything. Besides, she still had lots of sightseeing and exploring to do.

"Come on," Max said. "I'll treat you to dinner."

"Oh," she said, surprised. "I need to jump in the shower."

"Don't worry about it. We're not going anywhere fancy." There was an air of mischief about him as he set off down the garden, glancing back to check she was following.

"Okay," she agreed.

"You won't feel out of place where we're going, I promise."

She knew she had at least a few flecks of paint on her face and more in her hair, but decided it probably didn't matter.

At Hope Cove she waited on the seawall as Max had instructed. He appeared five minutes later and gave her a tray of fish and chips, then sat on the wall beside her.

"The best dinner around," he said. "And you're definitely not underdressed."

She picked up the wooden fork and tucked in with gusto. "This is amazing, thank you."

"You're welcome," he said. "Thanks for all your help with the house."

"I think it's me who should be thanking you. It's been fun. I didn't realise how much I needed a break from reality."

"Me too," he said thoughtfully.

"I haven't checked my phone all day," she said, surprised that it had only just occurred to her. "Phil reckoned I couldn't manage without checking in at work."

"Why would you check in with work when you're away?"

"It's not always so easy to switch off."

"Ah," he said. "You're one of those people."

"What people?"

"People who think the company will fall apart if they're not there! What do you do, anyway?"

"I'm a magazine editor," she told him.

"That's understandable, then. If you take too much time off, people won't have magazines to read. Disaster!"

"You're such a tease," she said, popping another chip into her mouth. "I still can't believe how my week's turning out. Isn't it weird that I just met you and ended up helping you paint?"

He shook his head and swallowed his mouthful of fish. "It doesn't feel weird at all. It feels like I've known you forever." He held her gaze for a moment and then resumed eating.

Elizabeth's appetite had vanished. She moved her attention to the waves rolling onto the shore while she waited for her heart rate to return to a normal rhythm.

When Phil called that evening and asked about her day, she found herself omitting critical details because they were too difficult to explain: Max, and painting the cottage next door. Instead, she said she'd enjoyed the sunshine, and she'd walked into the village and had fish and chips for dinner. She wasn't actually lying.

And when she went to bed with those annoying pangs of guilt, she told herself it was all entirely innocent, and it wasn't a big deal that she hadn't told

Phil the truth about her day.

The painting was all finished anyway, so she wouldn't be spending any more time with Max.

Chapter 17

Elizabeth beamed when Max appeared at the kitchen window the next morning. "Don't tell me the cottage needs another coat of paint?"

"No," he said. "I promise I'm not going to rope you into any more work."

"Phew!"

"I wondered if I could take you to lunch later? A proper lunch, not chips on a wall."

"Erm…"

"I wanted to thank you properly for all your help."

"You don't need to," she said. "I was happy to help."

He leaned on the doorframe. "You'd be doing me a favour. The restaurant at the golf club does great food, but I hate eating out alone."

She glanced out of the window as though something had caught her eye, stalling for time. Should she really go out for lunch with another man?

"The food's amazing," Max said. "We could head up to the driving range too, if you fancy it. Not sure I can manage a round of golf, but I wouldn't mind a few swings."

There was a little voice in her head which was adamant she should be saying no. She was engaged and it really wasn't appropriate for her to spend so much time with Max. But it was hard to resist when he was such easy company.

"Lunch sounds good," she said, ignoring the voice in her head. "But I'll pass on the driving range. I'm more of a crazy golf kind of person."

"I'm sure you're teasing me with the crazy golf. I bet you've got a wardrobe full of fancy golfing outfits and would show me up on the green."

"I wouldn't," she assured him lightly.

"I'm still not sure I believe you! Anyway, I've got some stuff to do first. Is a late lunch okay? We could walk up there."

"Sounds lovely."

The pesky voice in Elizabeth's head insisted she shouldn't be going out for a lovely walk and fancy lunch with an attractive man who wasn't her fiancé. But she convinced herself that it was innocent. Max only wanted to say thank you, and it did solve the problem of eating out alone. They were both spoken for, so there wasn't any harm in it. Surely.

That's what she kept telling herself when she drove over to pick up her beautiful painting from the gallery, and as she enjoyed a cup of tea and a scone loaded up with strawberry jam and cream. She'd had a good natter with her friend in the café who Elizabeth learned was the owner of the place and called Verity. It was another pleasant morning and Elizabeth marvelled at how warm and welcoming the people in Hope Cove were.

***

"Are you sure you don't want to spend half an hour at

the driving range?" Max asked when they approached the clubhouse.

"I'd really rather not."

"Please…" He stuck his bottom lip out. "I haven't swung a club in ages. It'll be fun, I promise."

His big blue eyes were hard to resist. "Go on, then. But we're getting the smallest bucket of balls. I'm hungry!"

The driving range was empty apart from an older guy at the far end. Elizabeth rolled her eyes when Max offered to give her some tips. Moving past him with a nine iron, she placed the ball on the tee. Her swing was perfect, starting at her hips and moving through her shoulders. Her backswing was crisp. The club swung neatly and connected with the ball to send it far out into the field.

"Oh," Max said, in obvious surprise. "Beginner's luck?"

Elizabeth couldn't help but feel smug. He'd been right about the golf outfits; she had several. Phil had insisted she learn when they first got together, to ensure they had a hobby in common. She was a natural and it irked Phil that after only a few months of lessons she was more skilled than he was, even though he'd been playing since childhood. He also took the game very seriously. Elizabeth enjoyed golf for the fresh air and social aspects, whereas Phil tended to be competitive.

"Why didn't you want to play?" Max asked. "Did you think it would hurt my ego?"

"It's not that," she said, wincing slightly as she put the club aside. "My arms are agony from the painting. I was worried I'd struggle to lift a knife and fork, never mind swing a golf club."

"Why didn't you say so?"

"I didn't want to seem like a wimp!" She rolled her shoulders to release some of the tension. "I'll just watch you."

"You might be able to give *me* some tips," he said sheepishly.

"I see. You wanted to show off!" She gave him a playful nudge when she passed him. "Now you're embarrassed that I'm better than you?"

"Who said you're better than me?"

"Come on, then. Show me what you've got!"

He also had good form. After the first couple of balls he relaxed and forgot he had an audience. His swing was effortless. Elizabeth enjoyed watching him and completely forgot how hungry she was until they returned the clubs and ambled over to the restaurant.

The terrace of the restaurant had a fantastic view of the golf course to one side and the English Channel to the other. It was clearly a popular dining spot, as most of the tables were occupied. They were shown to a table and spent a few minutes inspecting the menu before ordering.

They clinked their glasses together when the drinks arrived and chatted easily. After watching Max at the driving range, Elizabeth announced she thought they were an evenly matched golfing pair. Her brain quickly flashed up an image of a relaxed day on the course with him. It was like watching an old-fashioned film reel, the images flicking quickly past. It was something that would never happen, of course. It was already Wednesday and she'd be back to real life soon.

"What's wrong?" Max asked when the food arrived.

She smiled quickly. "Nothing. I'm fine."

"You're a terrible liar," Max said. "Something's bothering you."

She shook her head. "Honestly, I'm fine."

"You're lying to me a lot today."

"When have I lied to you?"

He popped a mouthful of lamb in his mouth and chewed slowly, watching her with amusement. Finally, he swallowed and said, "Crazy golf."

She was about to protest, but instead her face creased with laughter. "Okay. That might have been a lie. But just a white lie!"

"You've never played crazy golf, have you?"

"No," she said.

"I'll probably never believe anything you tell me ever again."

Elizabeth's laughter fizzled out. She couldn't help but think about the fact that she'd be home again soon and there'd be no more joking around with Max. Coming to Devon alone had caused her so much worry, and now she was worrying that time was going too fast. She shifted her focus to her food and tried not to think about it.

"Do you play often?" she asked a few minutes later, as they watched a couple of golfers strolling along the fairway in the distance.

"No," he said. "I used to play with my dad, but he died a few years ago."

"Sorry," she said softly.

His eyes met hers and his warm smile returned. "Thanks. We were really close. And all my favourite memories of him seem to be from times at Hope Cove. I keep wishing Mum wasn't selling the cottage."

"It must be hard." Again, she wondered why he didn't buy the place himself. He hadn't answered when she'd asked him before but somehow she didn't feel she should probe him on the subject.

He sat up straighter. "Sorry. I'm not the most cheerful company, am I?"

"I don't mind." She was enjoying finding more about him.

They bumped shoulders regularly as they ambled along the narrow path on the way home. Conversation was light and even silly. Elizabeth couldn't remember laughing so much in ages. They stopped for ice cream at South Milton Sands. The beach was packed – no wonder, on such a beautiful day in the school holidays.

When they finally reached the little bay that Elizabeth had come to think of as theirs, the sun hung just above the horizon. The path wound down to the small beach and they had to watch their footing.

"The water looks fantastic," Elizabeth said.

"It does," Max said. "Fancy a dip?"

She gazed out at the tranquil water, sorely tempted.

"I'll get my swimsuit," she said.

Her phone rang five minutes later, as she was heading out of the back door in her bikini. It was Phil. His presentation would be over, and hopefully he'd be more relaxed. She reached for the phone, then hesitated. Quickly, she replaced the phone on the kitchen table, leaving it to ring, and went outside.

Hannah Ellis

Chapter 18

Elizabeth shivered as she waded slowly into the water, eventually working up the courage to submerge herself. Her breath caught as the cold water enveloped her and she waited for her body to get used to it.

"It's fine after a few minutes," Max assured her. He dived under the water, and she followed as he swam further out. "Definitely good for your poor aching muscles," he said when he reappeared. "I can't believe you talked me into painting the windows."

"It wasn't me! It was all Conor's idea."

"You backed him up!"

"It was fun." She swam around him. "You enjoyed it too. Admit it."

He stood up in the water. They'd swum out a fair distance, but the water was still only up to his chest. "Okay. It was fun. I'm glad you helped."

Her heart rate increased when he looked at her. His eyes were so blue, it was hard not to stare at them. "Are the sunsets here always this stunning?" she asked, changing the subject. As she stood on the seabed, her left foot landed on a jagged shell and she hopped for a moment until Max reached out to steady her. She held on to him while she reached to brush the shell from her foot. When she regained her balance, she realised how close they were and hastily moved away.

"It's absolutely stunning," she called to him as she swam, remarking again on the sunset. She had to say something to break the tension. At that moment, with his hand on her arm, all she'd wanted to do was kiss him. And that was why she'd had reservations about going out for lunch with him. She enjoyed his company far too much.

How on earth had she convinced herself that it was okay to spend all her time with him? And go swimming with him at sunset? What had come over her? She was always so in control. Always rational and logical. But since she'd arrived at Hope Cove she'd been anything but.

They swam for a little longer until Elizabeth started to shiver and Max insisted they go and warm up. "The towel was a great idea," Max said as Elizabeth wrapped herself up on the beach. "You could've brought me one."

"You're a big boy," she said. "You need to learn to look after yourself." She cringed at her choice of words, given that he was standing in just his wet boxer shorts. He was no doubt smirking, but she carefully avoided eye contact. Why had her brain gone there? It was only an innocent comment. She was losing the plot.

They walked quickly up the beach, slowing when they reached the path.

"I'm going to get the fire going, if you want to come over for a drink," Max said.

"That sounds great." Actually, it sounded perfect, but she knew she should decline. It would definitely be inappropriate to spend the evening in front of the fire with him.

"I'll get showered and come over," she said after a pause.

The warm shower was bliss, and she slipped straight into her pyjamas when she got out. Her senses had returned. She knew she couldn't go over to Seaside Cottage. Something had shifted and everything felt wrong. She shouldn't be spending all her time with Max when she was engaged to Phil.

Phil! She remembered the phone call she'd missed and felt awful. She'd ignored his call to spend time with Max. What on earth was going on with her?

His phone only rang once before Phil answered.

"Sorry," she said. "I was on the beach and only just saw your call."

"Don't worry. I haven't been home long."

"How was the presentation?"

"It went well," he said. "I think things are calming down again so hopefully next week will be quieter. It's a big relief to get that over with. When are you back? Friday? I thought about driving down but I've still got a few things I need to do in the office tomorrow."

"That's fine. Don't worry." She hesitated. "Actually, I was thinking about coming home earlier. Will you have time for dinner with me if I drive back tomorrow?" That would be the sensible thing to do – go back home to her fiancé where she belonged.

"Probably," he said. "But don't feel that you've got to rush back for me. We can have dinner on Friday night."

"Traffic will probably be crazy on Friday too," she mused, trying to talk herself into it.

"Come tomorrow, then."

"I think I will. By the way, you'll be very proud of me; I've not checked my work emails once."

"Wow," he said. "That's impressive. What's keeping you so distracted?" His words were light and jokey but the question unnerved Elizabeth and she felt a rush of guilt.

"Just the beach and the sunshine," she replied quickly.

"I bet there's no internet," Phil said. "Is that why you want to come home early?"

"I wanted to see you," she said, sounding tenser than she'd intended. "But if you're going to tease me, I won't bother."

"Don't be daft. I want to see you too. Come home tomorrow."

"I'll let you know when I'm setting off."

They wished each other goodnight and hung up.

She looked out of the window and down into the garden of Seaside Cottage. There was a glow from the living room window and she imagined the fire – and Max. She considered going over for a drink. She'd said she would, after all. Max would be waiting for her. Instead, she picked up the phone again and called Karen.

"I need you in serious and sensible mode," she said firmly.

"Okay," Karen said. "What's up?"

"It's the guy in the next cottage," Elizabeth said. "Max. I have a crush on him."

There, she'd said it. It was out in the open. She was recognising the problem and taking control.

"I don't know what to do."

"Oh! I hate that you want sensible advice…"

"Please," Elizabeth said.

"Okay, okay. I guess you need to stay away from him." There was a definite hint of eye-rolling to Karen's voice, but otherwise it was exactly what Elizabeth needed to hear.

"It's so difficult. I keep telling myself it's innocent, but I definitely have a crush on him. He invited me over for a drink this evening, but I shouldn't go, should I?"

"A drink at his place?"

"Yeah, we went for a swim while the sun set, and he was going to go and light the fire. He invited me to join him."

Laughter erupted down the phone. "Oh, my God!" Karen shrieked. "I thought you were talking about a harmless flirtation. But sunset swimming? Drinks by the fire? No, you need to stay well away. And this is my actual opinion, not me being sensible because you've asked me to."

"Really?"

"Who am I speaking to?" Karen asked. "This isn't you. Do not go over there. Drinks in front of the fire after a sunset swim pretty much always end with sex, and you're not a cheater."

"I'm not going to have sex with him. It's just a drink."

"Fine. But please call Phil and get his opinion on the matter before you go over there. If it's so innocent, I'm sure he won't mind."

Elizabeth rubbed her eyes. Karen was right.

"This is something *I'd* do," Karen said, "not you. And I'm divorced, by the way, so that's a clue as to how these things turn out."

Elizabeth knew just how badly Karen had been hurt by her divorce, and knew she would never seriously advise anyone to do anything to jeopardise their relationship.

"I know, I know. I just really like him. And it's so lovely to spend time with someone who isn't constantly looking at their phone or their laptop."

"Only because he's trying to get in your knickers!"

"It's not like that. He's a good guy. He's got a girlfriend. I think they're engaged." She'd gathered that much from Conor but hadn't specifically asked.

"Really?" Karen said. "Stay away from him, anyway. Sounds like he has a crush on you too."

"Do you think so?"

"Oh, wow. You really like him, don't you?"

"No," Elizabeth said sulkily. "I love Phil. I'm just having a crisis."

Oh, flipping heck, was she actually having a mid-life crisis? An affair with a younger man? A year younger surely didn't classify him as a younger man. And it wasn't an affair!

"I'm going to go home tomorrow. See Phil. Sort my head out."

"That sounds like a good idea," Karen said. "Stay away from this Max guy. You'll only end up getting hurt."

"Thanks," Elizabeth said. It was sage advice that she shouldn't have needed to ask for. She flopped onto the bed when she ended the call.

For the first time since she'd arrived in Hope Cove, sleep didn't come easily. Her mind whirred for hours before she finally fell asleep.

Chapter 19

She'd hoped to catch the sunrise on her last day in Hope Cove, but after falling asleep so late, Elizabeth didn't wake until mid-morning. She packed her bag and then went to say goodbye to Max. She'd make it quick and painless and be on her way.

Did she really have a crush on him? It was probably just the lovely meal and the romantic moonlit swim that made her feel that way. She'd say goodbye to him and get back to Phil. Not a problem. She was cool. She was calm. She was just saying goodbye.

He was in the kitchen making coffee, and smiled when she put her head round the door.

"Morning," he said. "Sleep well?"

"Yes. I was worn out. I only meant to sit for a minute after my shower and I went out like a light."

She got the distinct impression he knew she was lying. There was a moment of awkwardness before they spoke at once.

"Sorry," Elizabeth said. "You go."

"I was going to say you only just caught me; I was going to head out for a drive since the painting's finished."

That was her cue to say she was leaving. Say goodbye, wish him well and get on her way. But her brain and mouth seemed to be having some sort of disagreement.

"You could come with me if you want," he said. There was vulnerability in his eyes and he backtracked quickly. "But you've probably got plans. I've taken up enough of your time…"

"No," she blurted out, "I'd like to come. But I thought you might like some time alone."

He held a cup of coffee out to her. "Not really."

"Where are we going, then?" she asked. Their fingers brushed as she took the cup.

"You'll see. I just need a quick shower first."

"I don't really like surprises!" she called after him, but she was intrigued nonetheless.

***

The winding roads snaked through the countryside and Elizabeth looked out over green fields separated by crumbling old walls. They passed farmhouses and a few villages. For a while they drove with a large wooded area to their left and Elizabeth peered between the dense trees.

"Where are you taking me?" she asked after half an hour.

There was mischief in Max's eyes. "To visit my dog."

"You have a dog?"

"Kind of," he said.

"How can you kind of have a dog?"

He didn't reply but soon stopped the car at a wooden gate. Beyond it, a long driveway ran up to an old stone farmhouse. Smoke plumed from the chimney. A sign by the gate read *Oakbrook Farm: Boarding Home for Dogs.*

"We're here," Max said.

"So you really have a dog?"

"No. Not really." He frowned and then laughed at Elizabeth's puzzled expression. "I always wanted a dog. When I was a kid, I begged my parents for one, but Mum isn't a dog person. Dad used to bring here. I'd always have a favourite dog and I used to tell people I had a dog but it lived on a farm. I didn't realise when I got sympathetic looks that people assumed my dog had died and my parents had fed me the old line about a farm. As far as I was concerned, I really did have a dog who lived on a farm."

"And you still visit?"

"Yes!"

"But you're a grown man! Why not just get a dog if you want one so much?"

Elizabeth realised the reason why when Max frowned. "Still not allowed one," he said, rolling his eyes. "Come on."

The reminder of his girlfriend made Elizabeth's chest tighten. At the same time she realised she hadn't messaged Phil to tell him of her plans. But he wouldn't be expecting her back until the evening anyway. She'd drive home later and message him when she set off.

A dog howled as they walked up the long driveway, and a figure appeared on the porch as they neared the house.

"I should warn you, the owners are slightly eccentric," Max said. "They're actually family. My aunt and her partner. That's why I still visit."

Three dogs bounded towards them. A beautiful golden retriever arrived first, forgetting to stop and crashing into Max's leg.

"Hey, Charlie!" he said, bending to stroke the happy dog. Two smaller dogs barrelled in next and vied for Max's attention. He greeted them joyfully as they jumped around him, tails wagging furiously. Elizabeth crouched beside Max, chuckling as the smallest dog jumped up to lick her face. "That's Macy," he told her. "She can be a bit over-affectionate." Elizabeth laughed and put a hand on Max's shoulder to steady herself as she reached to rub behind Macy's ear.

"I take it you're not the one who's allergic?" a voice said loudly.

A grey-haired woman loomed over them. She stood confidently, with her hands on her hips and a grin on her face.

"Hi, Annette," Max said, standing to hug her. "This is my friend, Lizzie."

"Definitely not allergic," Elizabeth said, extending her hand.

"No one really is," Annette said. "Pet allergies are a myth made up by—"

"All right, all right!" Max said. Apparently he'd heard that before. "Is there any coffee going or what?"

"Doesn't seem two minutes since we were feeding him milk and biscuits," Annette said, shaking her head and moving towards the house. "Wendy!" she shouted. "Come and see who's here."

Another woman limped slowly outside. She wore a cross-body handbag and walked slightly hunched over. Her hair had obviously dulled with age but was

118

still a striking shade of copper. She looked weary but brightened immediately at the sight of Max. She wrapped her arms around him. "Next time, let me know you're coming. I've got a doctor's appointment – I was just heading out."

"Sorry. It was a spur of the moment thing," he said. She finally registered Elizabeth and smiled warmly at her, waiting for an introduction. "This is Lizzie," Max told her, without explanation. "Lizzie, this is Wendy."

Wendy's curiosity was only evident in the slight dip of her eyebrows. "Nice to meet you, Lizzie. Sorry, I'm afraid I'm in a rush."

"Are you sure you're okay going alone?" Annette asked when Wendy gave her a kiss on the lips. "I could drive you."

"I'm fine," Wendy replied, patting Annette's cheek. "Stop fussing over me." Wendy turned back to Max. "Come again soon, won't you?"

He followed her to her car. When Annette went inside, Elizabeth wandered over to sit on the porch, beaming and fussing over the three dogs that surrounded her. As soon as she stroked one, another would tussle to move into its place.

When Elizabeth looked up, Max was watching her. The intensity of his gaze made her stomach flutter.

"Annette went to get coffee," she said as he joined her. When he sat beside her, the little dog, Macy, jumped into his lap. Max stroked the excitable pup.

"She's so cute," Elizabeth said, reaching out to stroke her. When Max's fingers brushed hers, she didn't think much of it, but the second time he stroked her hand instead of the dog, she knew it was no accident.

She pulled away. She knew she should have gone home that morning. But part of her was glad she hadn't.

Standing quickly, she put some distance between her and Max, lingering at the edge of the patio. It was a large property, bordered by a wooden fence and dotted with sturdy old trees. Beyond the fence, fields rolled away in every direction, all beautifully green. From the house there was a path worn into the grass leading to a barn a little way off. Dogs could be heard barking occasionally, but otherwise it was peaceful.

"Won't they ask questions about me?" Elizabeth asked finally. "Isn't it weird that you're visiting with me and not your fiancée?"

"Jessica's allergic to dogs," he said. "She's never been here."

"But surely they'll wonder…"

"Yes," he said. "They'll want to know everything."

"Aren't you worried that they'll say something to your family?"

"I'm the only one who has anything to do with Annette and Wendy since Dad died. There was some feud years back between them and my mum, so none of the rest of the family has anything to do with them. My dad and I were the only ones who ever came out here. Besides, I'm allowed to have friends, aren't I?" Again, his gaze was far too intense, as though he was daring her to comment on their friendship.

"Coffee!" Annette announced, breaking the

atmosphere as she arrived carrying a tray loaded with three mugs and a plate of biscuits.

"I assume there are more dogs here somewhere?" Elizabeth asked. Taking a biscuit, she dunked it into her coffee – something she wouldn't usually do.

"Oh, plenty!" Annette said. "I'll show you around later."

"They're out in the stables," Max said.

"In the *stables*?"

"It's a doggy paradise here. Kennels just wouldn't do!"

Annette swiped playfully at Max. "It's a barn, really, but it was used as stables when we bought the place," she explained. "We thought it would be nice to keep it as it was – with a few adjustments."

"The dogs that stay here get spoiled rotten," Max said. "They cry when their owners come back for them."

"No, they don't!" Annette said. "Okay, some of them do."

"It's a beautiful place," Elizabeth said, looking out over the fields. "I'd love to live somewhere so quiet." She'd always thought of herself as a city girl but she really meant what she said. She imagined herself living somewhere so peaceful. Yes, she could definitely see it – but what she actually imagined was living at Hope Cove.

"What?" Max asked, breaking into her thoughts. She hadn't realised she was smiling.

"Nothing," she said. "I was daydreaming. Sorry."

"It's a great spot for daydreaming," Annette said, her warmth and easy nature putting Elizabeth at ease.

"How did you end up here?" Elizabeth asked. "I

mean, how did you get into the kennels business?"

"It's what I'd always wanted to do. Not exactly this, but I always wanted to work with animals and I wanted to live in the country. I met Wendy when we were in our twenties. She wanted the same as me. At that time she had an office job and hated it. We found this place going cheap. Once upon a time, it was a working farm and we were even tempted to give farming a go when we bought the place. We had dreams of keeping cows and chickens and living off the land! We soon came to our senses and decided dogs were enough for us. So we kept the name, Oakbrook Farm, and kidded ourselves that we were farmers with our measly little vegetable patch." She stopped and looked around. "I have everything I want, right here."

"That's amazing," Elizabeth said.

Max set his mug down. "Come on. You need to see the rest of the place."

The dogs went crazy when the barn door opened, and Annette immediately calmed them with her soothing voice.

"It's gorgeous," Elizabeth whispered as she ventured in. The stalls were red brick with the original stable doors still in place. The front of each stall had a large Perspex window and the dogs pushed their noses up to look out. Small blackboards hung on each door with the names of the dogs written neatly in white chalk.

Max followed Elizabeth as she peered into each stall, greeting the dogs by name.

"I'm gonna take these two out for a run," Annette

called, releasing a couple of dogs. "Look at the husky at the end, Max. She's beautiful – and a big softie. You'll love her."

"They all have an outdoor enclosure too," Max said, pointing to a door at the back of one of the stalls. His pride in the place was evident in his tone. When they reached the far end, he unlatched the door to the stall belonging to Talia, the husky. She was stunning.

"Hello!" Elizabeth said, approaching the dog who sat obediently and lifted a paw. "Aren't you lovely?" She took her paw and looked into her stunning blue eyes. "She's got the same eyes as you," she said as Max crouched beside her.

He raised an eyebrow. "I'm not sure how to take that…"

"It's a compliment! She's got beautiful eyes."

Max had that look again. Smouldering and intense. It made her stomach flutter.

Talia nudged her head against Max and he shifted his focus to the dog, stroking her head and her back.

"Come on," he said after a few minutes. "There's somewhere else I want to show you."

Chapter 20

There was a spring in Max's step as he led the way to the back of the barn and hopped over the fence behind. "Won't be long," he shouted to Annette, then held out a hand to help Elizabeth. She felt completely at ease on the farm, and was glad Max had invited her along.

They stopped at the top of the hill. "See the house there?" Max said, pointing to a little house that stood halfway down the hill on the left. "My friend Sam lived there. We used to go off exploring together. Sometimes, I'd stay for a weekend and we'd run around the fields, climbing trees and playing in the stream."

"It sounds amazing."

"I'll show you the stream," he said, heading down the other side of the hill.

"What happened to Sam?"

"He still lives there. He moved away for a while, then came back and bought the place from his parents. He's a good guy – he helps Wendy and Annette out a lot. And he's still one of my best friends."

They came to the small stream that ran through the valley. It was bordered by scattered trees and Elizabeth sat on a rock by the trickling water.

"I can see why you liked playing here," she said,

taking it all in. "It's a kid's paradise."

"I hardly ever venture down here any more. Occasionally, I'll come and walk the dogs this way. It's still one of my favourite places."

He quietly surveyed the area with an air of contentment and nostalgia. It must have been a great place to play. Elizabeth didn't remember ever having the freedom to explore the outdoors as a child. There had always been an adult supervising play.

When Max caught Elizabeth watching him she snatched her gaze away.

"Shall we head back?" he asked.

"Okay." She stood, then looked around once more. "Or maybe we could go a bit further? I'll be back to city life soon – I may as well make the most of the countryside."

"Suits me," he said. "Why did you have to mention going home? Back to the real world. And work!" He sighed. "I'd rather not think about it."

"What do you do?" she asked, realising she still didn't really know.

"I'm a lawyer," he said, falling into step beside her. "Just not the big hot-shot kind!"

"And you work for a cosmetics company?"

"Yes," he said. "I'm an in-house legal consultant."

"Do you enjoy it?"

"Yeah," he said. "It's okay, and I work with good people. There's generally not a lot of stress."

"And you can take time off when you want?"

"Not really. It's the same as any job. I took holiday time this week." He paused. "But it's not the sort of place where you're expected to put the job before everything else in your life."

She followed Max across the stream via a couple of stepping-stones. "That's why you changed jobs?"

He nodded. "When I worked for the law firm, it was crazy. And I was so caught up in it, I didn't realise how crazy it was. Then my dad died and I spent a lot of time in discussions about how much time was reasonable to take off. It was a bit of a wake-up call. I don't want to work with people who have no compassion."

Elizabeth's eyes narrowed. "So what's your priority now? If it's not work?"

"Good question. I had great intentions of spending time here. Wendy's struggling with arthritis and I'd like to help out. But it's quite a trek from London, and Jessica's never keen to come." He went quiet. "I ought to make more effort. Annette and Wendy have always been good to me. They're my favourite family members."

"Do you want kids?" She blurted out, unable to stop herself. She felt herself blush. Why had she asked him that? Her mouth seemed to run away with her around Max.

His mouth twitched into a half-smile. "Yes. Maybe that's why I wanted work to take a back seat too. My dad was always there for us. Mum worked a lot." He paused. "She was the hot-shot lawyer whose footsteps we followed in."

"So you'll be a stay-at-home dad?" she asked, amused and impressed by the idea.

"I don't know," he said. "But I definitely wouldn't be against it. We'll see. Why are we talking about me so much? What about you? Kids?"

"I'm not sure. I can't really imagine having kids. I'd have to give up my career and I'm not sure I want to do that. Does that sound selfish?"

"A little," he said lightly. "You couldn't convince Phil to be a stay-at-home dad?"

The thought of it amused her. "No."

Max's phone buzzed to life and he pulled it from his pocket.

"Is that work?" Elizabeth asked.

"No," he said, frowning. "Jessica."

Elizabeth's smile dropped slightly before she composed herself. Why should she care that his girlfriend was calling?

"I'll meet you at the top of the hill," she said, and then set off at a good pace, giving him some privacy. She walked briskly, and was out of breath when she reached the crest. Sitting on the grass, she took in the view. You could see for miles. Mainly fields, with narrow roads weaving between. Not too far off was a village with a scattering of buildings and a church with a spire. It was all very pretty.

"Sorry," Max said when he approached a few minutes later. He sat down and sighed. "I didn't tell Jessica about you. I should have, but it was hard to explain, and then the longer I went without mentioning it, the harder it was to say something."

"I didn't mention you to Phil either. It seemed difficult to explain." Idly, she plucked a daisy from the grass between them. "I can't believe I spent a week painting window frames with you! I might be having a mid-life crisis."

"Don't people usually buy a sports car or have an affair?" he asked, confused.

"Yes!" she said enthusiastically. "That's what I told my sister. She thinks that Phil and me getting married is my mid-life crisis. Because we've been together so long and are only just getting round to it. Another of my little sister's crazy ideas. I'm not even old enough for a mid-life crisis."

"Really?" Max said, smirking.

She gave him a friendly shove and then stood up, reaching out a hand to pull him up. "Let's head back," she said.

"At least if the painting is your mid-life crisis you don't need to worry so much about your marriage."

"That's true," she said. Her face turned serious. "Why isn't Jessica with you this week?"

"She didn't fancy cleaning up the cottage. I can't blame her."

"Yeah," Elizabeth said quietly. She couldn't really understand, though; it was such a magical place, she couldn't imagine not wanting to spend time there. And she'd enjoyed helping Max. "Do you live together?" she asked, curiosity getting the better of her.

"Yes," Max said. "We're engaged."

"Oh, lovely," Elizabeth said, but her mouth went dry and she felt suddenly shaky. "Have you set a date for the wedding?"

"Next July," he said. "You?"

"May," she said.

They carried on back to the farm in silence.

Hannah Ellis

Chapter 21

Annette had a plate of sandwiches waiting when they arrived back at the house. It gave them a convenient excuse to stay longer and for Elizabeth to put off going home for a little while. They drove back to Hope Cove in silence. When the car pulled up at Seaside Cottage, she was filled with anxiety at the thought of going home.

In truth, it wasn't what she was going back to that was the problem, but what she'd be leaving behind. It wasn't just the peaceful surroundings and stunning scenery that had made her time at Hope Cove so special.

"Do you want to have dinner with me tonight?" Max asked as they stood in front of the house. "I was just going to throw some pasta together. Or have you finally had enough of me?"

Elizabeth bit her lip and tried desperately to collect her thoughts and think rationally. She was supposed to have dinner with Phil, although a glance at her watch told her it was probably already too late for that. She felt torn. A big part of her knew she shouldn't have dinner with Max – mainly because of how badly she wanted to.

"I'd love to," she said.

It was the wrong decision. She knew that, deep

down. But he was like a magnet pulling her to him and she couldn't do anything about it. "I need to call Phil … and jump in the shower. So I'll come over after that?"

"Great."

What on earth was she doing? she asked herself as she stood under the shower. Had she really fallen for another man? Butterflies stirred in her stomach. She *was* falling for him. It was stupid; she was engaged, for goodness' sake. And she loved Phil. What she should do was get in the car and go back to her fiancé, not have dinner with Max.

Unfortunately, her rational thoughts were being completely overruled.

Phil wasn't at all concerned when she called and told him that the day had got away from her and she'd be home tomorrow as originally planned. He was probably going to be stuck at work until late anyway, he told her.

At that point she should have called Karen again and got her to talk some sense into her. But she purposely didn't call Karen. Instead, she gave in to the part of her that desperately wanted to have dinner with Max.

And then, as if having dinner with a guy she had feelings for wasn't bad enough, she also decided that it would be okay to wear a pretty sundress. It was summer, so it was completely appropriate. It was only because it suited the weather, of course.

For a change, she decided she'd wear her hair down. It wasn't because she was making more effort than usual. Actually, it was no effort to leave her hair down. She wasn't wearing make-up either, so no one could really accuse her of going to any effort for Max.

She did spritz herself with perfume, because it's always good to smell nice.

It was all completely innocent, she told herself when she stepped outside and took a deep breath to calm her nerves. She enjoyed his company, that was all. It wasn't as if anything was going to happen.

She dithered at the back door of Seaside Cottage and then walked around the front instead.

"You look nice," Max said when he let her in.

"You too," she said. And he did. He looked great. He'd obviously made an effort. He wore jeans with a crisp white shirt, sleeves rolled up to reveal his toned forearms. He was all fresh and clean-shaven, and he smelled great. God, he smelled amazing. Why on earth had he put so much aftershave on? What was he trying to do to her?

A fire crackled in the grate in the living room. Even though Max had cleared out the cottage, leaving it fairly bare, it was still cosy and homely.

"I'm not sure it's really cool enough for a fire," he said, "but I like it. And it gets draughty here in the evenings. Make yourself comfy. Do you want wine?"

"Yes, please," she said, feeling awkward. Her emotions were all over the place, and there was a voice in her head shouting at her that she was an idiot and should go home.

That voice grew quieter with wine.

Soon, she was curled on the couch with her legs under her, having eaten a lovely meal of pasta and salad. She was completely at ease.

"So you're all finished with this place?" she asked. There was only really the furniture left.

"I think so." He rested an arm along the back of the couch. "Mum cleared out a lot earlier in the summer. Took all the things she wanted to keep. We were supposed to take anything we wanted and get rid of the rest. And paint the windows," he added with a flicker of a smile. "Mum's hoping whoever buys the place might like to buy the furniture too, but I'm not convinced. I think any buyer would want to modernise."

"It seems a shame," Elizabeth mused. She thought the furniture was lovely. It was mostly oak – solid and sturdy but not old-fashioned. The whole place was beautiful. "None of the family wants to take it on?"

"Nope," Max said.

"Sorry," she said quickly. "I didn't mean to depress you."

His phone rang then, making them jump. He went into the kitchen to answer it, and Elizabeth found herself straining to hear. She couldn't make out any words, but knew from his expression when he'd answered that it was his fiancée.

Elizabeth was gazing into the fire when he returned. The atmosphere had changed. "What's she like?" she asked solemnly. "Jessica?"

"She's kind," he said, settling back into the couch. "And sweet and funny. She's so full of life. Always on the go. She likes to organise people."

"She sounds amazing," Elizabeth said, twirling her wine glass at the stem.

There was a brief pause before Max spoke again. "It annoys me that she won't go to the farm," he said softly. "And she's only been here once."

"How could she not love this place?" Elizabeth

wondered aloud.

"She thinks it's drab."

"Drab?"

"That was the word she used."

Elizabeth surveyed the cosy living room with its roaring fire. She thought of stepping through the hedge at the end of the garden to be met with that incredible view. How could anyone describe it as drab?

"I wanted to buy the place," he said. "But she thinks that if we're going to buy a holiday home it should be somewhere in Europe with more reliable weather."

They fell silent. Elizabeth couldn't think of anything to say. She found herself suddenly nervous again.

Max took her left hand and inspected her engagement ring. "What's *he* like?"

Elizabeth let her hand linger in Max's and struggled again to find any words. "He's nice," she said eventually.

"Nice?" Max said, reaching for his wine.

Elizabeth frowned at her pathetic choice of word. "It's not a bad quality, is it?"

"Not at all."

She thought some more. Surely she could come up with a better adjective than nice? She was marrying him, after all. "He's handsome," she said. "And dependable."

Wow. She wasn't doing a good job of describing him.

"We're similar, I guess. Both work too much. We want the same things out of life…"

"Like what?" Max asked.

"This is starting to feel like an interrogation!"

"I'm just interested," he said. "I can't understand what sort of man would leave you to come here alone."

"Don't say that," she said quickly as a sense of panic crept through her. She knew she was walking on dangerous ground. She shouldn't have agreed to dinner. No good was ever going to come of it.

He persevered, his voice determined. "So what is it you want out of life? What big plans do you have?"

She shot him a warning glance, hoping he'd get the message and back off.

"Sorry," he said. "I've probably had too much wine."

"It's okay." His questions weren't actually the problem; it was the answers that made her uncomfortable. And the way her emotions had become such a jumbled mess over the course of the week.

"So what happens after tomorrow?" he asked gently. "Can we keep in touch?"

Tears pricked her eyes. "No," she whispered, "I don't think we can."

"I thought you might say that."

"I think I should go." She moved to get up, but he laid a hand over hers.

"Sorry," he said. "I didn't mean to make you feel uncomfortable."

"You didn't." It was her own feelings that were making her uncomfortable.

He seemed sad. Without thinking, she reached up and ran her fingers through his hair. When their eyes locked she felt like she was being torn apart. She knew they couldn't stay in touch, but the thought of never seeing him again made her feel sick. Briefly, she closed her eyes and all she was aware of was her racing heart and his soft hair in her fingers.

The fire crackled loudly. She knew she should leave, but couldn't bring herself to move. He didn't flinch when she leaned towards him.

His lips were soft against hers. It was only a fleeting kiss. Barely anything really, just a gentle brush of lips before she came to her senses and pulled back.

"Sorry," she said.

"Don't be."

He followed her to the front door. She'd just touched the handle when he reached for her elbow. Their lips met again as soon as she turned. His hands were on her face and in her hair. She didn't even try to resist, instead pushing her body closer to his until he pinned her against the wall. He kissed her desperately, and then his mouth dropped to her neck and her collarbone. His kisses made her skin tingle.

"Stop," she said, breathlessly. She couldn't do this. "Stop."

After one last kiss on her shoulder, his eyes came up to meet hers. Their bodies remained together and she rested her cheek against his. "Sorry."

"I don't want to leave and never see you again," he whispered, his breath tickling her ear.

She kissed his cheek and breathed in his scent. "I need to go," she said tearfully.

"I don't want to say goodbye to you tomorrow."

"Max," she said, her voice firm and pleading at

the same time. *This was all wrong.*

He took a step back, as though she'd slapped him.

"I'm sorry," she said again. Then she fled without looking back.

Chapter 22

Back at Seaview Cottage she stood in the hallway thinking about what she'd done. She should never have gone over there. It was a stupid, irrational thing to do. She knew things had gone past platonic with Max, and yet she'd gone to see him anyway.

For a while, she wondered if he might follow her. Then, briefly, she thought about going back to him – and not to apologise. His kisses lingered, and part of her wanted more. A big part of her, if she was honest. But none of this was real, she told herself. It was just a silly little holiday romance. Not even that. In the real world she'd never fall for someone like Max. No, she thought, in the real world she'd be with someone like Phil. Dependable, reliable Phil, who wanted the same things out of life as she did.

In the end, she trudged up to bed but couldn't switch her thoughts off and had another night of staring at the ceiling while her mind raced. When she finally fell asleep it was with thoughts of Max – and his kisses.

She was awake again after only a few hours, filled with anxiety at the thought of saying goodbye to Max. What if he really thought there was something meaningful between them? What if he tried to convince her to leave Phil?

And what if he didn't? What if he said it had been the wine talking? What if he wished her well and they went their separate ways?

What if she never saw him again?

Tears stung her eyes.

She set off to watch the sunrise over the beach, hoping it would help her figure things out. There was only the thinnest line of orange stretched across the horizon when she arrived at the top of the beach, but within minutes the sun's rays had burst gloriously across the sky. Everything glittered and glowed: oranges and pinks and yellows filled the sky and splashed onto the water.

Then she saw him sitting on the beach. She wasn't sure how she'd missed him, but it had been dark when she'd arrived, and she wasn't expecting him. He sat gazing at the spectacular display in the sky.

Tears rolled down Elizabeth's cheeks. She could go to him, wrap her arms around him, kiss him… That was what she wanted to do. She didn't want to leave. She wanted to give everything up. They could buy his mum's house and live there together.

Her thoughts were running away from her. She looked back at the cottage. The easiest thing to do would be to get in her car and leave. No goodbyes, no questions, no discussion. She could go and get on with her life. Pretend the week had never happened. But when she turned to catch one last glimpse of Max, she knew she couldn't do it. If she really wanted to go home and get on with her life, she had to say goodbye. She had to draw a line under this. Whatever this was.

He flashed her a sad smile when she reached him.

"You stole my sunrise spot," she said.

"I know, and I don't even have coffee."

She sat close beside him and instinctively leaned her head on his shoulder. It felt so natural to be close to him and… oh, God, did he bathe in aftershave or what? Why did he have to smell so delicious? She didn't ever want to move.

They stayed that way for a while, watching the sunrise and saying nothing. She knew that once she started talking, it would all come to an end. And she wanted to drag things out a little while longer.

"I'm sorry about last night," he said finally.

"If anyone should be sorry, it should be me. I knew I shouldn't come over last night. And I did kiss you first. And I was the one who kept turning up all week."

"To be fair, I kept inviting you places. Even though I knew I shouldn't."

"I don't want to discuss whose fault it is," she said softly. "And I don't want to be sorry for any of it."

He looked at her. "But you are going home today?"

"I have to. I need to get back to my life."

"Okay," he said, his face suddenly void of emotion.

She wasn't sure what she'd expected him to say. But part of her thought he'd argue, ask her to stay. Put up some sort of fight. But he had a fiancée too. He had as much to lose as she did. Why had she thought she would have meant more to him?

"I'm not sure what to say," she said.

"Goodbye?" he suggested.

"You seem angry."

"I'm trying to make things easier for you."

Tears pooled in her eyes. "It doesn't feel easy."

"Will you at least take my number?"

The tears spilled over, rolling down her cheeks. "If I take your number, I'll end up calling you."

"That's what I'm hoping," he said sadly.

"I love Phil," she said. "I have everything I want. I just need to get back to my life."

"Okay."

"You love Jessica," she argued. "You have everything you want too. We can't mess all that up. We'd just end up hurting everyone. We barely even know each other."

"I know," he said, taking her hand and entwining his fingers with hers. "I'm sorry." With his other hand he reached up to brush her tears away. "I know we've only just met, but I feel like I've known you forever. This week has been amazing. I don't want to just walk away."

"But what would we do?" she asked, pulling away. "Just give everything up and run away together?"

"What if we did?" he said.

She laughed manically and struggled for words. What he was suggesting was ridiculous. "We can't," she said. "I can't risk everything for a holiday romance."

"But what if it's more than a holiday romance?" His voice was pleading and she couldn't bear it. "Running away together is crazy, I know, but we should at least stay in touch. See how things work out."

"I'm not going to have an affair with you," she said angrily. "This week has been bad enough. It should never have happened."

"Maybe it was supposed to happen," he said.

She shook her head sadly. "I have to go," she said, kissing his cheek. She lingered too long and when she went to pull away her lips brushed his, and then she was kissing him again. She couldn't stop. Didn't want to stop. Finally, she forced herself to pull away.

"I have to go. I'm sorry. I'm so sorry."

She hurried up the beach, not trusting herself to look back.

Chapter 23

The drive home was horrendous. Her mind drifted constantly to Max and she kept having to wipe away tears so she could see the road ahead. She should have stopped; her driving wasn't safe. But she knew that if she stopped she might turn around and go back to Max.

She needed to get home. When she was back with Phil and her real life, everything would feel normal again, she was sure of it. That's what she kept telling herself, but the closer she got to home the more she hated the thought of it. She didn't want to see Phil and she didn't want to be back in the home she shared with him. She wanted to be in Seaside Cottage with Max.

She'd known saying goodbye to him would be difficult, but it had been even worse than she'd imagined. Would he really have ended his relationship with Jessica for her? She hadn't seriously thought he'd want things to go any further. They were both engaged. What he had suggested was irrational and reckless. She was absolutely right to walk away.

Fresh tears appeared as she remembered how hurt he'd looked. Had she made a huge mistake?

She inhaled deeply and told herself to get a grip. Max would have come to his senses by now. He was probably already on his way back to Jessica. Back to the idiot who didn't like dogs, or cottages by the sea, and who obviously didn't know how lucky she was.

Get a grip! she told herself again, this time more sternly.

It was late morning by the time she reached her home in Oxford. Phil came to the door to greet her. She was surprised to see him, and wished she'd made more of an effort to compose herself first. "I thought you'd be at work," she said.

"I decided to work at home today," he said. "I wanted to be here when you got back."

She was surprised by how pleased she was to see him. Somehow she'd convinced herself she was returning to something awful. But it was as though she'd stepped into a parallel universe. They had a beautiful house, with lovely things. And there was Phil. Good old familiar Phil. It was a relief to see him. When he put his arms around her, she couldn't help the tears that came.

"What's wrong?" he asked gently, rubbing her back.

"I don't know," she said, her words muffled by his shoulder.

He led her into the living room and to the couch. All she could do was apologise.

"Stop saying you're sorry, and tell me what's wrong." He was full of concern. "Why are you so upset? Did something happen?"

"No," she said. "I don't know what's wrong. I just feel so emotional. I'm sorry."

"It's okay." He brushed her hair back and pulled

her to him again. "I'm sorry. I should have been there with you. I hate that you were alone all week."

"Yes," she said quietly. "It would have been better if you were there." Everything would have been different if he'd been with her like he was supposed to be. She'd have had a lovely sunny break and then gone back to her life. Her world wouldn't feel like it was falling down around her.

"You look different," Phil said. "What happened to you?"

Surprised by his words, she went back into the hallway, stopping in front of the mirror. She stared blankly at her reflection, wondering who she was looking at. He hair hung to her shoulders, streaked with highlights from the sun. Her skin glowed with a light tan. She looked like a surfer. She wasn't wearing a scrap of make-up. In fact, she hadn't even showered that morning, and the shorts she'd pulled on were splattered with paint. She hadn't noticed, just dressed in whatever she found first.

"I need to shower," she said, moving to the stairs. "I got straight in the car this morning. I won't be long."

After a long shower she slowly put herself back together: immaculate, expensive clothes; her hair twisted at the back of her head and held in place by a clip and a ton of hairspray; then make-up. It was such a familiar routine, and she wondered why it suddenly felt so foreign.

Afterwards, she remained at the dressing table for a while, looking in the mirror and feeling nothing but confusion. She could do this, she told herself. She could go back to her life and carry on as though the past week hadn't happened.

Phil made coffee and they sat together at the kitchen island. Elizabeth felt she was seeing everything for the first time. It was a lovely house: neat and ordered, everything in its place. It could've been a show home. She thought of the painting of Hope Cove, which was still in the back of her car, and wondered where she would hang it.

"So?" Phil said, looking at her over his coffee. "Are you okay?"

"Yes. Sorry. I don't know what came over me. I'm fine." But she didn't feel fine at all. She smiled weakly, wishing she had the guts to tell Phil the truth and go back to Max. But he'd be gone by now, back to his life and his fiancée.

Phil kissed her and she forced herself to kiss him back. After a moment she pulled away, wittering about work and how much she would have missed.

"I should probably start going through my emails," she said with false cheer.

"You really haven't checked them all week?"

"No."

"There wasn't any internet at the cottage, was there?" he said with a smirk. "There's no way you could keep away from work for a week otherwise. Tell me the truth."

"Okay," she said, holding up her hands. "You got me. There was no internet." She was lying too, but that seemed like a minor misdemeanour compared to the cheating.

"Knew it!" His expression was mock serious as he wrapped an arm around her. "It sounds like hell on earth. How did you survive a week? It's no wonder you're emotional!"

She managed a small smile.

"I'll make us some lunch," Phil said. "Go and check your emails."

In the study, Elizabeth took a few calming breaths and opened her laptop. Her email inbox was full of unread messages. While it should have been overwhelming, she found it comforting. It was something to focus on, and that was exactly what she needed. When Phil brought her a sandwich, she forced another smile. She could do this.

By the time she slipped into bed that evening, she was feeling much more positive … until Phil snuggled up to her and nuzzled her neck. Instantly, she thought of Max. She missed him so much.

She tensed as Phil persisted. "Don't," she said, edging away from him. For a moment he seemed to be waiting for her to say something more, then finally he retreated to his own side of the bed, mumbling a sarcastic apology. Tears came to Elizabeth's eyes.

When Phil fell asleep, Elizabeth listened to the rhythmic sound of his breathing. Tears streamed down her face and soaked into her pillow. Thoughts of Max consumed her, and all she wanted was to be back at Seaside Cottage with him. She wondered how long it would take for her life to feel normal again.

It was hours later when she finally fell asleep, exhausted.

Hannah Ellis

Chapter 24

Elizabeth woke on Saturday with a heaviness that seemed to pin her to the bed. She didn't even attempt to snap herself out of it, just lay on her bed, hating everything. Mid-morning, Phil put a coffee on her bedside table. He sat beside her and the mattress sank under his weight.

"You okay?" he asked.

"I feel like I'm coming down with something," she said. Another lie.

"Need anything?"

"No. Thanks. I'll get up in a minute."

She showered and dressed, and put her hair up and her make-up on as she usually would. Funny how it felt so depressing and unfamiliar.

"Feeling better?" Phil asked when she found him in the kitchen.

"Yes. I was just tired."

"Do you want to do something today?"

She shrugged and perched on a stool.

"We could go for a round of golf?"

She spluttered out a laugh that sounded slightly manic.

"What's so funny?" Phil asked, his eyebrows darting together.

"Nothing." She rubbed at her temples. "Sorry."

She was trying to forget about Max, but everything reminded her of him. Had he ruined golf for her forever? And sunrises? And painted window frames? She chuckled again and shook her head at how ridiculous she was being. "Sorry. I don't feel like golf."

"Gonna let me in on the joke?"

"I was only thinking about how much work I missed, but I thought you'd tease me."

"A week without the internet seems to have had a terrible effect on you," he said lightly. "But if you want to work, it's fine. I've got some stuff to do too. I just thought it would be good to spend some time together."

She reached up and kissed his cheek. "How about we get some work done and then go out for dinner this evening?"

"Perfect," he agreed.

"I need to run into the office," she said. She didn't, but she needed to get out of the house and knew the office would be empty – and a good place to hide away on a Saturday afternoon.

"No problem. See you later."

She got a coffee and a sandwich at the café near work and then went to sit at her desk. She stared at the computer screen without even turning it on. It was weird being there at the weekend when everything was quiet. Whenever she was in the office things were manic, even when they weren't approaching deadlines. That was the vibe of the place, and she'd always found it exhilarating, but now she wondered whether it was necessary.

After a while, she went over to look out of the

window at the busy street below. When she got bored of the view she went outside and headed for a nearby park. She wandered in circles for hours and was sitting on a bench when her phone rang. It was going dark and she'd forgotten all about dinner with Phil.

"Sorry," she said, quickly. "I'm leaving now. It's not too late for dinner, is it?"

Part of her hoped it was. All she wanted to do was go to bed and shut out the world. She glanced at her watch, a delicate gold piece which her parents had given her for her last birthday.

"How about Romano's?" Phil suggested. It was their favourite Italian restaurant. "We could meet there."

Elizabeth stood up, then wondered where she'd left her car. "Perfect," she said. "I'm walking out now, hopefully traffic won't be too bad."

Thankfully, she hadn't strayed too far, and reached her car quickly. When she pulled up at a red light ten minutes into the journey, she felt weary. It was starting to feel as if her week in Hope Cove had been a dream. It didn't feel real. She struggled to comprehend that it was only yesterday that she'd left Max.

Her mind took her back to the previous morning, sitting on the beach watching the sunrise, snuggled up to him. Then an image of him laughing over dinner came to her and made her want to cry. Memories flashed through her mind: Max playing golf. Max reaching out to her as she stumbled in the sea. His cheeky grin as he looked down at her from the ladder. His lips on hers...

A car horn blared and she hurriedly fumbled with

the gear stick. The engine stalled and she inhaled deeply, swiping tears from her cheeks and getting herself under control. She waved an apology at the car behind and finally pulled away.

Trying hard to push all thoughts of Max aside, she drove to the restaurant on autopilot. It wasn't just hard for her to believe it had really happened; it was also hard for her to believe she was the same person. She felt like a stranger in her own skin; an intruder in her own life. All she wanted to do was forget about Max and her minor detour from reality. She wanted her life back to how it had been a week ago when everything made sense and she was perfectly happy. She had been happy a week ago, hadn't she? Before Max? She couldn't actually remember.

Focus on Phil, she told herself as she arrived at the restaurant. Pulling the visor down, she checked herself in the mirror, running her fingers under her eyes to remove smudged mascara and reapplying her lipstick.

This was her life and she'd worked hard to get where she was. She wasn't about to ruin it all because of a stupid crush. That's what she told herself throughout dinner, while Phil filled her in on his week. She nodded along and did her best to smile in appropriate places. But somehow, she couldn't bring herself to care. Her appetite had disappeared and she only managed half of her seafood pasta, pushing the remainder around her plate while Phil droned on.

She couldn't figure out if he hadn't noticed that she was somewhere else entirely, or if he was politely ignoring the fact. Surely he noticed a difference in her? Maybe he assumed that if he carried on as normal, she'd go back to normal. Maybe she would.

"Sorry, what?" she said, tuning in to Phil again. "A promotion?"

"Yes."

"And it's where?"

"Paris," he said impatiently. "I told them it was impossible, of course. What would you do in Paris? But it got me thinking. It would be great for my career. I'd be Principal Consultant for a new project with one of the biggest clients in France. And it'd be a fantastic experience. They pay all the relocation costs. Imagine us strolling around Paris at the weekends…"

She frowned. "But we couldn't move to France, Phil. My job is here. Our lives are here."

"I know," he said. "It just sounds so amazing."

"Would you really consider it?" she asked. "If it weren't for my job."

"It's a great opportunity," he said. "I was flattered they asked me."

She shook her head and leaned back in her chair. Of course she wouldn't move to Paris, and she was surprised Phil found it even remotely appealing.

She spotted a toddler in a high chair at the other side of the room. He was banging a spoon on the table while his parents ignored him completely and carried on eating and chatting as though they didn't even hear the racket.

"It's a bit late to bring a kid out, isn't it?" Phil said, following her gaze.

"I suppose."

She dragged her gaze back to Phil, who'd resumed eating his pizza.

"Do you want kids?" she asked flatly.

"What?"

"We haven't talked about it recently, and I wondered…"

"Is this why you've been acting so strangely?" he asked. "You want a baby?"

"No." Her eyes welled up and she wasn't sure why. "I don't think so. I just thought … we always said we didn't want children, but what if I changed my mind? Hypothetically."

He sighed. "I suppose, if you really wanted a baby…" He paused, flustered. "If you *really* wanted one."

"If I *really* wanted a baby you wouldn't say no?"

"I suppose not. Are we still being hypothetical?"

"Yes," she said, irritated. "But you definitely don't want kids?"

"I've no burning desire for them. I'm not sure where a baby would fit into our lives. We work so much."

"I would have to give up work, I suppose."

"For a while, at least," he said.

"I'd never make editor-in-chief," she mused.

"There's always options," he said. "Nannies and things. I'm not sure."

"Right," she said, sighing in annoyance.

"I'm not sure what you want me to say," Phil said tensely.

"I don't want you to say anything."

They descended into a stony silence and Phil finished off his pizza.

Elizabeth wasn't sure why she'd felt the need to bring up children. It wasn't as though she suddenly felt her biological clock ticking and had been hit with an overwhelming longing for children. One thing had become clear to her, though: if she were going to have children, she'd want to have them with someone who wanted them too, not someone who'd go along with it if they had to. Someone who'd only be doing it to keep her happy.

She'd want to have a child with someone who would be excited by blue lines on a stick, and who'd sit and whisper to her growing belly. Someone who'd want to spend time with their kids, not farm them out to a nanny.

Her mind drifted to Max, sitting on the hill at the farm and telling her he'd happily be a stay-at-home dad, and that his family would be his priority, not work.

"Are you okay?" Phil asked, interrupting her thoughts. "Where's all this come from?"

A muscle in her cheek twitched. "I don't know. I just had lots of time to think while I was away."

He grinned widely. "I'm telling you, no good comes from not having the internet. Time to think, indeed!"

She smiled, tight-lipped. He was only trying to lighten the atmosphere but, honestly, if he mentioned the internet one more time she thought she might just bash him round the head.

Hannah Ellis

Chapter 25

Going to work on Monday was a relief. Elizabeth was sure that once she got back into her old routine and caught up with her life again, she'd be swept away with it all and be back to normal before she knew it. Her stupid crush would soon be a distant memory – a moment of madness she would look back on with amusement.

"What are you doing?" she asked Emily, the mousy intern, who was in Elizabeth's office, sitting at her desk, tapping on her computer.

"Oh, God. I'm so sorry. I'm going."

"Get out of my chair," Elizabeth said, slowly but firmly.

She hadn't yet decided if she liked Emily, and anyone who crossed her today probably wasn't going to come off well. So far Emily hadn't seemed suited to work at the magazine. She looked constantly terrified, and Elizabeth didn't have the time or inclination for handholding. Also, Emily was Josie's friend, so that didn't endear her to Elizabeth. It almost felt like having a spy at work, and she wondered what Emily reported back to Josie. Not that she really cared.

"I'm sorry," Emily said again, frantically tapping at the keyboard. *What on earth was she up to?*

"Just get out," Elizabeth said again.

"My computer crashed on Friday," Emily explained. "So I just nipped in here to use yours quickly. But I think I might have left something open. I just need to—"

"You need to get out of my chair," Elizabeth said, reaching across her to take the mouse. She was intrigued now. "Go!" she said, nudging Emily out of her chair.

"Just close the file," Emily said frantically, pointing at the computer screen.

"I think I can manage that, thank you." Elizabeth shooed her out of the room. What was the big deal? She frowned at the Word document open on the screen. Was Emily trying her hand at journalism? It didn't look like a magazine article…

"Hey!" Karen said as she stuck her head in the room. "Come in my office?"

Elizabeth stood to follow. Then, on impulse, she moved back to the computer, saving the document and emailing it to herself before closing the file.

"Welcome back!" Karen said, in her office. "Please don't go away again. I don't like it when you're not here."

"I'll bear that in mind," Elizabeth said, smiling. "Should I talk to Heidi about the horoscopes?"

"It's fine," Karen said, dropping into her chair. "I spoke to her."

"Oh, God. Did you fire her?"

"No, I did not. I politely and tactfully suggested how things could be improved."

"Really?"

"Yes!"

"Good. What else have we got going on?"

"I take it you went through your emails at some point?" Karen asked, frowning.

"Yeah. Over the weekend."

"Great, so you're already up to speed."

"Yep," Elizabeth said, trying to remember what any of her emails had been about. Her mind had gone blank.

"I need you to go over the Winter Getaway section fairly urgently…"

Elizabeth zoned out. Maybe she should plan a winter getaway with Phil. Except it was hard to think of winter when it was still August. That was the trouble with the magazine industry – issues had to be planned months in advance. Besides, another holiday was the last thing she needed. What she should do is immerse herself in work. That would be the best thing. If only she could concentrate for long enough.

Karen was staring at her. "Are you okay?"

"Yeah. Still in holiday mode, I guess. I was miles away."

"Nothing happened with you and that guy, did it?"

"No." Elizabeth laughed, but it came out weak and pathetic. "Of course not."

"When did you come home?"

"Friday."

"I thought you were coming home on Thursday. Something happened, didn't it? You slept with him."

"No," she said forcefully. "Nothing happened."

"So why did you stay longer?"

"I didn't. I always planned to stay until Friday."

"Until you got a crush on the hot guy next door."

161

She stood abruptly, irritated by Karen's questions. "Please don't sit there accusing me of things I haven't done – and wouldn't do."

"Sorry," Karen said. "But you're acting very weird."

"That doesn't mean I slept with another man. And to be honest, you're my boss. Maybe you should act like it occasionally."

"Woah," Karen said, her features stony. "I'm your friend. I was asking as a friend, because clearly something is going on with you."

Elizabeth stood still, trying to figure out who was out of line. She couldn't get things straight in her head.

"I've got work to do," she said.

"Okay," Karen said coolly, leaning back in her chair. "If that's how you want to be."

Elizabeth strode back to her office and sat heavily in her chair. Her head dropped into her hands. What was she doing? It wasn't like her to be so short-tempered. On top of everything else, she now felt bad for snapping at Emily and Karen. She'd have to apologise later.

Taking a deep breath, she pulled herself together and dived into her work.

Chapter 26

She switched completely into work mode and shut everything else out. After making brief apologies to Karen and Emily, she did her best to limit her interactions for the rest of the week. When she did speak to anyone she kept it business-like and formal. Work kept her distracted and she bounced from one task to the next in an almost robotic state. She arrived at the office early and went home late. If she stayed focused on work, she could keep thoughts of Max from creeping in.

It almost worked. Except he was there in her head right before she fell asleep at night and as soon as she woke up in the morning.

On Friday afternoon, when most of her colleagues were leaving for the weekend, Elizabeth headed back to her office with a coffee, determined to get a few more hours in before she left.

"I've got wine in my office," Karen said when they passed in the hall. She'd given Elizabeth a wide berth since she'd snapped at her on Monday. "Tempted?"

She felt a pang of guilt. She missed her chats with Karen, but at some point she was bound to start asking questions again and Elizabeth couldn't deal with it. It was easier to keep to herself until she was more emotionally stable.

"Sorry. I've got a couple of things to finish, and then I need to get home to Phil."

"Okay," Karen said, looking at her intensely. She was obviously dying to say something else, but Elizabeth made a dash for her office.

She jumped at the sight of Josie swivelling in her chair.

"What are you doing here?" she asked, shooing her out of her chair.

"Waiting for Emily. We're going for drinks. Thought I'd call in and say hi to my favourite sister!"

"Hi," Elizabeth said dryly, hoping that would be the end of the conversation. She took a sip of coffee and then set it aside.

"You wanna come for a drink with us?"

Elizabeth snapped her head to Josie, surprised by the invitation.

"No," she said frostily. "I've got work to catch up on."

"Did you get behind on your week off?"

"Not really." Elizabeth glared at her. "Did you want something?"

"No." Josie moved to the door, shaking her head. She stopped in the doorway. "Are you still annoyed with me about the shoes?"

"What shoes?" Elizabeth asked, with her eyes on her computer screen.

"The wedding shoes…"

Chills ran through Elizabeth and she froze.

"I know you think I was just trying to annoy you," Josie said. "I'll wear the beige shoes if you want. They hurt my feet, that's all."

"Wear whatever you want," Elizabeth whispered.

"What?"

"I don't care what shoes you wear," she repeated. "I've got work to do."

"Sorry," Josie muttered. "I'll go then."

Elizabeth stared at her computer, but could sense Josie hovering. "Are you okay?" Josie finally asked.

Elizabeth bit her lip. Josie being nice to her was more than she could deal with. She was trying so hard to quash her emotions. Now she felt like they would erupt like a geyser just because her sister asked her if she was okay.

"I'm fine," she said, turning and smiling tightly. "Have fun with Emily."

Finally, Josie left. The door to the office had barely clicked into place when Elizabeth let out a sob. She felt as if she was drowning. The wedding that she'd been so excited about felt overwhelming and extravagant. Why had she been so consumed by her wedding day? It was just one day. One day when people would look at her and congratulate her and envy her. But it was all a big joke.

Shaking her head, she tried to laugh at herself. Why was she being so irrational? An image of Max filled her head and she wanted to scream. She wiped her eyes and tried to focus on work, but only managed to stare numbly at the computer screen.

She barely registered the knock at the door.

"Me again," Josie said cheerfully as she made her way quietly into the office, waving a bottle of wine.

"I thought you were going out with Emily?"

"I said I'd meet her later. I thought we could have a drink and talk weddings!"

Elizabeth glanced up. Josie might have had the best intentions, but Elizabeth really wasn't in the mood for company. "I don't want wine. And I don't want to talk about the wedding." She hoped Josie would get the message and leave, but instead her sister's eyes filled with tears. *Great.*

Josie ran out of the door and Elizabeth fought her instinct to go after her. It didn't matter; Josie shot back into the room seconds later.

"What did I ever do to you?" she demanded.

Elizabeth sighed. "I don't have time for your temper tantrums, Josie." Actually, she didn't have the energy for other people's emotions. It was hard enough battling through her own.

"Well, I am so sorry for interrupting your perfect little life!" Josie turned to leave again. "Have a great evening, Liz!"

The way she spat the name stirred something in Elizabeth. *It's Lizzie!* she wanted to scream.

"Just because I don't treat you like a princess!" Elizabeth shouted, standing and daring Josie to come back and argue. She desperately needed someone to scream at or she might explode.

"What?" Josie asked weakly.

"You don't like that Mum and Dad think of you as their little princess, but I see you for exactly who you are: a spoiled brat with no direction, no responsibilities and no regard for consequences."

"That's not true."

Elizabeth laughed scornfully. "You don't have a job. Mum and Dad pay your rent!"

Tears rolled down Josie's face. Elizabeth retreated, knowing she was right but not sure why she

166

felt bad about it.

"It's all so easy for you." Josie's voice quivered with quiet anger. "You've known what you wanted to do since you were a kid. You had everything planned and then everything fell into place. Lucky you! You have no idea what it's like not to know what you want out of life. And to make it worse, my perfect sister has it all figured out and constantly looks down her nose at me." She sniffed loudly and walked out of the office.

Elizabeth stayed in the silent room for a long time. For the first time ever she felt that perhaps she could relate to Josie.

What if all the things she'd been striving for weren't what she wanted after all?

Hannah Ellis

Chapter 27

The shops were busy on Saturday morning. Elizabeth trudged around three shoe shops before she found what she was looking for: white Converse with a smattering of glitter. She didn't see what all the fuss was about, but then, on a whim, she plucked another pair off the shelf – classic white ones – and asked the shop assistant for a pair in her size.

Bouncing up the stairs to Josie's apartment, she was surprised by how comfy the shoes were. They didn't look too bad either. When Josie had buzzed her in to the building she'd sounded surprised – no wonder, really. Elizabeth never visited. Josie greeted her with a scowl at the top of the stairs.

"What do you think?" Elizabeth asked, looking happily at her new shoes.

"I think you're a complete bitch," Josie said, marching back into her apartment. The door banged shut.

Elizabeth winced. That hadn't gone to plan. "I bought you some too!" she shouted, then waited hopefully.

The door opened a crack. Elizabeth held out the shoe box and eased the lid open. With a squeal of delight, Josie flung the door open and grabbed at the shoes.

"I love them!"

Elizabeth smiled sheepishly. "Peace offering."

"For the wedding?"

"You can wear them now," Elizabeth said with a sigh. "I'll get you new ones nearer the wedding."

"Oh, thank God! I don't think I could wait. Thank you! You're the best." She flung her arms around Elizabeth.

"That was easy. Have you got any coffee?"

Josie grimaced. "Not to your standards. Just instant stuff. And the place is a mess."

"It'll do," Elizabeth said, determined to clear the air with Josie. Their argument the previous evening had left her unsettled, and she kept remembering her mum's comment that it was she who caused the distance between them, not Josie. It probably wouldn't kill her to try to get along with her only sibling.

Josie switched the kettle on and randomly tidied up as they moved through her small apartment.

"You don't have a cleaner, then?" Elizabeth sat on the couch as Josie tried on her new shoes. "You're not such a princess after all."

Josie opened her mouth, then caught the teasing in Elizabeth's eyes and laughed instead. She scuttled out when the kettle clicked and returned a couple of minutes later with two cups of coffee.

Elizabeth copied Josie and put her feet up on the coffee table, showing off her new shoes. They rocked their feet, the bright white trainers swaying in unison. They sat in companionable silence for a few minutes before Josie spoke. "What's going on with you?" she asked hesitantly, clearly worried that she was going to ruin their newfound truce.

"How do you mean?"

"You've been acting strangely. You were so uptight about the wedding that I was worried you were going to explode. Then you went away on your own for a week…"

The reminder of the week with Max filled Elizabeth with sadness, and she worried Josie could see it.

"And now you've bought me shoes!" Josie said. "Something's not right."

"I don't know," Elizabeth said honestly. "I might be going a bit crazy."

Josie nodded. "That's good." A slow smile spread across her face. "I could cope with you being a bit crazy sometimes. It would be a nice change, Little Miss Sensible!"

"The trouble is, I don't have the luxury of going crazy. I have commitments and people expect me to be… Well, they expect me to be me."

"Who cares what anyone expects? Do what you want."

"It's not that simple," Elizabeth said, trying not to get irritated.

"Okay." Josie crossed her legs on the couch and sat up straighter. "If you could do anything you want, right now, what would you do?"

"I don't know." What a ridiculous question. People couldn't just do what they wanted; that wasn't how the world worked. Her mind drifted regardless. She'd go and pack a bag, then she'd drive to Hope Cove and find Max. Of course, he wouldn't be there so it was a crazy idea. He'd be sitting in his cosy kitchen at home, enjoying brunch with his fiancée. The thought made her nauseous.

"Tell me!" Josie said excitedly. "You have something in mind, I know it. Tell me what you'd do if you threw caution to the wind and went for it."

"I wouldn't do anything," Elizabeth said, standing abruptly. "I've spent far too long being Little Miss Sensible to start throwing caution to the wind."

"Are you going?" Josie asked, disappointed.

"I'd better get back to Phil," she said, hating the thought but needing to escape. "Thanks for the coffee."

"Thanks for the shoes," Josie called after her.

***

It wasn't long before Elizabeth wished she'd never left Josie's couch. Phil followed her around the house, asking her a string of mundane questions. No, she hadn't had any more thoughts about sightseeing trips for their honeymoon. Yes, she would call his mother to update her on wedding plans. No, she didn't want to go out for dinner. Why wouldn't he just leave her alone?

"I've actually got a bit of work to finish," Elizabeth said finally. "I'm afraid I'll be holed up in the study all afternoon. Why don't you see if your dad fancies a round of golf?"

He gave her a peck on the cheek. "Great idea."

She told him to have fun and went up to the study until she heard him leave. Having the house to herself for the afternoon felt like the ultimate luxury. She lay on the couch staring at the ceiling, contemplating how everything had gone wrong. She missed Max so much. There really was a part of her that longed to get in the car and go and find him. Except then what? Would he actually leave his fiancée and run away with her? It was absurd. But if she could go back to that last morning on the beach, Elizabeth knew she wouldn't be able to walk away again. She'd agree to anything; no matter how outlandish it seemed. If she'd known then how much she'd miss him, there was no way she'd have left.

If only she'd taken his number. She'd call him now, just to hear his voice. Tears dripped slowly down her cheeks and she wiped at them angrily. What was she thinking? Was she really considering giving up the life she'd worked so hard for? Could she walk away from her job? From Phil? From her home? And if she did, would she be happy?

What she needed to do was stop taking things for granted and being so negative. She had a great life and she needed to focus on all the positives. She'd make more effort with Phil and remind herself how lucky she was. Jumping up from the couch, she decided she'd go shopping and cook a romantic meal for that evening.

Everything would be fine.

Chapter 28

After some consideration she made baked salmon, flavoured with lemon and black pepper, with new potatoes and asparagus. It was a relatively simple dish but she was proud of it nonetheless.

"Why did you cook?" Phil asked when he arrived home. "I'd have taken you out for dinner."

"I felt like eating at home," she said. "I might start doing more cooking. I quite enjoyed it."

She waited while he chose the right wine to go with the salmon, then they sat down together in the kitchen. The plan had been to set the table properly, with a cloth and candles, but in the end that had seemed frivolous and silly. Phil would probably make some annoying comment about it.

"How was golf?" she asked.

"Great. The weather was fantastic. The course wasn't too busy. Can't complain at all."

"How's your dad?"

"He's all right. Slowing down, but that's age for you. By the way, Mum wants you to call her. She wants to talk about flowers for the wedding. If you haven't booked the florist yet, she knows someone, apparently."

"Hmm," she replied, focusing on her food. "I had a voicemail from her. I'll call her later."

"Have you booked a florist already?"

"No."

"Great. Mum will be happy. Don't forget to call her."

"I won't."

"This is nice," he said, nodding at the food. "Maybe a little more lemon next time."

She ignored him.

"If you're going to do more cooking, maybe you should do a course."

She shook her head in exasperation. "Thanks for the vote of confidence."

"No, it tastes fine. I just thought if it's something you're interested in…"

"Can we not make such a big deal out of me cooking dinner?"

"Sorry," he muttered.

They ate in silence for a while, the meal punctuated by the scrape of cutlery on the plates and the extractor fan – which Elizabeth had forgotten to switch off – humming gently in the background.

"How was work this week?" Phil asked. "All caught up after the holiday?"

Her heart raced. The holiday. Max. She was trying so hard not to think about it, but her mind took her back there time and time again. "Work was fine," she said. "Good to be back."

"I bet Karen missed you."

"Yeah." Even though she'd apologised to Karen for her little outburst, things had remained tense between them all week. "We had a bit of an argument."

"Really? What about?"

"Work stuff. Nothing important. But there's an awkward atmosphere now."

"You should talk to her and clear the air. It's no good having an atmosphere at work. Especially with the amount of time you spend there. And Karen's been a good friend."

"She has. You're right. I should talk to her."

"And you need to stay in her good books if you plan on taking her job."

"You make it sound very underhand," she said. "Karen knows I want her job. And she's happy for me to take over when she retires."

"Speaking of bosses, did I tell you I was at Dennis's house last week? I went round to go over everything before the presentation."

Elizabeth nodded. "How's he doing?"

"He's okay. Staying away from the office will be the hardest thing for him. Anyway, they'd just got a wood burner installed. I was thinking we might get one in the living room."

Her forehead creased. "We don't have a chimney."

"We could get one installed."

"It sounds like a lot of disruption."

"It'd be lovely and cosy in the winter. I thought you'd like the idea of cuddling up to me in front of the fire."

"It does sound nice." Her heart was racing again, and it occurred to her that she wouldn't do well on a polygraph test at that moment. The idea of cuddling up in front of a fire *was* lovely. But not with Phil.

Her thoughts scared her. She was marrying Phil in a matter of months. Surely she shouldn't feel indifferent towards him?

"I'll do some research," he said.

After they'd finished, she took the plates to the sink, glad of something to do.

"Stick them in the dishwasher," Phil said.

She hadn't even noticed she'd begun to wash up, but she had the urge to be busy. Phil came and wrapped his arms around her waist. "Why don't we watch a film? It'd be good for you to relax."

"I'm fine," she said, bristling when he kissed her neck. "I'm going to tidy up here, then I've got some work to do."

"I thought you worked this afternoon?" he said, moving away from her and topping up his wine.

"I went shopping, and cooked. I've only got a bit to do, but I'd rather get on with it. You watch a film."

"Okay," he said, before disappearing into the living room.

Elizabeth felt strangely exhausted when she sat down in the study and opened her laptop. She didn't have anything specific to do but she wanted to be alone, and Phil wouldn't bother her if he thought she was working.

Her fingers seemed to work alone, typing Max's name into a search engine. Of course she didn't know his last name so she typed 'cosmetics company' and 'lawyer' instead. Then she hit delete as she realised how crazy she was being. If she really wanted to find him, she could. His aunts at the farm would be a better starting point than an internet search with his first name. Or she could go back to Hope Cove and ask around the locals. Someone would surely have contact details for his mum, since she had a house there. Or she could drop a note through the door of Seaside Cottage.

Again, she was left wondering what she was really hoping for. She'd only known Max for a week – she couldn't turn her life upside down because of him. The irrational thoughts were driving her crazy and she needed to get them under control.

After closing the search engine, she scrolled through her personal emails, and was puzzled by an unopened email from herself. It had an attachment. The document that Emily had left on her work computer. On a whim, she opened it and began reading.

From the word count it appeared to be a full-length novel, and Elizabeth soon found herself completely absorbed in it. It was hours later, when the words began to blur on the screen and she kept having to blink to focus, that she realised how much time had passed. It was almost midnight. Phil had put his head round the door at some point and said he was going to bed. Without taking her eyes from the screen, she'd told him she'd join him soon.

When she finally slipped into bed beside him, he was fast asleep.

Chapter 29

On Sunday, Elizabeth slept until mid-morning. Phil was heading into the shower when she got up.

"I thought I'd make brunch," she said as she passed him on the landing.

"More cooking? Are you ill?"

"Ha ha," she said dryly. "I'll just make it for myself then, shall I?"

"I'm only teasing. I'll take whatever's going."

She made a fruit salad, placing it on the table alongside the yoghurt. There was orange juice in a carafe, and part-baked rolls were browning in the oven. She was also making a ham and cheese omelette.

Her laptop was open on the kitchen island and she kept glancing over to read Emily's novel. She couldn't decide if Emily had written it or if it was some editing project that she was working on. Either way it was good, and Elizabeth was enjoying it immensely.

"What so funny?" Phil asked when he wandered in to find her bent over the computer.

"Oh, nothing," she said, turning quickly to take the bread from the oven. "I'm just reading something, and it's funny." She dropped the rolls into the waiting bread basket and added it to the table.

"Work?" he asked, as she went back to the omelette. She was fairly sure it was overcooked, but never mind. He kissed her cheek. She smiled at him – a proper smile – and remembered how much she used to love him. They had been happy together, once upon a time.

"No," she said. "A little side project. It's nothing."

He looked intrigued but didn't ask any more about it.

"This is great," he said, moving to the table.

It was all pretty simple but made for quite an impressive spread. To anybody looking in, they'd appear to be a perfect couple enjoying a delicious brunch together. Unfortunately, conversation was stilted, and Elizabeth's lack of appetite meant she only picked at the lovely-looking breakfast. But no one could say she wasn't trying.

***

Emily was wide-eyed and twitchy when Elizabeth beckoned her into her office on Monday morning. She'd never get far in the magazine business, Elizabeth realised. She lacked the edge she needed to get ahead.

"Don't look so worried," Elizabeth said, directing her to sit down.

"Okay," Emily replied, swallowing hard.

"I want to talk to you about the document you left open on my computer last week. You wrote that?"

"Yes. Sorry about that. I should've checked it was okay to use your computer. I just thought—"

"I don't care about you using my computer. You wrote a novel?"

"Yes," Emily replied, seeming confused by the question.

"It's really good."

"Oh, no, it's not." She paused and her eyebrows shot upwards. "Did you read it?"

Elizabeth nodded slowly. "Yes."

"All of it?"

"I couldn't put it down." She'd spent all day Sunday reading it and it had been a lovely distraction. "I thoroughly enjoyed it."

"It's just a soppy romance…"

"It's not!" Elizabeth said. "It's so much more. It's funny and it's clever and it made me laugh, and cry. It reminded me how much I love to read."

It was the first novel she'd read in years, and it had felt so good to get lost in the story. She'd also been reminded of why she worked where she did. Reading had been a huge part of her life as a teenager. She always had a book on the go; wouldn't leave the house without one. She'd decided on writing as a career and studied journalism at university.

Somewhere along the way she'd found she was good at editing, and even did an internship at a publishing house. For a while she'd imagined herself editing novels for big-name authors and pointing out the bestsellers she'd edited as her claim to fame.

Then she got the job at the magazine and forgot all about editing actual words. Now she spent her time managing people and budgets and layouts – tasks that seemed so far away from her earlier goals. She'd stopped reading for pleasure too. She never had enough time.

"No one else has read it," Emily said, her eyes sparkling with tears. "I didn't dare show it to anyone."

"You should." Elizabeth felt an odd sense of pride. "Show it to the world." She looked earnestly at Emily. "Honestly, you should try to get it published."

"No," Emily said, shaking her head. "It's not ready for that."

"It needs a bit of a polish," Elizabeth said. "And I wondered if you might let me do that for you…"

"I can't afford an editor," Emily said quickly.

"I wouldn't charge you."

"Really?"

"Really. I'd like to."

Before she knew what was happening, Elizabeth had been enveloped in a bear hug and Emily sniffed into her shoulder. "Thank you," she said.

When Emily left Elizabeth's office she passed Karen, who was on the way in.

"What's wrong with her?" Karen asked. "You haven't fired her, have you?"

"No. She's fine."

"Okay," Karen said, puzzled. "Are you all right?"

"Yeah. Have you got a minute?"

"Of course." Karen smiled widely and closed the door behind her.

"I owe you an apology for last week," Elizabeth said.

"You've already apologised," Karen said. "It's fine. I'm worried about you, that's all."

"I feel that things are still a bit tense between us. And it's my fault, I know. I just…" Elizabeth paused and took a deep breath. Maybe it would help to talk things through. "When you asked about the guy in Devon, I got so upset because you were right. Kind of."

Karen gave her a sympathetic smile. "What happened?"

"Not much," Elizabeth said with a shrug. It wasn't true. She hadn't slept with him, that was what she was getting at. But a lot had happened. "I spent all week with him, and somehow I convinced myself that there was no harm in it – that it was innocent." She gave a frustrated sigh. "Now I can't stop thinking about him."

"Are you still in touch with him?"

"No. I told him that I was engaged, and happy, and didn't want to risk messing that up."

"Good," Karen said quietly. "Did you tell Phil?"

"I don't know what I would say. Should I tell him I kissed another guy? That I really like the other guy and can't stop thinking about him? That I'm not sure I love *him* any more? That I can't help thinking we should call off our wedding?" Tears dampened her eyes. "I don't know what to do."

"I know I like to joke about Phil being a weasel, like all men! But, honestly, Phil's a good guy. You two are great together. Don't throw that away for a fling."

"I know. But I'm so torn. Being with Phil feels like such hard work. I feel like we disagree about everything. I spend all my time biting my tongue around him."

"Relationships *are* hard work," Karen said. "I wish I'd worked harder at my marriage."

"But don't you also think that you just married the

wrong person? What if Phil and I aren't meant to be together? Wouldn't it be better to figure that out now rather than after we're married?"

"But you love Phil," Karen insisted.

"I keep telling myself that, but I keep having these doubts. Like, we both said we don't want kids. And now that's panicking me. What if I change my mind?"

"You were always so sure you didn't want kids."

"I know. And I probably don't."

Definitely not with Phil. But what if she was with someone who wanted kids? Maybe she'd feel differently then.

"That's something you should discuss with Phil," Karen said. "But the fling with the guy at the beach isn't real. It's just exciting because it's new and different. You don't even know the guy properly. What would you do? Run away with him and start a whole new life?"

"No," Elizabeth said, her mouth twitching into a smile. She'd been telling herself it was crazy but it sounded even worse when you said it out loud. "Everything feels a bit flat at the moment, that's all."

"You and Phil have been together a long time. Things are bound to go a bit flat. You'll get through this. Five years from now, you'll be happily married, you'll be sitting in my chair bossing everyone around, and you'll absolutely love it. Everything will be great. You'll see!"

"You're right," Elizabeth said, wishing she could feel as enthusiastic about her future as Karen was.

"I am," Karen declared. "Take my advice. Forget about your holiday fling, and focus on Phil and your wedding. You're getting married – it's exciting!"

"Thanks." It was what Elizabeth needed: a bit of a shoulder shake and a reality check.

With a fresh sense of determination, she fully intended to take Karen's advice.

Hannah Ellis

Chapter 30

After two weeks of determinedly following Karen's advice, Elizabeth felt exactly the same. Perhaps that's not true; things were arguably slightly worse. As well as the problems in her relationship with Phil, she was also finding work increasingly frustrating. Using it as a distraction wasn't as effective as it should be.

Being at the office was preferable to being at home, but she was only going through the motions. Nothing she was doing felt worthwhile or inspiring – with one exception. She'd been editing Emily's novel in her spare time – and she was loving the process. She wished she could devote more time to it.

She still thought of Max often, and missed him just as much, which was ridiculous. Utterly ridiculous. Karen had been right about their fling; it didn't mean anything. She wasn't going to run happily into the sunset and start a new life with Max.

Yet something niggled at her. What if her feelings for Max weren't the cause of the problems in her relationship with Phil? What if the problems had been there before Max? Maybe, deep down, she'd already had doubts about marrying Phil, and Max had merely highlighted those doubts.

For someone who was usually so sure of herself, she was having difficulty keeping her thoughts and feelings straight. She'd tell herself everything was fine, and then five minutes later feel like getting in her car and just driving away. Anywhere. It didn't matter where. She just wanted to keep driving and never stop.

It was suddenly Friday again and she'd promised Phil they'd spend some time together over the weekend. Everyone else had left the office and she stared at her computer screen, dreading going home. She felt she was living a lie, and she wasn't sure how much longer she could keep it up.

Phil would be wondering where she was.

She'd taken to driving into work. The time it added to her commute didn't bother her at all; it gave her time alone, which was increasingly what she craved. When she got in the car that Friday evening, her desire to avoid going home was so strong that she shot off a quick message to Phil saying she had to visit Josie, but wouldn't be long.

***

Josie didn't answer the intercom but when another resident left the building, Elizabeth slipped inside and went upstairs. She banged on Josie's door, panicking that she wasn't in. When Josie finally answered, she was wrapped in a towel.

"I was starting to think you weren't home," Elizabeth said, barging in. "I could have been anyone, by the way. You could have let a madman in. Don't just open the door when someone bangs on it. Have you got no sense?"

"Never mind the madman," Josie said. "I've let a

mad *woman* in. Lesson learned. What's wrong with you?"

"Everything," Elizabeth said, stalking through to the living room. "I might seriously be a mad woman. I'm going crazy. What am I doing?" She pulled her blazer off roughly and threw it across the room as if it was trying to attack her. "I hate my stupid clothes!"

"Okay. You're scaring me. Sit down."

"But I hate them," Elizabeth said, kicking off her black patent stilettos.

"Liz! You need to calm down!"

"Don't call me Liz! I hate it. Everyone keeps calling me Elizabeth or Liz and I hate it."

Josie's mouth twitched into a half-smile as she dropped onto the couch. "You know that's your name, don't you? Because now you're really worrying me…"

"But I hate it." Elizabeth scowled. "And I hate my life."

"Since when?"

"I don't know," she said. But she did know, of course: she knew exactly when everything had gone wrong.

"Well, what exactly do you hate?" Josie asked.

"All of it! Work…" She couldn't bring herself to say Phil, but he was there, on the tip of her tongue. Hate was a strong word, and she was certain she wouldn't hate him at all if she didn't have to spend any time with him, but that wasn't ideal since she was marrying him. "Everything," she said sadly.

"I'm supposed to be getting ready to go out," Josie said, sounding decidedly unmoved.

"Sorry," Elizabeth said, wondering why she'd felt

the need to visit Josie with her problems. But she didn't feel like leaving. "Have you got wine?"

"Nothing up to your standards," Josie said flatly.

Elizabeth rolled her eyes. "Please."

With a sigh, Josie stood and went in search of wine. She returned moments later with a pair of mismatched glasses brimming with cheap white wine.

"You're not supposed to fill it so full," Elizabeth said as she carefully manoeuvred the glass to her lips, gulping at it to lighten the load.

"Whatever." Josie took a long sip. "You seem like you need it. I'm going out. I need to get ready." She glanced back as she left the room. "Your phone's vibrating around the kitchen, by the way."

"That'll be Phil," Elizabeth said, with no intention of answering it.

Halfway through her wine, she stood and wandered through the apartment, taking in the mess. She picked up a photo from a cluttered bookshelf: it was of the two of them on a beach when they were kids, wearing matching polka-dot swimsuits. Another photo on a different shelf was of them with their parents, gathered around a birthday cake with six candles, and Josie in the middle of blowing them out.

The only photos in Elizabeth's apartment were some elegantly framed black and white ones of her and Phil, taken by a professional in a studio. It suddenly seemed an odd thing to do – posing for photos instead of taking them in a natural situation. She lingered on another photo: a selfie of Josie and Emily, presumably on a night out, all dressed up and grinning into the camera. Emily looked completely different. She always seemed so nervous in the office, but she and Josie seemed ready to take on the world. Their joy radiated out into the room.

Walking to Josie's bedroom, she pushed gently at the door. Josie stood in front of the mirror holding up two tops. "The grey one," Elizabeth said.

"Thanks." Josie threw the grey top on the bed and pulled on the sequinned one instead. She grinned cheekily at Elizabeth, then admired herself in the mirror. She wore ripped jeans that somehow looked okay dressed up with a decent top. Her make-up was minimal – as always – and her brown hair fell just below her shoulders.

Her eyes darted to Elizabeth when the doorbell rang. "I feel like I should invite you along…"

Elizabeth shook her head. "I'm not in the mood for a night out."

"Thank God for that." Josie said mischievously. "We're meeting some guys and I don't really want you cramping my style!"

"Do you mind if I stay here for a bit and finish this?" Elizabeth asked, holding up her wine.

"Make yourself at home." Josie turned back briefly. "Next time bring your own wine!"

Chapter 31

Elizabeth hadn't intended to stay overnight at Josie's place. But the messy flat had suddenly felt homely and warm. It was cosy. Not unlike Seaside Cottage, she thought, somewhere towards the bottom of her second glass of wine.

There was a romantic comedy on TV which kept her entertained for a couple of hours, and when that finished, she stared at the ceiling until she fell asleep on the couch.

She stirred briefly in the early hours, when Josie stumbled home, but quickly fell back to sleep. Her head was foggy when she woke, and she dozed on and off for a while before finally venturing into the kitchen for coffee. She couldn't face checking her phone for Phil's missed calls and messages. After a few sips of coffee, she imagined him worrying about where she was and got her phone out, texting to tell him she was fine and had just fallen asleep at Josie's. She couldn't bring herself to apologise for worrying him.

It was mid-morning when she nudged Josie awake.

"Jesus, Liz!" Josie shouted, almost falling out of bed in shock. "Are you trying to give me a heart attack? How did you get in?"

"I slept on the couch."

"Why?" Josie asked, rubbing her eyes and trying to wake up properly.

"I just fell asleep."

"You could've at least made me breakfast," Josie grumbled, snuggling back into her pillow.

"You've got no food in," Elizabeth said. "But I'll take you out for breakfast."

"I won't be able to move for a while."

"Oh, come on. Jump in the shower and you'll feel fine."

With a groan, Josie dragged herself out of bed. "Life was easier when you didn't want to know me," she mumbled as she headed for the shower.

The comment wasn't intended harshly, but it bothered Elizabeth nonetheless. Why had she always been so irritated by Josie? She found it hard to understand Josie's flighty attitude, but Josie wasn't a bad person. And why couldn't Elizabeth overlook her flaws and just accept her for who she was? Maybe she was jealous of Josie. Josie had always been so carefree, while Elizabeth worried about every little thing.

She also resented that, as the baby of the family, Josie was always handed everything on a plate, while Elizabeth had to work for what she wanted. When she churned it all over in her mind, it seemed so petty. She vowed she would try harder with Josie.

It wasn't until they were in the car that Josie asked where they were going.

"You can have a little nap if you want," Elizabeth told her, avoiding the question.

Josie was suspicious. "I feel like I'm being

kidnapped. How far are we going exactly?"

"It's a little bit of a drive," Elizabeth admitted. "But we'll stop for breakfast on the way."

"I thought breakfast was the destination…"

Elizabeth's features wrinkled in uncertainty. "How long is it since we did anything fun together?"

Josie shook her head. "Fine. Kidnap me. Just wake me up when it's time for breakfast." She closed her eyes, clearly too hungover to cope with Elizabeth being sentimental.

Apart from a quick stop for breakfast, Josie slept for the whole drive. Elizabeth sang along to the radio and felt more content than she had since her holiday.

They arrived in Hope Cove early in the afternoon. It was three weeks since she'd been there with Max, and she wasn't sure why she'd suddenly felt the need to go back. But once she'd had the idea, she couldn't stop thinking about it. She parked the car by the seawall and got out, taking a lungful of sea air. Automatically, she reached for the clip holding her hair neatly in place. Her hair fell around her shoulders and she shook it out in the breeze.

"Where are we?" Josie asked, squinting.

Elizabeth's gaze didn't shift from the sea. "Hope Cove."

"Okay," Josie said slowly, shaking her head in confusion. "What are we doing here?"

"I thought a day at the coast might be fun," Elizabeth said, beaming.

She felt different. Like she'd inhaled happiness. It was something she hadn't felt for a while. She caught Josie taking in the view. When Josie turned to her, they grinned at each other before breaking into spontaneous laughter.

"Let's go for a walk," Elizabeth said after they'd calmed down. She set off up the hill and then took the coastal path.

"How do you know your way around here?" Josie asked, falling into step beside her sister. The fresh air seemed to be curing her hangover, and the spring was back in her step as they made their way along the path at a good pace.

"This is where I came on holiday," Elizabeth said wistfully. "You know, when Phil had to work and I went alone."

"It's a long drive for a day trip," Josie remarked. "What's so special about it? "

"You're not allowed to ask questions all day," Elizabeth replied. "You'll ruin it."

Josie nodded and they continued in silence.

When they reached the door in the hedge at Seaside Cottage, Elizabeth only gave it a cursory glance. She wanted so badly to push it open and wander up the garden. She longed to find Max sitting on the patio, sipping coffee and smiling at the sight of her.

Instead, she veered off the path and down to the beach.

"Where are you going?" Josie asked, hurrying to keep up.

"Let's go and sit on the rocks," Elizabeth said, happily leading the way in long strides.

She clambered up the rocks, and found a good spot to sit and gaze out at the sea. Grey clouds rolled overhead, threatening rain. Elizabeth wasn't the slightest bit worried about the weather. Nothing could ruin her mood. It was exhilarating sitting on the rocks with the waves beating nearby. Occasionally, the sea would pound the rocks so fiercely that spray would shoot up and land on Elizabeth in a fine mist.

"This place is amazing," Josie said, finally catching up and taking a seat on the smoothest rock she could find. "It's gorgeous."

"I love it here," Elizabeth said.

Josie picked idly at a limpet that would never budge from the rock it had claimed as home. "I know I'm not supposed to ask questions," she said. "But what's going on with you?"

Elizabeth contemplated acting as though she had no idea what Josie was talking about, but she didn't have the energy to pretend.

"I feel like I don't know who I am any more," she said slowly. "I keep thinking I want to stop everything – just draw a line under my life and try something new. I have everything I always thought I wanted, but I'm not happy. So I'm not sure what to do. I've tried ignoring it … but that approach doesn't seem to be working."

"Wow," Josie said. "I wasn't expecting that."

"Sorry," Elizabeth said. "Do you think I'm crazy?"

"No. It's probably the most sensible thing I've ever heard you say. If you're not happy, then you need to change something. Life's too short to be unhappy."

"I keep thinking that if I keep going in to work every day, if I keep living my life, it will get better. And maybe it's easier to carry on the way things are and be miserable than it is to try to change things.

Who's to say I'd be any happier?"

Josie shook her head. "What would you do," she asked, "if you could have anything? What would be your ideal life?"

Elizabeth appeared to contemplate the question, but she knew the answer immediately. It surrounded her. From their vantage point, the first floor of Seaside Cottage was visible over the hedge. She could see the top half of the upstairs windows with their bright white frames.

What if it was her house?

What if it was hers and Max's?

She went back to watching the waves hit the rocks. "What if what I want is impossible?"

"Nothing has ever been impossible for you," Josie said. "Whatever you want, you always get it. It's bloody annoying, to be honest! But if you set your mind on something, things usually work out."

"Not this time," Elizabeth said, struck by a sudden wave of reality. Max had gone back to his life – he probably hadn't given her a second thought. She'd let her feelings for him affect her too deeply.

"It's not like you to be so defeatist," Josie said, standing when Elizabeth did.

"I'm just being realistic," she said. "What I want is completely unrealistic. I'll make some changes, but I need to be realistic too."

When she jumped from the rocks back onto the sand, for a moment her heart stopped. A man walked along the path further up, and she was convinced it was Max. As he came into focus, she laughed at herself. "I really think I'm going crazy," she said, marching up the beach. If it had been Max, what would she have said to him?

She paused on the path and dithered for a moment.

"What are you doing?" Josie said in a stage whisper as Elizabeth opened the door in the hedge.

She checked the coast was clear and then slipped into the garden. "Come on," she said to Josie.

They ran along the garden like a couple of giggling schoolgirls.

"What are we doing?" Josie demanded as they hid beside the kitchen window with their backs to the house. "This is trespassing, you know?"

"It's not the first time!" Elizabeth peeked in the window and when she saw no sign of anyone, she leaned onto the glass, cupping her hands to peer inside. There was no one there. No signs of life.

She tried to open the back door, only to find it locked. Down the side of the house she caught sight of a For Sale sign in the front garden. Tears filled her eyes and she rattled the door again, as if it might magically open. Sadly, she rested her forehead on the windowpane.

"Liz," Josie said softly, "what's going on?"

"Nothing," she replied, but the tears wouldn't stop. He should be there. In her head it was the only place that Max existed. When she thought of him he was always there in the cottage, and he should be there now. She wanted to tell him that she'd been an idiot to go back to Phil. That they should have stayed in touch. That she should have given up everything for him.

"I'm worried about you," Josie said, gently patting her arm. They'd never been affectionate and she was clearly unsure how a hug would go down.

"I'm fine," Elizabeth said, wiping her eyes with her sleeve. "I'm an idiot. But I'm going to be okay."

Her mind tortured her on the walk back to the village, teasing her with the thought that Max could be just around the corner. Back in Hope Cove she kept imagining he was there too. It was both an exhilarating thought and a slow torture.

She knew Josie would love Hope Cove Gallery, and watched as she flitted about the shop exuberantly.

"It's all beautiful," Josie said to the woman on the counter. "There's literally nothing here I don't love."

"I knew it would be right up your street," Elizabeth said.

"Oh! I want this," Josie said excitedly, stopping in front of a display.

"Really?" Elizabeth asked, dropping her voice to a whisper. "It's some sea glass on a piece of string…"

"It's gorgeous," Josie said, unhooking it from the wall. "I'll hang it in the window. It'll look stunning when the light catches it."

When they stepped back into the street, the sun had come out. Elizabeth squinted and wished she'd brought sunglasses. "How can you afford to buy sea glass when you can't afford to pay rent?"

"I do a bit of freelance work now and again," Josie said as they wandered slowly back down the quiet street, past the brightly coloured cottages. "Just online typing jobs and stuff. Gives me a bit of pocket money."

"Shouldn't you use that for rent?"

"If I used it for rent I'd have no money for food or nights out… or sea glass!"

Elizabeth had a lot more to say on the subject but didn't want to spoil their day out so bit her tongue.

"Why didn't you buy anything?" Josie asked.

"I bought a painting last time I was here."

Josie beamed. "What's it like?"

"I can show you later. It's in my car."

"Your car? Why on earth is it in your car?"

"I just keep forgetting to take it out," Elizabeth said. That wasn't actually true. The painting taunted her constantly. At first she'd convinced herself that she was waiting until she'd decided where to hang it, but there was much more to it than that. Every time she looked at the picture she was transported back to Hope Cove and her week with Max. She wasn't sure she could face that every day in her house. Then there was Phil. She didn't want to share her beloved painting with him. She didn't want his opinion on it; didn't want him looking at it. It was completely irrational but that was how she felt.

A voice called out. It was Verity, the owner of the café. She was standing outside the café in her familiar apron, waving madly. "A batch of scones have just come out of the oven!"

"It's as if you knew I was coming," Elizabeth said. She crossed the street and introduced Verity to Josie.

"How long are you here for this time?" Verity asked.

"Just a day trip, unfortunately."

"You got lucky with the weather," Verity said, glancing up. The grey clouds had passed right over. "Here, take a seat in the sunshine. What can I get for you?"

"A pot of tea and a couple of scones will do nicely, I think."

"Coming up!"

"The view is fantastic," Josie said. They were sitting at the same table Elizabeth had sat at on her first morning in Hope Cove, with a perfect view of the bay.

Verity appeared with their order five minutes later.

"I saw Seaside Cottage is up for sale," Elizabeth remarked casually.

"Just went on the market a few days ago." Verity nudged Elizabeth's shoulder. "That's right, you helped with the redecorating, didn't you?"

Elizabeth ignored Josie's puzzled expression. "Yes. A little bit."

"You must have done a good job," Verity said jovially. "They've whacked a good price tag on the place…" She glanced around, before leaning in to whisper the asking price as though she was giving up a state secret. It actually sounded quite reasonable to Elizabeth. "It'll be snapped up regardless, I'm sure."

"Probably," Elizabeth agreed. "Have the owners been around much?" She spread jam on her scone and hoped she sounded as casual as she intended.

"Gosh, no, I don't know when last I saw Charlotte. She always was an oddity anyway. Pleasant enough but not a particularly warm woman, if you know what I mean. Now her husband, on the other hand, he was a character. Lovely man."

Elizabeth nodded and smiled. "You're not in touch with Charlotte, then?"

"Oh, no. I know her to say hello to, but that's

about it. I've only seen her a handful of times since they stopped using the cottage themselves and started renting it out." Verity greeted a couple of customers and scuttled away to take their order.

Elizabeth had no idea why she'd asked if Verity was in touch with Charlotte. What was she expecting? That she could pass on a note for Max?

"Are you sure you were just here for a week?" Josie said, breaking her thoughts. "You sound more like a local, gossiping away!"

"I wasn't gossiping," Elizabeth insisted.

"What was all that about redecorating?"

"I just helped out with a bit of painting, that's all."

"At the cottage we were at before? What's so special about the place?"

Elizabeth bit her lip. "You're not allowed to ask questions, remember? Just eat your scone," she ordered, smiling. "They taste divine."

Josie did as she was told. When they'd finished their tea and scones, they bid Verity farewell and returned to the car. Josie insisted on seeing the beautiful watercolour hidden in the boot of the car, and while she fawned over it, Elizabeth went to take one last look at the view in real life. Her emotions were such a mess. Overall, she'd enjoyed revisiting Hope Cove but it was hard too, as she'd expected. The place was full of bittersweet memories and the promise of a life she could never have.

"Let's go home," Elizabeth said.

She'd tortured herself enough in Hope Cove. Now it was time to get back to Phil, and deal with the torture that her life had become.

Hannah Ellis

Chapter 32

When she finally arrived home, Phil's smile was as fake as the ones she'd been giving him over the past month. How had they got to this? She knew he was suspicious of her. When he'd called Josie earlier that day, it hadn't been because he couldn't reach Elizabeth, as he'd said. He was checking up, obviously not believing that she really was with Josie.

Elizabeth was angry with him constantly, but she also felt sorry for him. None of this was his fault, after all. He was the collateral damage in the mess she'd made.

"Did you have a good time?" he asked with fake cheer.

Her forced smile matched his perfectly. She had arms full of shopping bags and he took a couple and followed her into the kitchen.

"It was surprisingly nice to spend some time with Josie," Elizabeth said. "I realised I don't make enough effort with my family so I invited them over for lunch tomorrow: Mum and Dad and Josie. I called at the supermarket, thought I'd cook a roast."

"Lovely," Phil said, but his confusion was evident. To be fair, her recent foray into the world of cooking was completely out of character. She'd never been interested in cooking, or in entertaining at home.

She'd been more inclined towards restaurants and being waited on.

To her, a relaxing evening always meant going to a restaurant or wine bar. She'd never truly felt relaxed at home. Glancing around her immaculate house, she felt annoyed by the lack of anything sentimental. Josie's apartment was littered with all kinds of knick-knacks, and the place had Josie written all over it.

If your home was a reflection of yourself, what did that say about her? she wondered. That she was cold, sterile, generic? The only thing she had of any sentimental value was locked in the boot of her car.

"So what did you get up to with Josie?" Phil asked, interrupting her thoughts. He perched on a bar stool, looking stiff and tense. She pretended not to hear the accusatory tone in his voice.

"Watched TV and drank wine yesterday and then went for a drive today." She wondered how vague she could get away with being. Her brow furrowed as she continued, and she made a conscious effort to try to distract him from asking questions about exactly where they'd been. "We had a lot of fun, actually. It was great to spend time with her without arguing for a change."

Phil drummed his fingers annoyingly on the kitchen counter. "Why was she suddenly so desperate to see you? And without giving you any warning. She can be very selfish sometimes."

Elizabeth tensed. She paused in unpacking the shopping and glanced at Phil. It was an effort not to defend Josie, but she was determined to avoid arguing with Phil. Once she started, she wasn't sure she'd be able to stop. There was so much brewing inside her:

things she wanted to say to him, but knew she shouldn't. He hadn't done anything wrong. It was all her.

She placed the chicken in the fridge, her movements calm and controlled. "She was panicking about the hen weekend," Elizabeth said, the lie falling easily from her tongue.

"Surely *she*'s not organising it? I'm surprised you'd even want a hen night."

"It might be fun," Elizabeth said. And who else did he think would organise her hen night? She wasn't exactly swarming with friends these days. It was another thing that had started to bother her. Her social life was non-existent. Especially since she and Karen had stopped going out for drinks in favour of drinking wine at the office. She used to have friends – what had happened to them? She had a couple of school friends she was still in touch with and saw occasionally: Jen and Becky. But when she thought about it, she couldn't actually remember the last time she'd spoken to either of them. They both had kids and when they had begun to insist they met at each other's house instead of at coffee shops and bars, their friendship had fizzled out. She remembered leaving Jen's place once with snot on her shoulder and squashed banana on her sleeve and vowing never to go there again. What a great friend she was!

Work was the problem, she supposed. She'd put it above everything else, and it was only now occurring to her that it wasn't a good thing to do.

"I'm not sure what Josie's idea of *fun* would entail," Phil said. She hated the derogatory tone he'd adopted to speak about Josie. Then she remembered it was exactly how she would have spoken about her until recently.

"She was thinking about a weekend at a spa hotel. All very civilised."

"Well, maybe I underestimated her," he said. "So that's where you've been today, then?"

"What?" she said, puzzled.

"Checking out spas?"

"Oh. Yes! We checked out a few."

He paused, and she could tell he knew she was lying. The atmosphere, which was frosty to begin with, turned even cooler. "Did you find somewhere?"

"I'm leaving it up to Josie…"

She moved to kiss him, feeling suddenly nervous at his questions. And her lies. Why was she lying? Kissing him did nothing to lighten the atmosphere, as she'd hoped. Instead, she was acutely aware that when she kissed Phil she felt absolutely nothing. It was as if she didn't know him any more. It was like kissing a stranger.

She was sure he felt it too.

At least Elizabeth had the luxury of knowing what the problem in their relationship was. If only she knew how to fix it.

Chapter 33

The smell of roasting chicken had an amazing effect on the house. The place felt suddenly homely. Elizabeth searched through the cupboards as though she was in someone else's kitchen. She couldn't decide which pots and pans to use for what. Cooking was enjoyable, nonetheless. Something for her to focus on – and far better than rattling around the house with Phil.

"Can I help with anything?" Phil asked when he joined her in the kitchen.

She moved to the stove to check nothing was bubbling over, then adjusted the heat when she saw that nothing was even boiling.

"It's all under control," she said brightly. "But you can be in charge of drinks."

Happy with the task assigned him, he headed to the pantry which he'd converted into a wine cellar. He'd just reappeared with a bottle of white in one hand and a red in the other when the doorbell rang.

"Can you get it?" Elizabeth said, trying not to feel overwhelmed.

"The world has gone mad!" Josie announced, walking into the kitchen a moment later in a pair of faded jeans and a scruffy T-shirt. "I know you said you were going to cook, but I assumed you had a person who'd come in and do it for you. That poor little old lady who cleans for you, maybe…"

"Mrs Wilkinson's services don't extend to cooking," Phil said, following Josie in, their parents right behind him.

Josie raised her eyebrows in amusement and Elizabeth flushed as she moved to greet her parents. She was slightly embarrassed that they'd asked Mrs Wilkinson to cook for them when she first started cleaning for them.

"What kind of potatoes are you doing?" Josie asked, peering into the pans on the stove.

Elizabeth shrugged. "I just put them into the water."

"Let's roast them," Josie said, moving them off the heat. "Where's your roasting tin?"

"I already used it for the chicken," Elizabeth replied.

Josie found another in no time and splashed it with oil before putting it in the oven to heat up.

"How long's the chicken been in?" Josie asked. "It looks like it's nearly done."

"It should need another half hour, I think," Elizabeth said, joining her by the oven. She wished she'd thought of roast potatoes.

"Well, this is really very strange," their mother said. "My two girls working together in the kitchen and no one screaming at anyone."

Their dad chuckled beside her. "Give them five minutes!"

But there was no arguing: everyone got along well and it was a pleasant atmosphere. They ate in the dining room, and Elizabeth was surprised by what a success her meal was. Perhaps it had a lot to do with Josie's help; still, she was pleased with it all.

They'd finished eating and were sitting round the table sipping wine when her dad asked her how work was going.

"Okay," Elizabeth replied unconvincingly.

"You work too hard," her mother said.

"I don't mind working hard."

"If that's a dig at me, I'm going to pretend I missed it," Josie said.

Elizabeth smiled at her. "It wasn't."

"What's the problem, then?" her dad asked.

"I don't know." She paused and mulled the question over. "I've just been there a long time and I don't really feel like I'm going anywhere. It doesn't excite me like it used to."

"I thought you were aiming to run the place one day."

"I am," she said. "I was. I don't know."

"Paris is still on the table," Phil said casually. "If you feel like a change!"

Her brow furrowed and she shot Josie a weary glance while her parents peppered Phil with questions about the possibility of a move.

"We're not moving to France," she said finally. Why on earth had he brought it up in front of her family?

"It sounds like a great opportunity," her dad said.

"But I'm not moving to France," she said, laughing at the absurdity of it, then glaring at Phil. "I might be a bit fed up with work but it doesn't mean I want to pack up and relocate to a different country! And what do you think I would do in France?"

"I know, I know," Phil said. "It's not realistic."

"It'd be lovely to visit you in Paris," her mum said.

Elizabeth shook her head. "It's not going to happen. Besides, I've been working my way up the ranks at the magazine for ten years. I'm not about to walk away now."

"Of course," Phil said. "And you'll soon be editor-in-chief. I'm talking nonsense. I can't even speak French."

Elizabeth felt deflated. Talking about becoming editor-in-chief no longer excited her. She'd spent so long aiming for it, it had become ingrained in her. Increasingly, the thought filled her with a sense of dread.

She was grateful when her dad redirected the conversation. "How's your new intern getting on?" he asked. "It was good of you to get Josie's friend a job."

"Emily's doing fine. I'm not sure it's something she'll want to do long term, but it's good experience for her." She turned to Josie. "You know she wrote a book?"

"Hmm," Josie said, picking at a tooth with her tongue. "I was a bit annoyed with you about that."

Elizabeth's eyes narrowed as she frowned. "Why?"

"You shouldn't have read it," Josie said calmly.

Elizabeth went on the defensive. "She shouldn't have left it open on my computer."

"Maybe she shouldn't have used your computer without asking," Josie said, fiddling with her wine glass, "but you still shouldn't have read her book. She's private about it."

"She shouldn't be. It's very good."

"You could have just asked her before you read it. She was upset that you'd read it without asking."

"She was glad I read it," Elizabeth insisted. "I'm editing it for her. I'll save her a fortune in professional editing."

"Well, she might be happy that you're editing it but she was still shocked that you read it like that. It was embarrassing for me, trying to make excuses for you."

Elizabeth could hardly believe her ears. "*I* embarrassed *you*?"

"Do you always have to argue?" Phil said. "I thought you'd got more civilised recently."

Josie ignored him, coolly keeping her eyes on Elizabeth. "Why is it so unbelievable that I could be embarrassed by you? You shouldn't have read the book without asking and I find it strange that you still can't see you shouldn't have done it."

"Josie," their mum said with a sigh, "don't argue with your sister. She's just cooked us a delicious meal."

"Little Miss Argumentative," Phil said, doing his best to keep his voice light.

"Shush, Phil," Elizabeth said.

"Well," he said, "she knows exactly how to wind you up and she does it every time. It's very immature."

"Josie…" Their mother glared at her in the same way she'd done to coax an apology from them when they were children.

"Okay," Josie said with a shrug. "I'm sorry. I wasn't trying to be argumentative. I was only saying."

"Well, let's get tidied up, shall we?" Phil said, collecting everyone's plates.

Elizabeth stayed where she was and kept her eyes on Josie. Her sister didn't seem angry, and she hadn't looked like someone trying to start an argument. They'd been getting on so well and it was odd that she'd want to argue for no reason.

When Phil rolled his eyes behind Josie's back, it annoyed Elizabeth.

"Josie's probably right," she said thoughtfully.

"Surely not," Josie said with a mocking ring to her voice.

Elizabeth couldn't help but laugh. "You're right," she said. "I should have asked before I read it. I thought I was doing her a favour."

"You are," Josie said. "I didn't say you didn't have good intentions."

"Sorry," Elizabeth said sincerely.

Their mother patted Josie on the shoulder and beamed at both her daughters.

They all drifted through to the kitchen together, carrying plates and dishes, then started to tidy up. Phil topped up wine glasses, then perched on a barstool.

"So you have the hen night all planned, Josie?"

Josie squinted at Phil in confusion, but recovered as soon as she caught Elizabeth's horrified look. "I don't think it's appropriate to discuss with men in the vicinity."

Phil's smile didn't reach his eyes. "You stole my fiancée away for half the weekend. You can at least tell me what you've been plotting."

"Sisters are allowed a secret or two, aren't they?" Josie said.

Phil tensed in annoyance. He was playing games, Elizabeth thought: using Josie to try to catch Elizabeth out. It was unnerving. Once again, Elizabeth reminded herself that it wasn't Phil's fault. He was muddling through and trying to figure out what was going on.

"I told you," she said quickly. "It's just a spa weekend. Nothing wild!"

"That's a good idea," her mum said. "I like the sound of it."

Elizabeth wandered back to the dining room to collect the last of the dishes.

Josie followed her. "What was that all about?" she whispered.

"Long story," Elizabeth replied, glancing nervously at the kitchen.

"Next time you might want to give me a heads-up so I can follow the lies."

"Sorry," Elizabeth said, feeling completely and utterly exhausted.

Chapter 34

Karen knocked on Elizabeth's door shortly after she arrived at work on Monday.

"How's things?" she asked.

"Fine," Elizabeth said. Since their chat about Max, she'd been pretending that Karen's little pep talk had worked and she was now back to her normal self. Everything was great – or so she kept telling Karen. She didn't want to hear again how she should make more effort with Phil. Making more effort with Phil was killing her.

"I'm glad you're doing better," Karen said. "Just a pre-wedding wobble, I'm sure."

"I guess so," Elizabeth agreed. "All okay with you?"

"Yes," Karen said, then sighed as she sat. "But Heidi's causing problems again. You're going to have to step in with your tact and diplomacy. I thought it might be easier if we went back to writing the horoscopes ourselves. That used to be fun."

"No way," Elizabeth said. "I'm not doing it. What's wrong with Heidi?"

"She's so inconsistent. Hang on…" Karen tapped at her tablet then held it up for Elizabeth. "That's Sagittarius."

Elizabeth glanced at the page of writing. "It seems

a little long."

"It's far too long, and very specific." Karen skimmed it. "*If you've been thinking of buying a new pillow, now is the time.* Seriously? Where does she get this from? *Wear yellow shorts for luck.* This will be in December's issue. Who wears shorts in December?"

"I'll talk to her," Elizabeth said. "But it's quite funny."

"Except some people take this stuff seriously. Some poor love is going to freeze to death going out to buy a new pillow in yellow shorts!"

"Nobody takes horoscopes seriously," Elizabeth argued. "Except maybe Heidi."

"What are you? Aries?" She dragged a finger over the tablet. "Let's see…"

"I don't want to know."

"Oh!" Karen said dramatically. "Heidi has six words for you. Six! It's like it's the last one she wrote and she got bored."

"Go on then," Elizabeth said, amused. "Hit me with it."

Karen adopted her best mysterious tone. "*Take a chance. Make a change.*"

"No," Elizabeth said adamantly. "It does not say that."

"Seriously. Look." Karen turned the tablet and Elizabeth shook her head.

"That's crazy," she said.

"I know. So you'll talk to her?"

Elizabeth covered her mouth but the laughter bubbled up and she couldn't stop it.

"It's not *that* funny," Karen said.

"It is." She swiped at tears. "It's hilarious."

Karen went serious. "I'm worried about you."

"Don't be," she said, taking a deep breath and trying to get herself under control. "I'm fine. I'll talk to Heidi."

Karen left the office quietly but her words floated in Elizabeth's head: *Take a chance. Make a change.* The hysterical laughter came again in an uncontrollable wave. She wasn't sure when it switched to crying, but she felt pathetic and it took a while before she composed herself enough to get on with some work.

The words niggled at her all day. She thought horoscopes were nonsense, but at the same time it felt like the universe was giving her a sign. It was exactly what she wanted to do: make a change. How long could she keep going as she was? It felt like she was fighting for something she didn't even want.

She struggled to focus on work and instead found herself mulling over the practicalities of leaving her job. And leaving Phil. She had money saved. He could buy her out of the house and she wouldn't ask much more from him. Financially, she was in a good position. If Josie knew how much money Elizabeth had stashed away, she'd wonder why she worked at all, never mind at a job she didn't enjoy.

For the first time she could remember, Elizabeth left work early. She headed straight for Josie's place.

"What's wrong now?" Josie asked when Elizabeth marched in.

"Well, I hate my job for a start," she said, moving to the living room. "I really hate it."

"There's an easy fix to that."

Elizabeth took a seat on the couch with Josie. At some point on the drive over, she'd changed her mind again, the rational part of her brain telling her that she shouldn't leave her job and Phil. That she was being crazy.

"I know! Quit my job! But it's not that easy. I have a great job. And in a few years I'll be editor-in-chief. How can I just leave?"

Josie pulled her legs under her. "I'm not saying it's not a great job. But maybe it's not the right job for you…"

Elizabeth tried to interrupt but Josie talked over her. "And I'm not saying it's easy to leave your job, but maybe you still need to do it, even though it's hard."

Elizabeth pouted. "When did you get so wise?"

"Probably about the same time you went crazy!"

They smiled at each other and Elizabeth wished that all her problems could be solved sitting on her little sister's couch. "It's not just the job," she said quietly.

"Phil?"

Biting her lip, she realised she needed to tell Josie the truth. She had to force the words out. "It's Max."

"Max?" Josie threw up her hands. "Who on earth is Max?"

"A guy I met. Remember the week I went to Hope Cove?"

Josie nodded.

"Well, I met someone."

"Okay," Josie said, clearly surprised by the revelation.

"I thought it was just a fling. Not even that – more

like a crush. But I can't stop thinking about him."

"What about Phil?"

"Well, Phil's great, isn't he? And clearly I'm a horrible person!"

"Oh, Liz," Josie said with a sigh, "don't be like that. Phil's a good guy, but that doesn't mean he's right for you. If you're not happy—"

"You're simplifying everything," Elizabeth snapped. "It's all so easy for you, isn't it? Don't like your job? Leave it! Fed up with your fiancé? Leave him and find someone else!"

Josie glared at her, her eyes wide.

"I'm not sure why I came here," Elizabeth said, getting to her feet. "I don't know why I thought you could give me advice."

"Oh, sit down," Josie said, her voice light. "You knew exactly what I would say, and it's what you want to hear. If you'd wanted someone to tell you to stop moaning and get on with things, you'd have gone to Mum or Karen. But you came here, so sit down and let's make a plan!"

"I can't." Elizabeth's face crumpled and the tears came. "I'm not like you. I can't give up everything I always wanted because I suddenly want something else. It doesn't make any sense."

Josie pulled her back to the couch. "What's your biggest worry? That you'll quit your job, leave Phil and end up alone and homeless?"

"No!" Elizabeth wiped at her tears. "I can get another job. And I've got savings."

"So what's your real fear?"

"That I'll never see Max again," she said. She took a deep breath. It was a relief to talk about him and be honest about her feelings. Generally, she wasn't even honest with herself when it came to Max.

"Right, well, what with the internet, it's a small world these days. We can find him."

"What if he doesn't feel the same? He's engaged too. What if he's happily moved on with his life?"

"We can find that out on social media, easy-peasy!" Josie reached for her laptop. "What's his last name?"

Elizabeth shook her head. "I don't know."

Josie frowned. "Liz, the internet's good, but it's not that good! Give me a clue. Where does he work?"

Elizabeth shook her head again. "At a cosmetics company."

"Really?" Josie said, raising her eyebrows.

"He's a lawyer at a cosmetics company."

"That sounds more your type. Which cosmetics company?"

"I don't know."

"We're a bit stuck, then. I didn't even know it was possible to fall in love with someone without stalking their social media pages. You're a freak, you know?"

"I didn't say I was in love with him," Elizabeth said, but the ache inside her was back. She frowned. "You need to help me! What do I do?"

"I have no idea," Josie said. "Stick with Phil?"

"No!" Elizabeth said. "I'm quitting my job. And leaving Phil…" She paused and took a deep breath. "And then I'm going to find Max. Somehow."

Josie let out a triumphant cheer.

Chapter 35

Elizabeth didn't go home on Monday evening. Instead she chatted with Josie, and composed her resignation letter. What on earth would Karen say? Elizabeth was dreading the conversation, but at the same time she felt a giddy excitement that she was going to go through with it all: leaving her job, leaving Phil, looking for Max. She wasn't a hundred per cent sure about the last one, or at least wouldn't let herself think too much about it. She didn't want to get her hopes up. He was engaged, after all.

Elizabeth and Josie stayed up chatting and laughing into the early hours until they finally fell asleep on the couch.

When Elizabeth called home to shower and change the next morning, Phil was waiting for her, lurking like a jailer, trying to appear nonchalant as he asked why she'd stayed at Josie's. If she told him quickly, it would be over and done with. Like ripping off a plaster. *I'm leaving you. Sorry. Goodbye.*

It couldn't be that quick, though, and it was going to be complicated. She owed him an explanation, but she didn't know where to start. Instead, she told him she was in a rush, but insisted she would talk to him properly that evening. Definitely. She would tell him everything, then pack her bags and leave. It was going to be an interesting day.

Her determination turned to nerves when she walked into Karen's office armed with her resignation letter. She kept it well out of sight at first, and had to listen to Karen rattling on about deadlines and meetings, and other mundane issues.

"I actually wanted to talk to you…" Elizabeth said gravely, taking a seat and hoping that Karen would take the hint and sit down. Thankfully, she returned to her desk and dropped into the swivel chair.

"Sounds serious."

"It is," Elizabeth said. It was hard to know whether to blurt it out or build up to it. Karen would probably prefer the direct approach. "I'm going to be leaving…" She tripped over her words and, when Karen looked puzzled, she realised she hadn't been as direct as she'd wanted. "Quitting, I mean. I'm quitting my job. I've got my notice here…" She waved the envelope. That was more to the point.

Karen shook her head and frowned. "You're what?" She reached for the envelope and scanned the letter, then sat holding it, staring at Elizabeth. "You're leaving?"

Elizabeth nodded. "I know you need four weeks' notice, but if it's possible I'd like to take two weeks' holiday and finish in two weeks."

Karen was lost for words, so Elizabeth filled the silence. "That would take us up to the next production deadline and I hoped that might be a good time. I don't want to leave you in the lurch…"

Quietly, Karen handed the letter back. "I think you should take some more time to think about this."

Elizabeth was stunned. "No," she said. "I've been

thinking about it for a while. I need a change."

"You've been distracted," Karen didn't make eye contact with Elizabeth, and seemed to be thinking aloud, "but I thought things were getting better."

"I guess I have been. It's not just work, to be honest. I've been doing some soul searching—"

"Is it the old biological clock? I know you mentioned kids before. You can have a family and a career. Don't let anyone say you can't."

"No." Elizabeth shook her head. For some reason, she'd expected this to be easier. "It's not that. I don't want kids." From out of nowhere an image popped into her head: sitting on the beach at Hope Cove with Max, his arm around her as they watched their kids jumping in the waves. She heard their giggles. Her chest tightened as she forced herself to focus. "I just need a change."

"Take some time off, then. A sabbatical. Recharge your batteries and then come back refreshed. I can keep your job—"

Elizabeth shook her head forcefully. She should be able to explain better. "I'm moving," she said.

"Where to?"

Elizabeth hesitated. Where was she moving to? And what happened to making a proper plan? 'Quit job and leave Phil' was fairly vague. Where would she live when she left Phil? What was she going to do for a job? She'd had one thought about that, at least. As she'd been editing Emily's book she'd been musing about editing for a living. It felt like a pipe dream, though. And she should probably worry about finding a place to live first.

Annoyingly, when she thought of where she

would live, Max sprang to mind again: cooking in the kitchen at Seaside Cottage while Elizabeth sat at the little table and watched him. It was ridiculous. She couldn't give up her whole life because of some silly romantic notions. Could she?

"I'm not sure where I'm moving to yet…"

"Did Phil get a new job?" Karen asked, looking increasingly puzzled.

"No. I'm leaving Phil," Elizabeth blurted out. Afterwards, she thought it might have been better to let him be the first to know, but never mind. "That's why I'll be moving. I'm having a whole new start."

Karen looked at Elizabeth as though she thought she was mad. At that moment Elizabeth would have agreed with her.

"It's not about that guy in Devon, is it?"

"No," she said. "Well, yes, in a way."

"I thought you'd put all that behind you."

"Not really, no."

"I think you probably need time to think this through," Karen said condescendingly. She gave the letter of resignation back again.

Elizabeth pushed it away. "I'm sorry," she said, pulling herself together and forcing confidence into her voice, "I know I sound unprofessional, but my mind is made up. I have thought this through. Please don't make this more difficult for me."

Karen looked hard at Elizabeth. "I thought you were going to be editor-in-chief."

"I was. But things change. It's not what I want now. And I can't pretend it is."

"I'll be sorry to see you go," Karen said. "But if you're sure…"

"I am."

"Then I wish you all the best."

"Thank you."

Karen's features softened. "We'll keep in touch, won't we? I'll miss you."

Elizabeth promised they would, and then slipped back to her office. For the rest of the day she tried to get on with work as normal, but it was hard to concentrate. She didn't want to slack off just because she knew she was leaving, but it was difficult to care about any of it any longer.

Her mind wandered; she couldn't help it. The thoughts she'd had about Max while she was in Karen's office left her feeling very uneasy. They were pure fantasy and if she was quitting her job and leaving Phil because of some crazy romantic ideas about a future with Max, she worried she was making a huge mistake. Her motives were all wrong.

By the time she reached home that evening, her thoughts were clearer, and she felt better. She wasn't doing all this so she could be with Max. She was doing it for herself. It was the right thing for her – regardless of whether she ever saw Max again or not.

Stopping to look up at the house before she went in, she felt nothing. It had never really felt like home and she wouldn't miss the place at all.

Phil was sitting in the kitchen, drinking a glass of wine. She suspected he knew what was coming. He must have some idea.

A forced smile flashed across his face when she joined him at the table, then quickly disappeared.

"Will you please be honest with me?" he said, holding a hand out to her. She took it and nodded.

"What's going on with you?"

She paused. Not because she didn't know what to say, but because she didn't want to say it. He'd been a huge part of her life for so long and she had no desire to hurt him.

"Are you seeing someone else?" he asked.

She shook her head and tears pooled in her eyes. "No."

"You said you'd be honest…"

"I'm not seeing anyone," she said sadly. "But I can't go on like this…"

"Like what?"

Tears rolled silently down her cheeks and splattered on the table. "I don't love you any more."

"Are you leaving me?" he asked.

She nodded sadly. "I'm sorry."

"Can you at least explain why?" he asked, far too calmly.

When she hesitated, his air of calm evaporated and he shot up from the chair. "If there is someone else, I'll find out eventually! I may as well hear it from you."

She watched as he paced the room. "I'm not leaving you for someone else," she said slowly. "But I am leaving you *because* of someone else."

He stopped abruptly. Elizabeth took a deep breath, hoping she could explain things to him better than she had to Karen.

"I met someone when I was in Devon."

He nodded. Obviously he knew that was when she'd changed. When everything had started to go wrong.

"Nothing really happened," she said, wincing.

Talking to Phil about Max seemed bizarre. "We just became friends. I haven't seen him since. I did feel something for him, though. More than friendship. I've tried to get on with things, but that week made me question so much about my life … and now I realise that I want something different. I'm not even sure what I want yet. But I need to find out."

He banged his fist on the counter. She flinched. Then silence filled the room. Phil moved to the window and gazed out over the back garden. Part of her wished he'd shout at her. Seeing him so upset was killing her.

"I quit my job," she said, needing to break the silence.

He moved back to sit beside her. "You really don't love me any more?" he asked. "There's no fixing this?"

She shook her head sadly. "No."

"So you don't know what you want, but you know what you don't want?"

She nodded. That was exactly it. The next chapter in her life was a complete mystery but one she needed to move on to. At that moment it was so daunting she felt physically sick.

She just hoped everything would work out in the end.

Chapter 36

Phil had been surprisingly calm about everything. After they'd talked, she'd thrown a few things into a suitcase and headed to Josie's. She'd collect the rest of her things later and they'd have to decide what to do about the house. They would have to cancel the wedding. Thank goodness they weren't already married, or things would have been much more complicated.

Elizabeth was lying awake beside Josie when her phone rang late that evening. She crept out of the bedroom to answer it. It was Phil. She was tempted to ignore it, but she suddenly felt compassion for him. She'd spent the last month panicking about her future with him and it was a relief now that he was part of her past. And it hadn't been an awful past; she didn't feel that she'd wasted her time with him. He'd been right for her at one time and they'd had a lot of good years together. She could look back fondly.

As soon as he spoke, it was clear he was drunk. He wasn't a huge drinker, and she only remembered a handful of times when he'd overdone it with the wine.

"You can't just leave," he said, slurring his words. Elizabeth sighed. Perhaps things weren't going to be as easy as she'd thought.

"I love you," he said. "We're getting married.

You can't leave."

She sank into the couch and pulled a blanket around her. "Things haven't been right for a while, Phil. You must have noticed. We grew apart. We focused too much on work and not enough on each other."

"I didn't grow apart," he said. "You did. And you need to come back. You're just confused…"

She shouldn't have answered the phone. It felt like this could be a long conversation that would never get anywhere.

"It *was* me," she agreed. "I changed. I want different things. And we can't be in a relationship if we want different things out of life."

"Whatever you want is fine. I want whatever you want."

"No you don't," she said firmly, not sure why she was bothering to argue when he was in such a state.

"Whatever you want, you can have."

"But you obviously want to move to Paris and further your career…"

"I was joking about Paris," he said, his words garbled. "We won't move to Paris. And if you want a baby, we can have a baby."

"I don't want a baby with you, Phil, and I don't want to discuss this now. You're drunk. Sleep it off and we can talk again when you're sober, if you want."

"I just want you to come home."

Oh God, he was crying.

"I'm really sorry," she said.

"Can't you come home?" he sobbed.

"No, Phil, I can't. I'm going to hang up now. Go

to bed, okay?"

The phone rang again a few seconds after she ended the call. She switched it off. She was doing him a favour. He'd be mortified the next day.

She stayed on the couch, feeling awful for Phil and wondering if she was doing the right thing. Of course, breaking up with Phil wasn't going to be easy. She had to give him time. Maybe they could even stay friends once he was over the shock.

Everything will be okay, she told herself before she finally fell asleep.

The next morning, she turned her phone on to find a barrage of messages and voicemails from Phil. She didn't listen to or read any of them. She'd call him later.

At the office, she dived into work for a few hours and then stuck her head out of her office to look for Emily.

"Psst!" she said, getting Emily's attention along with that of most of the other people in the room. "Come in here a minute."

"Is everything okay?" Emily asked, following her back into the office.

"Fine," Elizabeth said, swivelling in her chair. "I've started to edit your book."

"Really?" Emily said excitedly.

"Yes. I should have it finished in a couple of weeks."

"That's amazing."

"I need you to do something," Elizabeth said. "Once I've finished, you need to find an agent and get it published."

"Well, hopefully one day."

"Definitely," Elizabeth said. "I think it's great."

Emily frowned. "Why are you so keen?"

"I want it to be a bestseller so I can tell everyone I edited it!"

"What's going on?" Emily asked. She seemed decidedly unnerved by Elizabeth's good mood.

"I quit my job yesterday!"

"What? No way?"

"Yes," Elizabeth said heartily. It felt fantastic to tell someone else.

"But why? I thought you loved your job."

"I want to edit books," Elizabeth said. "It's so much fun. I need a change. I'm going to set up as a freelance editor and work on projects that interest me, like your book."

The idea had come to her as she lay awake, worrying about her future. The thought of going back to her original plan of working in a publishing house had been niggling her, but she knew her chances of getting a job were slim due to her lack of experience in fiction editing. Then she had the idea to set up on her own. She'd do the training and get some experience and, at the end of it, she'd be her own boss.

After sleeping on the idea, she was positive it was what she wanted to do. The more she thought about it, the more sure she was that it was the right thing for her.

"That's amazing," Emily said, taking a seat.

"I'm so excited," Elizabeth said. "And I'm excited for you too. Your book is so good. And it's going to be the first thing I list in my portfolio when I set up my business."

Emily laughed. "Maybe I will try to get published. If you're following your dreams, perhaps I should do the same. You're very inspiring today!"

"I'm glad," Elizabeth said happily. "Following your dreams is a great thing to do. I don't think it's going to be easy for me, though. First, I need to find more jobs to build up my portfolio."

"Would you do editing for free to get the experience?"

"Yes. I'll need to work for free to start with. That way I can get some experience while I do the training and get the proper credentials. I just need to find some authors."

"I know authors," Emily said eagerly. "And they'd fall over each other for free editing!"

"How do you know authors?"

"I'm in a few online writing groups and author communities. People are always asking for recommendations for editors."

"Seriously?"

"Of course. I can post in the groups and give people your email if they're interested. If you want me to?"

"That would be amazing."

"I'm going to be so popular," Emily said. "Free editing! You'll be inundated with requests."

"I hope so," Elizabeth said. It made everything seem real. She'd have to look in to training courses.

"I can't believe you're leaving," Emily said.

"Me neither. It's going to be weird, not being here. Maybe you should leave too. Focus on your writing. Write another book!"

"You're in a funny mood," Emily said, chuckling.

"I know. Now that I know I'm definitely leaving, I've completely lost my motivation. I wish I could leave today. I've got two weeks left but I think it's going to be the longest two weeks ever."

"I'm sure it'll fly by," Emily said, standing. "Now I'd better get back to work."

"Yes, you should." Elizabeth tried to be stern. "Back to work, Emily!"

Chapter 37

The week went surprisingly fast – probably because she had so much going on in her head. When she called Phil he was aloof, acting as though everything was fine, and pretending his drunken phone call had never happened. He politely asked her not to come to the house without calling first. Apparently he didn't like the idea of her walking in at any moment, and he'd rather not be there when she collected her stuff.

It was tempting to tell him it was still her house too and she'd do what she liked, but it seemed petty – and he was obviously very hurt and dealing with it the best he could. Besides, she had no desire to pop back for a visit and was in no hurry to collect her things.

When she woke on Saturday, Josie was snoring beside her, and when she went to the living room she found Emily fast asleep on the couch. They'd invited her to go out with them the previous evening, but she'd declined, opting instead to scour the internet researching website designers. She suspected she could set up a website herself but she needed something professional, and she thought it would probably end up being stressful. She'd emailed a couple of designers and was waiting to hear back from them.

The other thing she'd done was apply to become a

member of the Society for Editors and Proofreaders, the professional organisation for editors in the UK. It was exciting to browse their website and she'd already signed up for a couple of online courses. All she had to do was survive one more week of work.

Josie stuck her head into the room, grunted at her, mumbled something about coffee and disappeared again. So far, living with Josie was going surprisingly well. It was hard to believe that only a couple of months earlier they couldn't be in the same room together without arguing.

She'd have to find her own place, but with so much going on she didn't feel ready to start looking yet. Plus, at a time when so many aspects of her life felt uncertain, living with Josie made her feel secure. When she'd had an attack of 'what on earth am I doing?' earlier in the week, Josie had been there to calm her and tell her everything was going to work out brilliantly.

"Did you have a good night?" Elizabeth asked when Josie reappeared.

"Yeah, it was great," Josie said, her tone not quite matching her words. Elizabeth was thankful she hadn't gone with them. A hangover was the last thing she needed.

"How was your evening?" Josie asked.

"Productive," Elizabeth said. "I emailed a few website designers. Hopefully I'll hear back from them soon."

On the couch, Emily hadn't stirred. Josie shuffled to get comfy by her feet. "Can't you do it yourself?"

"Maybe, but I think it's probably better to let a professional do it."

"I could do it for you."

Elizabeth frowned. "I want it to be professional."

"It would be," Josie said with a laugh. She winced and held her head. "Ouch, too loud." She lowered her voice a little. "I can set up a website, no problem."

"I don't know."

Josie shook Emily's leg. "Em! We can set up a website for Liz, can't we?"

Emily stretched, then grunted. "What?"

"Liz needs a website for her freelance work. She was gonna pay someone to set it up."

"We can do it," Emily said. "It's easy."

"Really?"

"Yes," Emily and Josie said together.

"But we'll need bacon sandwiches," Josie said.

"And coffee," Emily added.

Josie sat up straighter. "You could pay us. Since you were going to pay a stranger…"

"I'm not paying you," Elizabeth said. "You can do it out of sisterly love."

"*I* can't," Emily said, grinning.

"Come on," Josie said. "I'm skint, and there's a gig we wanted to go to tonight…"

"Okay," Elizabeth agreed. "I'll pay for your night out. But the website needs to be good."

"Just get the bacon on," Josie said. "And give me your laptop!"

For two people with a hangover, they were very productive. Emily worked on Josie's laptop, searching for similar websites to get some ideas about how Elizabeth's could look, and Josie set up a WordPress account and browsed the website templates. They sat side by side discussing layout and fonts, tabs and graphics. They were surprisingly professional. Elizabeth hovered over them, asking questions and giving her input. It was a lot of fun.

The day flew by, and by late afternoon they had created a professional-looking website that Elizabeth would have been very happy to pay for. Treating Josie and Emily to a night out was the least she could do, she decided. She ordered pizzas to celebrate.

When the doorbell rang they were all in the kitchen, discussing possible tweaks to the website. Josie buzzed the pizza deliverer in. She'd not bothered with the intercom, and they were all surprised when Phil trudged up the stairs, not the pizza person.

"Hi," he said awkwardly. "I wondered if we could talk quickly?"

"We can go in the bedroom," Josie said, looking questioningly at Elizabeth.

"Thanks," Elizabeth said, and Emily and Josie hurried out of the way. Elizabeth gestured for Phil to come in, briefly wondering why she wasn't supposed to go home without calling first but it was fine for him to show up at Josie's unannounced. She decided it wasn't worth commenting on.

"How are you?" she asked.

"I'm fine," he said, without making eye contact. "How are you?"

"I'm okay."

"Good." There was a brief pause. "I've accepted the job in Paris. I wanted to let you know. They want me out there ASAP so I'd like us to decide what we're going to do about the house."

Elizabeth's eyes were wide. "You're moving to

Paris?" She shouldn't really have been surprised. It made sense when she thought about it. It was just so fast.

"Yes. I think it'll be good for me. Fresh start, and all that."

He was being so matter-of-fact about it that it made Elizabeth uncomfortable. They'd been together for so long, but now it felt like talking to a stranger.

"I wondered if you wanted the house?" he said. "You could buy me out. That might be the easiest... And I suppose you don't want to stay here indefinitely." His lip twitched as he glanced around at the messy room.

"I don't want the house," she said.

"Okay. Well, if you're sure... You don't need time to think about it?"

"No. I don't want it."

"In that case, I'll speak with the estate agent on Monday and get it on the market. You'll obviously need to clear out the rest of your stuff, and if you want any of the furniture let me know."

"I don't think I will," she said. She couldn't think of anything that she was very attached to. She just wanted a fresh start.

"Okay," he said. "In that case I'll organise selling the furniture too and we can split the money."

"Do you want me to take care of anything?"

"I'd rather get on and do it myself, if you don't mind. I've got some contacts and I think I can get things moving quickly. I'll keep you updated, of course, and call if there are any decisions we need to make together."

"That's fine," she said. "Thanks. When will you

go to France?"

"As soon as I can get everything in order with the house and tie up a few loose ends at work. Soon, I hope."

"I'm sure it'll be good for you." She sighed. "I really am sorry."

He shrugged, his features fixed in a frown.

"I'll call when I know anything about the house," he said. "But if you could come and pick up your things soon, that would be great. Tomorrow, maybe?"

"Okay," she said. "I'll come in the morning."

"You've still got your key, haven't you? I'll probably make myself scarce."

She began to cry. Everything was too cut and dried. "Will you keep in touch? Let me know how you get on when you're in France?"

"I don't think so," he said sadly. "Not at first, anyway. It's too hard for me at the moment. You understand?"

She nodded and bit her lip. Then he was gone.

The floodgates opened. Elizabeth sank onto the couch and sobbed. Josie came in a few minutes later and enveloped her in a big hug.

"He looked so sad," Elizabeth spluttered. "I can't believe I did that to him."

"He'll be okay," Josie said. "And you will too. You'll both be better in the long run."

When Elizabeth had calmed down, she told Josie about Phil's move and selling the house.

"I need to clear out my stuff tomorrow," she said. "It seems so final."

"I'll help you," Josie said.

"You'll be too hungover after your gig tonight!"

"We won't go out tonight," Josie said. "We'll stay in with you."

"No. You should go. I'm fine. I need some time alone to process everything."

"Okay. I can still help tomorrow."

At the doorway, Emily cleared her throat discreetly. "We're quite productive when we're hungover." She flashed Elizabeth a sympathetic smile. "We'll both help."

More tears came. It was a relief to have help. Elizabeth wasn't sure how she'd handle it alone. "Thank you," she said, smiling through her tears.

Chapter 38

With help from Josie and Emily, moving the rest of her stuff was fairly painless. She put several boxes into her parents' spare room and stacked several more in Josie's apartment. That evening she sat with Josie, staring at some reality show that Josie was addicted to. She was exhausted.

The framed picture of the beach at Hope Cove had finally been removed from the car and was propped against the wall in the living room. Josie went to get a drink in the ad break, and Elizabeth moved slowly over to the picture. Carefully, she removed the bubble wrap. Occasionally, she'd had a quick peek at the picture in the car but hadn't lingered on it.

Now, she was transported back to Hope Cove. Seagulls shrieked as they sailed on the salty breeze, and the smell of the sea filled her nostrils. She was sitting outside the café with the warm sun on her face and could hear Verity in the background, nattering with customers.

It was all so familiar. In her mind, Max appeared, sitting beside her and grinning widely. They were laughing about something.

"Are you okay?" Josie asked, snapping Elizabeth from her daydream.

"Would it be okay if I hang the painting somewhere?"

"Of course." Josie set her drink down. "I'll find my tools!"

The picture looked great up on the living room wall. Josie had hung her string of sea glass in the kitchen window and Elizabeth had been astonished the first time she'd seen it reflecting the morning sun. The glass seemed to glow and the colours beamed gloriously around the kitchen. When Elizabeth had remarked on it, Josie had shrugged, as though that was the way she'd seen it all along.

"Are you going to try to find him?" Josie asked, gazing at the picture on the wall.

"I don't know."

"If I were you I'd be stalking him by now."

"I know you would," Elizabeth said, amused. "I don't know what to do. He's got a girlfriend."

"I can't believe you didn't swap numbers. How did you leave things?"

Her mind took her back once again, and she was on the beach telling him it could never work, that it was just a holiday romance. With a deep breath she forced herself not to dwell.

"He wanted to keep in touch," she said, matter-of-factly. "He mentioned leaving his girlfriend. I said he was being ridiculous. I refused to take his number."

Josie stared at her.

"You don't need to tell me I'm an idiot," Elizabeth said.

"I'll keep biting my tongue, then!" There was a short pause. "I think you should find him. It sounds like he might not even be with his girlfriend any more if he was talking about leaving her."

"I think part of me is just terrified of finding him, and losing him all over again."

"At least you'd know," Josie said. "Do you think you'll ever stop wondering about him if you don't find out?"

"Probably not," Elizabeth admitted. "I'll think about it. I just want to focus on getting through my last week at work, and then I'll decide what to do about Max."

Josie was suitably placated by the plan. When her TV show finished she went to bed, leaving Elizabeth alone with her thoughts.

She gazed at the picture of Hope Cove and let herself daydream about being back there with Max. After a while she reached for her laptop. A quick internet search brought up the sale listing for Seaside Cottage. The photos of the cottage were stunning and she lingered on every one of them.

Another search brought her to the website for Oakbrook Farm: Boarding Home for Dogs. It was one of the most basic websites she'd ever seen. Maybe she should put Annette in touch with Josie to spruce it up. Strangely, there was an announcement on the home page that they were closed until further notice. The kennels had been busy when Elizabeth was there. She remembered the way Wendy had limped and Max talking about her ill-health. She hoped everything was all right. It was too late to call but she made a note of the phone number. She had no idea what she would say if she did call, but it was comforting to think that she could probably track Max down if she decided to.

***

Her final week at work went by in a blur. The week running up to the production deadline was always hectic, and Elizabeth was glad: it meant the week went fast. There was a cake on her last day, and a card, and a bunch of flowers. People were busy; there wasn't time for a lot of fanfare.

Then, before she knew it, she had begun the new chapter of her life. It was the last week of September, less than six weeks since her week in Hope Cove, and her life had changed so much. It was hard to believe that one week could completely alter the course of her life. If she stopped to think about everything she'd be completely overwhelmed. Thankfully, she had a lot to keep her occupied.

"I thought you might at least take a few days off," Josie said, arriving home on Monday afternoon. Elizabeth had spent the morning working through an online training course on fiction editing – the first of many courses she would undertake in the upcoming months. In the afternoon, she'd finished working on Emily's book. She'd also been emailing a few of Emily's writer friends and had booked in some other projects to edit, to give her more experience and hopefully garner some testimonials for her website.

"I need to keep busy," Elizabeth said. "How was the library?"

"Good. I found a couple of job possibilities and sent off my CV."

"You're sure you didn't go to the library to get out of my way?" Elizabeth asked, closing her laptop and putting it aside. Josie flopped onto the couch. "It is your place. I can always work in the library if you need space." Living together was working out well, but Elizabeth was concerned that now she wasn't working, they might get under each other's feet. Becoming so close to Josie was one of the positive changes in her life, and she didn't want to ruin it.

"No. It's fine. I often go to the library. It's a change of scene."

"I'm going to look for a new place soon. I promise."

"Don't worry about it," Josie said. "I like having you here. It's surprising how it's worked out, isn't it? You living here, I mean."

"Very surprising!" Elizabeth agreed. Her voice turned serious. "It was my fault we didn't get on, wasn't it?"

"I'd say so," Josie said, kicking off her shoes and putting her feet up on the coffee table. "You definitely weren't my biggest fan!"

"Sorry."

"I'm just glad we're friends now. And I'm glad you're so happy."

"Am I?" she asked, surprised by the comment.

"You're so relaxed now. Surely you can see that?"

"I suppose so." Elizabeth did feel more peaceful, and she was definitely hopeful. She just wasn't sure she was really happy yet.

"Anyway," Josie said, "I've got an interview tomorrow. Something really interesting. This could be a big break for me."

"What is it?"

"I'll tell you when I get the job. I don't want to

jinx it. It would be nice to start paying my own rent again. I don't mind taking handouts from Mum and Dad for a while, but guilt is setting in now."

Elizabeth still couldn't understand Josie's choices. She could never imagine being financially dependent on anyone.

"Don't get all judgemental," Josie said, as though she could read Elizabeth's mind. "It was Mum's idea for me to quit my job at the cinema and find something I enjoy."

"Is it so hard to find something else?"

"Not really. I've had interviews. Even got a couple of offers, but I turned them down."

Elizabeth shook her head. "Why?"

"They didn't inspire me," Josie said flatly. "I want to find something I can do in the long term. Something I love. I just can't figure out what."

Elizabeth picked up her cup of tea only to find it empty. "Have you ever thought of doing web design?" she asked. "You're good at that."

Josie had surprised her when they worked together on her website, showing a flair for the creative as well as the technical side of website design.

"Boring!" Josie said with a sigh. "Anyway, stop hassling me. You're the one taking up space in my apartment. It's your issues we need to address. When are we going on a Max hunt?"

Elizabeth kicked Josie gently. "We're not mentioning him! I've decided he was my wake-up call, that's all."

Josie sighed dramatically. "But he might be the love of your life! You're just giving up on him?"

"I'm not just giving up," Elizabeth said. "I've tried. His aunts have a dog kennels. I met them while I was in Hope Cove. So I looked up the number and tried to call, but they never answer. On the website it says the kennels are closed for business."

She'd been so nervous when she'd dialled and then utterly disappointed when it had come to nothing.

"Drive down there," Josie said adamantly. "Don't give up so easily."

"It would be completely embarrassing. They'd think I was crazy, arriving on the doorstep asking for his number."

"You're supposed to do crazy things for love!"

"It's also about a six-hour round trip. I feel like there must be an easier way." She paused, mulling things over. "His mum's house is for sale – the cottage in Hope Cove. I was thinking maybe I could get in touch with her somehow and enquire about it. I could have a chat with her and pretend I went to school with Max, ask how he's doing…"

"Okay," Josie said, unconvinced.

"Do you think the estate agent would give out her number?"

Josie shook her head and looked thoughtful. "I think his aunts seem like a better option."

"I told you, I already tried that."

"You just tried ringing them. Go there."

"I did!" Elizabeth said quickly, taking Josie by surprise. "Yesterday, when I said I was going shopping and meeting Karen for lunch. I drove down to Devon and knocked on their door. There was no one there."

It had taken so much determination to go there. She'd been a nervous wreck on the drive. Finding the place deserted wasn't just disappointing, but worrying too. It had been such a hive of activity the last time she was there, with all the dogs jumping around the place. This time it was eerily quiet, without a dog in sight. She'd even called at the local pub and asked about the kennels. The landlord told her they'd had to close for a while due to illness. It was what Elizabeth had suspected, and she was sorry to hear it. She remembered how fond Max was of his aunts, and how kind and welcoming they'd been to her.

"There must be another way of getting in touch with him," Josie said.

"I'm beginning to think it's just not meant to be. Besides, he hasn't been knocking down my door."

"He might be trying to find you, for all you know," Josie argued. Her face lit up. "Is your Facebook account searchable?"

"I have no idea. I told you, I never go on Facebook."

"Literally never?" Josie asked.

Elizabeth shook her head. "Never."

"So he might have messaged you and you've not seen it?" Josie said.

Elizabeth grabbed her phone. "Oh my God!" she said when she opened the Facebook app.

"Did he message?" Josie asked excitedly.

"Where did this photo come from?" Elizabeth asked, holding up the phone. Her profile picture was now a selfie of her and Phil. She was laughing as Phil kissed her cheek and she was squirming to get away from him. Phil had thought it was hilarious to snap a selfie when Elizabeth was ranting about how much she hated the selfie craze.

"Oh yeah!" Josie said cheekily. "I messed with your Facebook that day when we were shopping."

"My status says 'Can't wait to marry my hunk of a man'."

Josie giggled. "I told you I'd announce your engagement! I can't believe you haven't logged on since."

"People can't see all this, can they?"

"Just your friends," Josie said. "Unless you're an idiot and have your privacy settings on public…"

They exchanged a look. Elizabeth passed the phone to Josie.

"You're an idiot," Josie announced, grimacing as she investigated Elizabeth's privacy settings. "Why would you set it to public? Are you insane?"

"I told you I don't go on there," Elizabeth said, her voice rising an octave. "Why on earth did you mess around with my profile like that?"

"It was a joke," Josie said. "I presumed you'd change it!"

"Josie! I can't believe you did that."

"Let's not forget you were a cow to me back then," Josie said. Anger flashed over her face and was gone again, quickly replaced by amusement. "It could have been way worse. I'd started typing a status about your fetish for sweaty armpits, but thought you'd probably never speak to me again if I posted it."

Under other circumstances, Elizabeth would probably see the funny side. "What if Max did look for me?" she said gloomily. "He'll think I'm still engaged."

255

"Don't worry," Josie said, tapping on the phone. "I'll fix your Facebook page … and then we'll track him down and tell him you're free and single and completely in love with him!"

"Except we've already established that I don't know how to find him."

"You can try to get in touch with his mum, like you said. It might work."

"Maybe," Elizabeth said. There was a short pause, then her forehead wrinkled as memories unlocked themselves. "Her name's Charlotte. She's just moved to a nursing home. Fancy place…" She paused, staring blankly at the wall of the living room while she tried to remember. "Henley House."

Josie clapped her hands.

Elizabeth shook her head, almost wishing she'd kept her thoughts to herself. Would she really get in touch with his mum? What on earth would she say?

Josie reached for her laptop, grinning.

Chapter 39

Elizabeth went the next morning, knowing she wouldn't be able to stop thinking about it until she did. Henley House was located just outside Bath, an hour and a half's drive from Josie's place in Oxford. Elizabeth spent the drive arguing with herself about whether or not she should just turn around and go home. Was she really going to visit Max's mother?

She realised she had to. She had a flicker of hope whenever she thought about Max that wasn't going to go away. She needed to see him again, at least once. Even if it was just so she could put it all behind her.

The nursing home was an imposing building in a couple of acres of neatly kept gardens. Elizabeth manoeuvred into a parking spot and looked up at the grand house looming over her. She was filled with nerves.

It took some courage to ring the doorbell, and it seemed to take forever before she was buzzed in. The front desk was manned by a tall, dark-haired care assistant whose name tag announced her as Kelly.

"Hi," Elizabeth said, walking up to her. *Oh, gosh, she was going to sound like an idiot.* "I've come to visit one of your residents. Charlotte…"

"Mrs Anderson?" Kelly jumped in, saving Elizabeth the embarrassment she'd been expecting.

She hadn't known her last name. Hopefully there was only one Charlotte living there, or things could get awkward. "I think I saw her in the day room earlier. Is she expecting you?"

"No. She's not."

"Okay," Kelly said cheerfully. She thrust a clipboard and pen across the desk. "Sign in and we'll see if we can find her."

Elizabeth scribbled her name and signature, then trailed Kelly through the impressive entranceway and into a large living room, where residents sat around in armchairs.

"Mrs Anderson!" Kelly called, waving at a well-dressed lady sitting with another couple of elderly women. "You've got a visitor."

Charlotte frowned, obviously not recognising Elizabeth.

"Are you family?" Kelly asked warily. Elizabeth ignored the question..

"Hi," Elizabeth said when Charlotte walked confidently over to them. It was odd to think she was Max's mum. Elizabeth could see no immediate resemblance: her features were stern and her posture was straight and formal. She wasn't the frail little old lady she had expected. "I'm so sorry to bother you," she went on, extending her hand. "My name's Elizabeth. I'm a friend of your son…"

Charlotte's features softened and she dismissed Kelly with a quick nod. She lowered herself into the nearest chair and glared at Elizabeth.

"Sit," she said, patting the chair beside her. "You're making me nervous."

"Sorry." Elizabeth did as she was bid and perched

on the edge of an armchair.

"I'm sorry," Charlotte said when the silence stretched a moment too long. "I've usually got a pretty decent memory, but I'm afraid I don't remember you."

What on earth was she going to say? She'd had a script ready in her head but she couldn't think of it now. "As I said, I'm a friend of your son." Her heart raced at the thought of Max, and she searched for the words to explain why she'd come.

"Were you at the wedding?" Charlotte asked. "I'm sorry, there were so many people and I didn't know half of them…"

Elizabeth's insides turned to jelly and she felt sick and faint at the same time. "No," she said, hardly hearing herself as the sound of her blood rushing round her body muffled everything.

But he couldn't be married yet. He'd told her he was getting married in July. Something wasn't right.

Charlotte was looking at her expectantly.

"We're just acquaintances," Elizabeth said, trying to compose herself. "I don't know his wife at all."

Charlotte rolled her eyes. "You're not missing out! She's an acquired taste, that woman. The wedding was over the top, in my opinion. I'm all for spending money, but she seemed to have something to prove."

"Sorry," Elizabeth said, confused. "For some reason I had it in my head that the wedding wasn't until next year."

"They changed the date! Just like that. It was absurd, expecting everyone to come at the last minute. I've never heard anything like it. Apparently there'd been a cancellation. Max told me it was all *her* idea. Poor old Max – he thought it was as farcical as I did. Not that he'd ever say. He likes to keep the peace. I don't know where I went wrong, but if there's one thing my sons have in common, it's dreadful taste in women." She paused. "Sorry – once you get me talking about my boys, I can't stop."

"It's fine," Elizabeth said, feeling suddenly weak. She felt as if all the air had been sucked out of her. She twisted her hands together to stop them from shaking. She'd been so determined to find him, and it was too late. He was already married.

Charlotte looked at her with concern. "Do you need a cup of tea, dear?"

"That would be lovely," Elizabeth said, wanting to run away but fearing her legs wouldn't comply. "Sorry. I feel a bit funny."

Charlotte fussed and went to the other side of the room where large urns of tea and coffee were set up.

"Drink that and you'll feel better," she said when she returned.

"I'm so sorry to have disturbed your morning," Elizabeth said. "I didn't mean for you to be waiting on me."

Charlotte lowered herself into her chair. "If you don't mind me asking, why *did* you come?"

Elizabeth smiled sadly. Max was married. She'd left it too late and now he would spend his life with someone else. She tried her best to push the thought from her mind. She'd have plenty of time to dwell on it when she was away from his mother.

"I wanted to ask about your house," Elizabeth said, improvising. "The one at Hope Cove. I heard you were selling it. Is it still on the market?"

Charlotte sighed. "That's another subject I could talk about all day!"

Elizabeth was suddenly desperate to know about Seaside Cottage. It must have shown in her face, because Charlotte kept talking.

"I've had an offer on the place. A couple of offers, actually. I accepted one but now they're claiming the survey's shown problems with the roof. There's no problem with that roof. They want me to drop the price. And they've decided they don't want to keep any of the furniture and are insisting I get rid of it. I think they found out I'm in a home and decided I was a frail old lady they can take advantage of. Well, that's not going to happen! I told the estate agent he can tell them where to go. I'll go back to the other offer or put it back on the market. I'm not negotiating with people like that." She stopped, apparently realising she'd got carried away again. There was a brief pause, then Elizabeth spoke.

"I'd like to buy it," she said, bending to put her cup on the floor. She couldn't help the tears that came.

Charlotte chuckled, then stopped abruptly when she caught the pleading in Elizabeth's eyes. "Are you serious?"

"Yes," Elizabeth said, clearing her throat. "I'd take it without a survey. I'll take my chances with the roof. And I'd take the furniture too. I'll give you the asking price and you won't have any trouble from me."

"You'd buy it without even seeing the place?"

Tears rolled down Elizabeth's cheeks and she

stroked them gently away. "I visited Hope Cove recently on holiday," she said. "I loved it. The cottage and Hope Cove ... I have such wonderful memories. It was the best time of my life."

She swiped at her tears, wishing she could make them stop. "I know I seem like a wreck, but I'm honestly a good person and the cottage would be in great hands." She touched Charlotte's arm as determination seeped through her. "I promise I'd look after it."

Charlotte covered Elizabeth's hand with her own.

"Please don't make me beg," Elizabeth said.

Chapter 40

Josie was waiting when Elizabeth arrived home that afternoon. She bounded straight into the kitchen to greet her. "How did it go?" Josie asked, unable to contain her excitement. She'd always been an optimist, and Elizabeth hated to break the bad news to her. "I've got champagne in the fridge!" Josie said, beaming.

Elizabeth failed to hide her surprise. "Have you?"

"Well, cheap fizzy wine. Same thing, isn't it? Who cares? Tell me what happened before I explode. Did you find him?"

Elizabeth went into the living room and flopped onto the couch. "He got married," she said, sadly.

"What? No!" Tears filled Josie's eyes and her chin began to wobble. She sat beside Elizabeth. "Oh my God. I'm so sorry."

"Why are you so upset?" Elizabeth asked. She was trying hard to keep her emotions under control, but seeing Josie's tears made her eyes fill up too.

"Because you've never asked for my advice before," Josie said, crying. "And this time you did, and I messed everything up."

"Don't be daft." Elizabeth said, shuffling over for a hug. "It was still good advice. I needed to find out. Now I can move on."

"What will you do now?"

Elizabeth leaned back and stared at the ceiling. "I'm buying his mother's house and I'm going to live by the sea."

"Ha bloody ha! At least you've not lost your sense of humour."

Elizabeth started to chuckle and it quickly morphed into a full belly laugh. Josie watched her, confused.

"I'm serious," Elizabeth said when she calmed down. "I'm going to buy the cottage and move to Hope Cove. I can live where I want now I'm self-employed and working from home."

"Is this some twisted plot to get Max back?" Josie asked seriously. "Because having a fling before you're married is one thing, but don't mess around with a married man. That's bad."

"Oh my God!" Elizabeth said. "What kind of a person do you think I am? I'm not trying to get him back. I love it at Hope Cove, and I need a fresh start."

"So you're going to live in a tiny village where you don't know anyone? What will you do?"

"I'll be busy setting up my business, and I think there'll be a bit of redecorating to do, to make the place my own." She imagined what her life would be like at Seaside Cottage. It had been a rash idea to buy the place, but it felt right, and the more she thought about it, the more excited she was. "I'll read and go for long walks. I'll eat fish and chips on the beach, and indulge in lots of Verity's scones. In winter I'll have a log fire burning every evening…"

And she hoped that eventually she'd be able to do all of those things without being reminded of Max.

"But you'll be all alone," Josie said sadly.

"It might be good for me," Elizabeth said. "And maybe I'll get a dog!"

Josie sank back into the couch. "What's happened to my big sister?"

"I'm okay." Elizabeth patted Josie's leg reassuringly. "It's all going to work out fine. Wasn't it you who said that everything always falls into place for me? Well, it will this time too. Now, what about that wine?"

"I'll fetch it," Josie said, darting into the kitchen and reappearing moments later.

"Josie?" Elizabeth said as she took her first sip of fizzy wine. "Even if everything had gone to plan today, I was only hoping to get Max's number…"

"So?"

"Why would that call for champagne? Or something vaguely similar," she added, raising her glass.

"Any excuse for fizz," Josie said casually.

"There's something you're not telling me. Do *you* have news?"

"I wasn't going to tell you now. My good news is irrelevant when you've had bad news."

"Oh, don't be silly," Elizabeth said. "Tell me! You got the job, didn't you?"

"Yes!"

"Tell me about it, then," Elizabeth said, setting her wine down. "I can't believe you wouldn't even tell me about the interview."

"It wasn't really an interview," Josie said, then squealed, "It was an audition! I've got an acting job!"

Elizabeth was shocked. "What? How?"

"I've been taking drama classes for ages."

"I thought that was just for fun."

"It was to start with, but I'm quite good at acting. I joined an agency a while ago and I've had a few auditions. This time I got the part!"

"That's amazing," Elizabeth said, not entirely sure what to make of her sister's latest career path.

"I know," Josie said. "It's going to be on the BBC too. If it gets aired," she added. "But it will. So far they're just making the pilot, but it's going to be fantastic."

"What is it? What part are you playing?" Elizabeth asked, carried along by Josie's enthusiasm.

"It's a soap opera set on a military base."

"You're a soldier?" Elizabeth asked.

"No. I'll be playing a barmaid. I think this could be exactly what I've been looking for. It's perfect for me."

"I'll help you learn your lines," Elizabeth said.

"Oh, it's a non-speaking part," Josie told her. "To start with, anyway. I'll be what they call a recurring extra."

"Oh, right." Elizabeth tried not to look too deflated. "It does sound perfect for you."

"It's going to be amazing!" Josie said, raising her glass.

Elizabeth didn't have the heart to disagree.

Chapter 41

Elizabeth had promised to meet Karen the week after she finished work. Karen wanted them to meet on the same day each week, so they didn't lose touch. If she didn't get to see Elizabeth at the office, she'd said, she needed to see her socially every week. Knowing Karen's work schedule, Elizabeth didn't really see that happening, but she didn't like to say so. She'd assumed they'd keep in touch by email and text, with the occasional phone call and meet-up.

It was four weeks since Elizabeth had left work, and so far Karen had cancelled on her every week. Elizabeth didn't actually mind. She'd been busy herself, but things with the cottage were moving quickly and she wanted to tell Karen about the move in person and, if they carried on like this, Elizabeth would have moved before they managed to meet.

The phone rang as she was getting ready. She sighed when she saw it was Karen. Was she going to cancel again?

"Don't worry, I can make our meeting," Karen said quickly. "But I wondered if you'd mind a change of venue?"

"Not at all," Elizabeth said, relieved. "Where were you thinking?"

Karen hesitated. "Would you mind coming in to

the office?"

"You're not serious?"

"Please! I'm snowed under. I've got so much to do I'll be here until midnight. But I thought maybe you could bring me a takeaway and I can take a break for a gossip. It'll be like old times!"

"This is ridiculous, you know," Elizabeth said, thanking her lucky stars she'd left.

"I know. I'm sorry. As soon as things slow down, I'm taking you out for a slap-up meal. My treat."

"Oh great. Something to look forward to when hell freezes over…"

"That tone doesn't suit you," Karen said. "You coming or not?"

"Yes," Elizabeth said. "But only because I have big news. This is the last time I set foot in the offices of *MyStyle* magazine."

"Ooh, I'm excited about your news. Now hurry up – I'm starving. Chinese, please. You know what I like."

Elizabeth rolled her eyes, then threw her phone aside and continued getting ready.

It was strange walking back into the office. She'd expected to feel some sort of nostalgia: after all, she had worked there for over ten years. But all she felt was relief. Relief that she was only there for a visit, and not to work.

"You're the best," Karen said when she walked into her office. "That smells amazing."

"Nice to see you too!"

"Yes! Lovely! That's what I meant. Give me a hug." They embraced warmly. Elizabeth really was happy to see her old friend.

"I missed you," they said at the same time and then laughed.

"I'm so hungry," Karen said, taking the bag of food and opening it on her desk. "I don't think I stopped to eat all day."

"Is it really that crazy?" Elizabeth asked. "What's going on?"

"What do you mean, what's going on? This is what it's like! Have you forgotten already?"

"I must have," she said, but when she thought back, she could remember days when she'd been too busy to eat.

"Don't you miss it?" Karen said, tucking into her chow mein.

"Erm, no," Elizabeth replied. "I'm quite happy."

"I don't believe you," Karen said. "And I'm surprised you've not called me begging for your job back. I was sure you would."

"That definitely won't happen."

"What's the big news, then?" Karen said, seeming to calm down as she ate. Had she always been so manic? Perhaps it was just more pronounced now, since Elizabeth's life had shifted down a gear.

"I have lots of news," Elizabeth said. "But the main thing is, I'm moving to Devon."

Karen stopped with her fork to her mouth. "What?"

"I'm buying a cottage on the coast. It looks like we'll exchange contracts in a few weeks, and I'll move straight in."

Karen put her food aside and leaned back in her chair. "Is this to do with the guy you met there?"

"Kind of. I'm buying the cottage from his mum. It's nothing to do with him, though. I did go looking for him, but it turns out he's already married."

"So you decided to buy his house?"

"Not *his* house," Elizabeth said calmly. "His mum's. He's not in the picture."

"I should hope not, if he's married. But I don't get it. Why would you buy a place in Devon? And are you really going to live there?"

"Yes. I need a fresh start, that's why. And it's a beautiful place."

"There are a lot of beautiful places in the world, but you don't just up and move like that. Do you even know anyone there?"

"No. But I'll be fine. A change is as good as a rest and all that…"

"You're serious, aren't you?" Karen said.

"Yes."

Karen chewed on a nail. "It's a bad idea. Do you think you might need some counselling or something? Are you depressed?"

"No," Elizabeth said, unsure whether or not to be offended. "I'm fine. I'm happy."

"That's not rational behaviour."

Elizabeth sighed in annoyance. "It is rational," she said, sounding more irritated than she intended. "I wasn't happy with my job, so I changed it. I wasn't happy with Phil, so I left him. What I want to do is go and live on the coast. So that's what I'm going to do. Which part isn't rational?"

Karen raised her eyebrows, then carried on eating without a word.

"You could just be pleased for me," Elizabeth

suggested.

"This is really what you want?"

"Yes."

"Okay. Then I suppose that's all that matters. I just worry about you. It seems a bit drastic."

"I know, but it's what I want."

"I hope it works out," Karen said. "Now I'm really never going to see you, am I?"

"I'll visit," Elizabeth said. "And you could come and visit me?"

"You know I don't like to leave London. I get nervous outside the M25."

"I'm sure you'll make an exception."

"I might," she agreed. "I probably ought to see the place that caused all this trouble. See what all the fuss is about."

"I can't wait to show you around," Elizabeth said, wondering if Karen would ever make it to Hope Cove – and, if she did, how many times she would cancel before she made it there.

Hannah Ellis

Chapter 42

The sale of Seaside Cottage went through without a hitch. When Elizabeth enquired about getting the keys, she'd been amused by the email from the estate agent, which said the keys would be left on the kitchen table, unless she had any objections. She didn't, and was excited that she would be living in the sort of place where people didn't worry about locking their doors. It would be a big change, moving away from Oxford, but she was determined it would be a positive one.

She moved in on a damp day in December. There was no moving van or strong men lugging boxes, just Elizabeth and a carload of stuff. It had felt liberating to have a big clear-out when she left Phil. Her wardrobe had been culled, all her power suits and high heels shipped off to charity shops. She'd kept a few outfits in case she had to attend any business meetings, but now that she was working from home her wardrobe could be far more casual. Heck, she could work in her pyjamas if she felt like it.

The first time she walked back into Seaside Cottage, it hit her harder than she'd expected. She was haunted by memories, and missed Max fiercely. He was so firmly ingrained in her memories of the place that it was hard not to see him everywhere she turned.

The constant reminders of him made her heart ache. She kept telling herself she was being ridiculous. How could she miss him so much when she'd only known him for a week?

On her first evening – after she'd stopped unloading and unpacking, and dropped onto the couch – she was hit by a sense of doom. Buying the house was the most ridiculous thing she'd ever done, completely eclipsing the time she'd let herself into the wrong cottage and slept there without realising.

She wondered how she would make a life for herself in a tiny coastal village where she knew no one. Why had she ever thought moving there was a good idea?

She missed Josie too. Living with her had been such a comfort, and part of her wanted to go back and take refuge on her couch again, drinking wine and laughing while Josie convinced her she could have whatever she wanted from life. If it hadn't been for Josie, Elizabeth had no idea how she would have survived the past months. As a thank you, Elizabeth had left Josie the painting of Hope Cove. She knew Josie loved it and when Josie had protested that it was too much, Elizabeth had argued she didn't need it any more. She had the view from her window.

She hauled herself up to bed that evening telling herself that things would get better. It was bound to take some time to settle in to her new life. Once her business was up and running properly and she got herself into some sort of routine, she'd feel much better. She felt as if she'd taken a leap into darkness and was waiting to see where she would land. It was terrifying, but all she could do was take each day at a time and hope everything would work out in the end. She'd visit Verity in the morning and treat herself to a scone. A good old natter with Verity would surely make her feel better.

Unfortunately, it was pouring with rain the next day. She waited all morning for it to ease and when it didn't, she abandoned her idea of walking into the village and drove instead. The girl working in the café was busy on her mobile phone and Elizabeth had to wait a few moments before she acknowledged her. Apparently, Verity had gone to visit her sister in New Zealand for a couple of months, as she always did in the winter when business was slow.

Elizabeth felt deflated as she walked out of the café. The town had been bustling in the summer, and there always seemed to be people to chat to. The view of the bay was different now too. The grey clouds made a bleak scene as the wind and rain whipped at her violently. The waves rumbled as they pummelled the sea wall. It was still stunning, but in a completely different way. There wasn't a soul in sight and it wasn't surprising.

Hurrying to her car, she told herself again that everything would get better.

***

The next month felt like the longest month of her life. She spent Christmas at her parents' place in Oxford, with Josie. It was such a lovely time but it seemed to make her life at Seaside Cottage even more depressing. She remembered Max telling her that his girlfriend thought the place was drab, and she finally understood. It was exactly that. Everything seemed so bleak, and with each passing day she became more convinced that she'd made the biggest mistake of her life by moving to Hope Cove.

Somehow, she'd expected it to be easier to meet people. It was a small community and she'd thought she'd get to know the locals easily. So far, she knew the people who worked in the shop and post office by sight, and she was starting to recognise a few dog walkers, but she wasn't sure how to engage in any meaningful interactions.

There was a community notice board and she'd hoped to find some activities she could join, but her only real options seemed to be a bridge club or a knitting club, and neither appealed in the slightest. Instead, she threw herself into setting up her business, taking more online courses and working with as many authors as she could.

In mid-January, she hit rock bottom. She'd spent yet another day alone in the cottage, working. The wet, windy weather made her feel like a prisoner in her own home. Her new life wasn't anything like she'd imagined it would be.

She gazed into the flickering fire, and pulled a blanket around her. In winter, the cottage she'd always thought of as warm and cosy was cold and draughty. When the television couldn't hold her interest, she lay down on the couch to cry.

The next morning, she woke in the same spot, cold and stiff. She pulled on a thick woolly cardigan and slippers before she switched on the coffee machine. There were still a few boxes to unpack. It was hard to know whether it was worth unpacking, or whether she should admit she'd made a huge mistake and move back in with Josie. She could rent Seaside Cottage out just as Charlotte Anderson had done.

The knock at the front door startled her. For a moment, she thought it might be Josie, and decided she would never be as happy to see her little sister. It wasn't. An elderly lady stood at the front step holding a plate draped with a tea towel.

Puzzled by the early morning visitor, Elizabeth forgot to speak for a moment.

"I've baked you a cake," the woman said. "To welcome you to the area. Sorry it's taken me so long. I'm always so busy over Christmas. I just live a couple of houses down, towards the village."

Elizabeth automatically craned her neck in the direction, but the houses were all set back from the road, hidden away.

"I'm Dorothy Peters," the woman said, holding out the cake. "You can call me Dot. Actually, most people call me Dotty, but that always feels an odd way to introduce myself."

Elizabeth finally found her voice.

"Elizabeth Beaumont." A slow smile spread over her face. "You can call me Lizzie."

Hannah Ellis

Chapter 43

Elizabeth was surprised and amused to find herself at a group called Knitter Natter at Dotty's house the following Thursday. It was the knitting group she'd dismissed when she'd seen it on the notice board.

Dotty was determined that Elizabeth should come and meet some of the locals, insisting she'd go mad in the winter months if she didn't have friends in the village.

Since Elizabeth had already started to feel that she was going mad, she didn't need any convincing on that score. The isolation had definitely been taking its toll. She'd begun to resign herself to life as a lonely spinster – a recluse in a hidden-away cottage. But maybe it wouldn't be like that after all.

A grey-haired lady called Penny sat in the armchair in Dotty's front room. She'd briefly looked up from her knitting when she was introduced to Elizabeth but otherwise kept her head down, engrossed in the blanket she was working on. Luckily, Tammy the local postwoman had arrived a few minutes after Elizabeth and had kept the room alive with conversation as Dotty came and went from the kitchen fetching drinks and biscuits. Elizabeth had learned that Tammy had recently turned forty and had two children, who attended the local primary school.

It seemed that she was well known in the area, and involved herself in many community events.

"I always call in on Thursday mornings," Tammy told Elizabeth. "It's lovely to break up my round with a cuppa and a chat. You've got a good neighbour in Dotty," she confided when Dotty left the room to answer the door. "She'll help you settle in. You're on your own, are you?"

"Yes," Elizabeth said, not at all put out by Tammy's directness. She was more amused by the thought that she could quickly become the subject of local gossip: the city woman living all alone in the draughty cottage. Although, come to think of it, it was probably only her who had an issue with the draughts.

"We're tight-knit round here," Tammy said. "I'm sure you'll feel at home in no time."

"I think I will," Elizabeth agreed with a much-needed feeling of positivity.

"Hello!" a tall man said as he entered the room, a baby in his arms. He passed the baby to Tammy, who bounced it happily on her knee. "I'm John," he said, shaking Elizabeth's hand before dropping a changing bag in the corner and peeling off his coat.

"John's our resident stay-at-home dad," Tammy said. "He's got three boys, and Thomas here is the youngest."

"Sounds like you've got your hands full," Elizabeth said as she tickled the baby's cheek.

"They keep me busy," he agreed happily.

"I'd better get on," Tammy said, casually passing the baby to Elizabeth and saying a cheery goodbye to everyone. Elizabeth was slightly taken aback but relaxed when the six-month-old smiled up at her.

"Sorry," John said. "I can take him off you."

"It's fine," she said. "If I've got the baby, Dotty might stop trying to push knitting needles on me."

"Sounds dangerous," John said.

Dotty returned and handed John a coffee. "I'm a patient teacher," she said. "Knitting might seem old-fashioned and boring, but it's a useful skill to have."

"I think I'll just watch for now," Elizabeth said.

Dotty had just taken a seat and armed herself with her latest project – mittens for little Thomas – when a low voice rumbled from the back of the house. "It's only us!"

"Come on in, Bill," Dotty called back.

A beautiful chocolate Labrador arrived first. From the fuss everyone made of him, Elizabeth gathered he was called Perry. He had a good sniff around before settling down by Dotty's feet.

"Bill, this is Lizzie," Dotty said when a well-built older gentleman in a brown checked shirt wandered into the room.

"From Seaside Cottage," he said, shaking her hand firmly. "I've heard about you. Welcome to Hope Cove!"

"Thank you," she said as he settled himself next to her on the couch.

The room was getting crowded but the atmosphere was jovial, and Elizabeth was glad she'd been persuaded to join. It was comforting to meet some of the locals. They were a such a friendly bunch and Elizabeth couldn't help but feel more positive about the move.

She spent a pleasant couple of hours in Dotty's front room before insisting she needed to get some work done.

"I've got some pie for you," Dotty said as Elizabeth reached the front door. She disappeared for a moment and then returned with a plate covered in tin foil. "Chicken and mushroom. You're not one of those vegetarians, are you?"

"No, I'm not," Elizabeth said, amusement in her voice. "You shouldn't have, but thank you very much."

"There was too much for me, so you're doing me a favour. It's no fun cooking for one."

It was the most enjoyable Thursday Elizabeth had had in a while. She spent the afternoon in the little home office she'd set up in a corner of the living room. The fire roared behind her while she edited a children's book set in space. Time flew by, and she was surprised when she saw it was already dark outside. She'd intended to get out for a walk but decided she would have to put it off until the morning. Instead she put on her pyjamas and devoured Dotty's chicken pie in front of the TV.

On Friday, she set off for a morning walk. The sunrises that she'd loved so much in the summer were unremarkable in winter, but she always loved the view over the water, nonetheless. She stood for a moment, breathing in the salty air. Then, unexpectedly, she thought of Max. She imagined him standing on the beach, turning to smile at her. Her heart pounded and she was irritated with herself for ruining her mood with schoolgirl thoughts. Memories of him still popped into her head without warning.

She was startled when Perry, the Labrador, arrived by her side and sniffed her hand. Jolted from her daydream, she stroked the top of his head. Bill wasn't far behind and greeted her warmly. He invited her to walk with them, and then introduced her to every dog they passed. The names of owners often escaped him, he confided, but he never forgot the name of any dog he met.

"You should get a dog," he said when they arrived back at Seaside Cottage. "You're obviously a dog person, and this is a great place to have a dog."

"I'd like to," she said. "I'm just not sure how to start the process. I need to do some research…"

There was a twinkle in Bill's eye as he offered to help out.

By the end of the following week, there was another new resident at Seaside Cottage: Tilly the springer spaniel.

Hannah Ellis

Chapter 44

Elizabeth had never had a pet before and she was amazed at the difference it made to her life. What surprised her most was how much she talked to Tilly. The cottage had always been so quiet, but now there was constant chatter as she conducted a never-ending monologue for Tilly. The well-trained dog was bombarded with an assortment of conversations from mundane shopping lists to the problems with the latest book Elizabeth was editing. Of course she ended up telling Tilly all about Max too, and how she'd ended up living at Hope Cove. It was therapeutic to talk it all through, even if Tilly had nothing to say on the matter!

In her first months in Hope Cove, Elizabeth's parents came to visit a couple of times and they seemed to fall in love with the place almost as much as she had.

It was the middle of February before Josie came to visit. Elizabeth was dying to see her. She'd well and truly settled into village life by then. Things had definitely turned a corner since she'd met some of the locals.

"It took forever to get here," Josie complained, lugging her bag inside. "You wouldn't believe the traffic. I hope you've got wine? And what on earth are you wearing? You look like you've just stepped out of a hiking catalogue."

Elizabeth looked down. She'd been out for a walk with Tilly. Her jeans were splattered with mud, and her fleece wasn't something she'd ever have worn in her old life. She'd been shopping and had invested in good sensible clothing suitable for her twice daily walks with Tilly. She enjoyed dressing for the weather rather than worrying about what other people thought.

"And this is Tilly," Elizabeth said, pulling the excited dog away from Josie. She was generally a calm and obedient dog, and had settled into life at Seaside Cottage far more easily than Elizabeth had.

"She's gorgeous," Josie said. "I can't believe you got a dog. It's crazy."

"I think getting a dog is probably the least crazy thing I've done in the last six months!" Elizabeth said as she led the way into the cosy living room.

"This place is beautiful," Josie said enthusiastically. "Now I can see why you wanted to move to the middle of nowhere. It's lovely."

"It's okay now," Elizabeth said. "I'm getting settled. It was difficult at first."

"I should have visited earlier," Josie said. "I was busy filming."

"I know. And I want to hear all about it. Make yourself comfy and I'll get us a wine."

An hour later, they were huddled by the fire in their pyjamas, having made good progress on a bottle of pinot grigot.

"So you think you're going to stick at this job?" Elizabeth asked after Josie had regaled her with stories about working on a TV set. So far they'd only filmed the pilot, but Josie was still convinced it would be a hit TV show and she'd be working on it for years to come.

"It's my ideal job," Josie said. "I love it. Now stop asking about me. Tell me about you. I want to know what life is like here. Have you found yourself a hot man yet?"

"No!" Elizabeth said. "I'm off men."

"Aren't you lonely?"

"No." She glared at Josie. "When did *you* last have a man in your life? Are *you* lonely?"

"No, but I have a hectic social life!" She reached down to stroke Tilly. "Anyway, maybe there *is* a man in my life."

"You're seeing someone?"

Josie beamed. "Yes, kind of. I met him at work."

"Is he famous?"

"No. He's just an extra … but you have to tell me what's going on with you before I tell you any more!"

Elizabeth realised she wasn't getting anything more out of Josie until she filled her in properly, so she relented and told her all about the village: the people she'd met, the community spirit, the coffee mornings. Verity had returned from her trip too, and Elizabeth often visited her in the café. She was always fun to chat to.

Josie was highly amused when she heard how Elizabeth had been roped into baking cakes for a sale at the community centre.

"Oh my God. Did you poison anyone?" Josie asked.

Elizabeth laughed. "No. I followed a recipe and

they came out fine. I might do more baking."

"What's happened to you?" Josie asked. "I can't believe you're hanging out with a bunch of old people, and knitting and baking!"

"They're not all old," Elizabeth protested. "And I only managed to knit a scarf. It's probably the only thing I'll ever knit."

"What about work?" Josie asked.

"What about it? It keeps me occupied, and I'm starting to get a few paid jobs. I'm enjoying it and it keeps me fed and clothed. There's my office," she said, nodding at the desk in the corner.

Josie leaned back on the couch, beaming from ear to ear.

"What?" Elizabeth asked.

"It's so unlike you. Not so long ago work was your life, and now it's just an afterthought. You've really changed, haven't you?"

"I have," Elizabeth agreed. And it was all for the better.

"I wish you'd find a man," Josie said. "It's like the last piece of the puzzle is missing. You made all these changes in your life for Max and then—"

"Not *for* him," Elizabeth corrected her. "Because of him. None of it was *for* him."

"So you think you met him just to help you figure out what you really want in life? There was never going to be a happy-ever-after?"

Elizabeth shook her head. Josie could be so airy-fairy and romantic. "I don't think there is a reason for everything. I met Max. It was fun—"

"Then you changed every single thing about your life," Josie said, smirking.

Elizabeth couldn't help but smile. "Yes! And I will live happily ever after. Now tell me about your love life."

Josie spent the next hour telling Elizabeth all about Jack, the brown-haired, blue-eyed extra who worked alongside her. Apparently she'd fallen head over heels for him. Elizabeth ignored the jealousy that niggled at her. It was surely the wine that made her mind wander to Max. She'd become skilled at pushing thoughts of him from her mind, but when she finally went to bed that evening, she let herself remember. Tears rolled down her face before she finally fell asleep.

The weekend with Josie went far too fast. It was so lovely seeing her and having a proper catch-up. On Saturday they went for a long walk then had dinner at the restaurant at the golf club. On Sunday, Josie insisted on fish and chips before she left. Elizabeth had started being strict about how often she allowed herself the delicious treat, but couldn't say no when Josie was visiting.

"I want you to come and visit me soon," Josie said when she was gearing up to leave. "We can have a proper night out. And I want you to meet Jack."

Elizabeth assured her she wanted to meet him too, and promised she'd visit soon. It would probably do her good to have a break from village life, she realised. For a while, she'd been avoiding going back to visit Josie, worried that she wouldn't want to leave again. Now she was settled, and had Tilly, she felt much more secure.

Chapter 45

It was a month later when Elizabeth finally went to visit Josie for the weekend. It would be a welcome change to have a weekend back in Oxford, she thought. She could do some shopping and have a night out with Josie.

Tilly was the only problem. Josie's place wasn't pet friendly. Elizabeth knew there was no shortage of kennels in the area, but she didn't want to take her beloved dog to stay at any old kennels. Only the best would do for Tilly – and Elizabeth knew exactly where that was: Oakbrook Farm With Max's aunts. Once she'd thought of it, she couldn't get the idea out of her head.

She knew they were open for business again. Her last visit had left her with a bad feeling and she'd tried calling again, back when she was living with Josie. She'd ended up having a brief chat with Annette, pretending she was a dog owner enquiring about availability. She gleaned from the conversation that everyone was in good health again, and was relieved to hear it. She ended the call by saying she'd be in touch again to confirm – but of course that didn't happen.

It was strange to think of returning to Oakbrook. Any romantic ideas about finding Max were long gone, but the thought of talking to someone who knew him, and asking how he was, was a powerful draw. It was pathetic – she was well aware of that. But maybe if she heard how ecstatically happy he was, she could finally put him out of her mind.

But what if she found out he was miserable? That his marriage had been a huge mistake and he was already separated and filing for divorce?

She shook her head at her ridiculous train of thought. Of course she wasn't going to the kennels just so she could ask questions about Max. She would take Tilly there, because she knew Tilly would be well looked after.

She'd booked online and then called a few days before to confirm. Annette's voice was familiar, and Elizabeth felt awkward that she didn't explain who she was. She wasn't sure how to explain, though, and Annette might not even remember her even if she did mention her previous visit with Max.

The Friday that she loaded her weekend bag – and Tilly – into the car, the weather was glorious. Thank goodness spring is around the corner, she thought. Winter at Seaside Cottage had been bleak and testing, but having just about come through the other side, Elizabeth felt that things were looking up. If she could survive winter at Hope Cove, she could survive anything.

As she navigated the winding roads to Oakbrook, she chatted away to Tilly. She was looking forward to spending the weekend with Josie, and she would get to meet her new boyfriend, Jack, who Josie still couldn't stop talking about.

The gates of Oakbrook were open. Elizabeth

drove slowly up the driveway. Once again, she was hit by bittersweet memories but was determined not to dwell on them. It was only after she'd stepped out of the car and let Tilly out that she registered the familiar car in front of the house.

Oh no. No, no, no. It was Max's car. She was sure of it. Panic hit her like a blow to the chest, sucking the air from her lungs. Should she leave? What would she say to him? What if his wife was with him? Could she cope with that? She took a deep breath and wiped her sweaty hands on her jeans. Was she really about to see him again? After all this time?

Beside her, Tilly barked.

The front door opened silently. She thought her heart couldn't take the stress.

He was so familiar – exactly as she remembered him.

The automatic smile that appeared as he opened the door faltered slightly and then disappeared. After a moment he bent down to Tilly, stroking her head and neck.

"This is a surprise," he said, keeping his attention firmly on Tilly.

Elizabeth reached to stroke Tilly's back. "It is," she said, pushing a stray lock of hair behind her ear. "I didn't expect you to be here."

"I've been helping out a bit," he said. "Wendy's not been well so I'm trying to do as much as I can."

"That's nice," Elizabeth said, barely able to concentrate on his words. It was so good to see him again. Focusing, she shook her head and frowned. "I mean, sorry to hear about Wendy…"

He didn't say anything for a moment.

She stroked Tilly again, needing something to focus on. Would he ever stop staring at her?

"I'm sorry," she said, shifting her weight. "If this is too weird, I can just take Tilly away again."

His stare became even more intense and she felt uncomfortable. "Why would it be weird?"

"It wouldn't," she said quickly. "I just thought … I mean … I don't want things to be awkward but you're right, of course it's not weird." She couldn't seem to stop rambling and he didn't seem in any hurry to jump in and stop her. She laughed nervously. "The thing last summer … we probably both just had cold feet about our weddings. It was just a silly holiday romance. We shouldn't feel awkward."

Wow! She was such a babbling idiot.

There was a short silence before Max spoke. "I heard you bought Seaside Cottage," he said. "I wondered if I might bump into you at some point."

She winced. So he knew. How could she explain to him? So much had happened since she last saw him. He must have been shocked to find she'd bought the house. "It's been a crazy six months," she said lightly. He seemed to be waiting for an explanation. "Maybe I should have been in touch, told you about the house…"

"Why would you?" he said gruffly. "It's none of my business."

"No. But—" She paused, trying to figure out why he sounded so irritated. "Are you annoyed with me for buying the house?"

He shook his head uncertainly. "Yes. I'm annoyed. Why on earth would you buy the house? I don't get it."

"It was a bit of a whim, to be honest. But I love it. I don't know why you're so upset about it. If you wanted it so badly, you could've bought it yourself."

"I didn't want to buy it," he said angrily. "That's not the point."

"What is the point, then?"

"You don't get it, do you? I was ready to leave my fiancée for you and you walked away as if I meant nothing to you."

His words irritated her. She might have walked away, but he'd moved on pretty quickly himself. It could only have been a matter of weeks before he got married.

"So you're upset because I hurt your ego?" she snapped.

"No!" he shouted. "It was nothing to do with my ego."

She couldn't seem to keep her emotions under control and shouted back at him. "Of course I wasn't going to agree to run off into the sunset with you when I'd only known you a week! It was a ridiculous thing to ask of me. And why are you still upset about it? Surely it's irrelevant now?"

There was a moment when she wanted him to tell her that it wasn't irrelevant. That his marriage was a mess and he'd made a huge mistake. That he wanted to be with her.

He rubbed his neck and seemed to calm down. "I guess so."

"I shouldn't have come here," she said. "I'm just going to take Tilly back with me."

She'd opened the car door and called Tilly over to her when Max finally spoke.

"She's all booked in," he said. "And it's not my place to turn customers away."

Elizabeth was thoughtful for a moment. It would probably be easier if she took Tilly away again. She really hadn't expected to see Max, or for things to be so heated between them.

"I'm sorry I shouted at you," he said. "You're right, it's in the past."

"It's fine. I don't want to put you in an awkward position. I'll take Tilly…"

"I'd be in trouble with Annette and Wendy if you did that." His features softened and a smile appeared. The smile that she'd thought of so many times. "You don't want to get me in trouble, do you?"

Maybe it would have been easier if she'd left while he was still angry with her. Him being nice to her felt like a different kind of torture.

He gestured to the barn, and Elizabeth grabbed the bag of Tilly's things from the back seat before they started to walk there.

"Annette and Wendy must be grateful that you can help out," she said, searching for something to break the silence. "I bet they love having you around."

"I enjoy it," he said, glancing at her. "You know how much I love this place."

She did know how much he loved it, and how much it meant to him. All this time she'd been telling herself that she'd only known him a week and they barely knew each other, but she *did* know him. She felt as if she was meeting up with her best friend again after a long absence. She wanted to tell him everything that had happened since she last saw him.

There was so much she wanted to say, but she didn't know where to start.

They walked into the barn to be greeted by howling and barking dogs. Max held the door for her, and she relaxed slightly.

He shouted to the dogs, telling them to settle down. The noise gradually died down as they walked through the barn, glancing into the stalls as they went.

"Here we are," Max said when they reached Tilly's stall. The chalkboard hanging on the stable door already had her name scrawled on it. Max unlatched the door and they walked in.

"I probably brought too much," Elizabeth said as she began to unpack things. She pulled out a dog bed and an old towel that was Tilly's favourite for chewing and fighting with. "I brought her bowl," she said, setting it down next to the one already in the stall. "I don't know why. And toys," she said, tipping out an assortment of battered and chewed dog toys. "It's too much, isn't it?"

He was gazing at her so intensely that she blushed and looked away. He'd turned her into a blabbering, awkward wreck. She felt like a lovesick schoolgirl and it was embarrassing.

"It's fine," Max said.

Elizabeth crouched to rub Tilly's ears. "I've never left her anywhere before."

"I'll look after her," he said. "She's only with us a couple of days, isn't she?"

"Yes. I'm going to stay with my sister for the weekend. There's not really space for Tilly. No garden or anything…"

"I thought you didn't get on with your sister?"

Elizabeth couldn't hide her surprise. He actually remembered that? "We get on better now," she said, rattled. She'd told herself so many times that it had been a meaningless fling, but now she remembered the time they had spent getting to know each other.

"That's good," Max said.

"Yes. Things changed." She smiled at her understatement. So much had changed.

They left the barn and wandered slowly in the direction of the house, Tilly between them. Elizabeth's mind whirred with all the things she wanted to say. She wanted to tell him about leaving Phil and quitting her job. And about her move to Hope Cove. She had so many questions for him too. She wanted to know why he got married so quickly when he'd seemed so unsure about his relationship. It was so rash. The main thing she wanted to know was whether he was happy, or whether he regretted the rushed wedding. There was so much she wanted to say, but didn't feel she could.

Her heart raced when she opened her mouth to ask him about the wedding. She couldn't help herself.

"I met your mum," she said. "When I was buying the cottage. She told me all about the big last-minute wedding. She really likes to chat, doesn't she?"

"That's an understatement! She's still telling everyone that story. I keep telling her to stop going on about it."

"It's kind of crazy, though, organising a wedding in a few weeks. That must have been stressful."

"I'd say the wedding planner earned her bonus," he said jokily. "And it definitely caused a few family arguments, but that's nothing out of the ordinary for my family."

"I think your mum described it as a farce…"

He nodded vaguely and his eyes sparkled with amusement. "It's probably a fairly accurate description."

They fell silent until they reached the house. Elizabeth wished she'd not mentioned the wedding. What was she expecting? That he'd tell her it was a huge mistake and they'd already decided to get divorced?

"Can I ask you something?" Max said when they reached her car.

She nodded.

"Are you happy?"

She paused for a moment, thinking about her new life in Hope Cove. "Yes," she said. "I am. Are you?"

He refused to meet her gaze. "Oh, you know," he said with a shrug.

No, she didn't know. And she wanted to know. She wanted to hear everything about his life.

When he didn't say any more, she stooped to hug Tilly, stalling for time. Why couldn't she think of anything to say?

"I didn't expect it to be this hard to say goodbye," she said, her eyes damp. Of course, it wasn't really the dog she was struggling to walk away from. After all this time thinking of him, all she wanted to do was wrap her arms around Max and never let him go. She should never have walked away that last day on the beach.

"Will you be here on Sunday?" she asked, trying her best to sound casual.

"I'm not sure," he said. "Probably."

"Okay," Elizabeth said. "Well, maybe I'll see you then."

He tipped his head, then bent to the dog, holding her collar to stop her from following Elizabeth.

"It was good to see you again," she said. She really was the queen of the understatement. And also a bumbling wreck. "Even though you shouted at me. It was still really good to see you."

"You shouted at me too!"

He watched as she got in the car.

The ache in her chest began as soon as she pulled away. She couldn't believe she'd seen him again.

It was as if she'd opened an old wound. Now it hurt more than ever.

Chapter 46

"I saw him," Elizabeth said, lugging her bag past Josie and dropping it in the kitchen.

"Saw who?" Josie asked.

"Max."

Josie's eyes widened. Elizabeth opened the fridge and pulled out a bottle of wine. "I thought you had a job now," she said, studying the wine label. "You could've got decent wine."

"Glad to see living in a village hasn't changed you completely," Josie said. "Snob!" She reached for wine glasses and held them out to be filled up.

"You're practically a celebrity now, aren't you? Can't you afford to pay more than four quid for a bottle of wine?"

"I'm not a celebrity. I just hang out with celebs! And I don't see the point of expensive wine when cheap stuff will do the job just as well." She took a mouthful and then followed Elizabeth into the living room. "And why are we talking about wine, not Max? What happened?"

"He was there when I dropped Tilly at the kennels," Elizabeth said. "He's helping out there for a while."

"Interesting…"

"What's so interesting about that?"

"I had him pegged as more of a city guy: a 'wears a suit, drinks fancy wine' kind of person. Now I'm envisioning a farm hand…"

"It's not a farm; it's kennels. Although they look like stables – but whatever."

"Sounds like a farm to me."

"Anyway, he doesn't work there. He's just helping out."

"Did you know he'd be there?"

"No! I had no idea."

"I don't believe you, but never mind that. How was it?"

"Terrible."

"Because you realised you had a fling with a dirty farm hand?"

Elizabeth put her wine down and reached over to give Josie a playful shove. "He's not a farm hand!"

Josie giggled and leaned on the arm of the couch. "So why was it terrible?"

Elizabeth sighed. "Because he's as lovely as I remembered."

"That's bad?"

"He's married," Elizabeth said with a shrug. "So, yes, it's bad."

"But I thought you were happy with your new life?"

"I am happy," Elizabeth said. For a moment she was quiet. "I am. I love my new life. But seeing him threw me a bit. It was such a shock, and then it was just so lovely being with him again."

"What does he think about you living at the cottage?"

"He was angry," Elizabeth said. "He shouted at

me. Not just about the house but about last summer. I think it's a bit irrational considering he went and got married straight after."

"Does he know you left Phil?"

"I don't know. I didn't mention it. What's the point? It would just be awkward."

"I suppose," Josie said. "Will he be there when you pick Tilly up?"

"Yes, I think he'll be there."

"This is not good," Josie mused.

"It'll be fine. I'll just pick up Tilly and leave again. I can manage that. "

"That's not what I meant," Josie said with a smirk. "I was thinking it's not good because you're going to spend the next three days obsessing about seeing him again!"

Elizabeth laughed. "I'm not," she said as firmly as she could. She didn't even manage to convince herself, never mind Josie.

***

It was a lovely relaxed weekend. They did some shopping, went to the cinema, and spent lots of time lazing around Josie's apartment in their pyjamas. On Saturday evening Josie insisted they get out and hit some bars like the young, free and single women they were. Elizabeth's protests that she wasn't that young any more fell on deaf ears. It was fun in the end, and Elizabeth was glad Josie had insisted.

Josie's boyfriend, Jack, didn't show up all weekend, even though Josie called and texted him. He called her back once, and Josie gushed down the phone. Apparently he needed to spend some time with the lads. Josie was understanding. Far too understanding, Elizabeth thought. She had a bad feeling about Jack, and it worried her that Josie was so besotted with him. Josie wouldn't hear a bad word about him, so Elizabeth left the subject alone. It would work itself out one way or another.

Josie's prediction about Elizabeth turned out to be right: Elizabeth's mind wandered often to Max, rehashing their brief encounter at the kennels and then worrying about seeing him again when she picked Tilly up. It was a nervous excitement which caused an internal battle. Because she shouldn't be nervous or excited about seeing him again. Both emotions were inappropriate.

She was a bundle of nerves as she left Josie's apartment on Sunday. When she pulled up outside the kennels, the gates were closed so she parked on the road. She sat for a moment, taking deep breaths and checking herself in the mirror. He was married. She was being ridiculous. All she needed to do was make polite conversation for a few minutes, then take Tilly and leave. Why was she making such a meal of it?

Annoyed with herself, she finally got out of the car and made her way up the drive. She waited for Max to stride confidently out of the house like he'd done before. But there was no sign of him. In fact, there was no sign of anyone.

When no one answered when she knocked, she walked down to the barn. She called hello at the door and caught sight of Annette coming towards her with Tilly beside her. Elizabeth's smile was automatic as she bent to greet the excited dog. She'd missed Tilly.

Annette had a huge grin on her face. "Remember me?" she said.

"It's lovely to see you again," Elizabeth said. "And thank you for taking care of this one for me." She bent to stroke Tilly again.

"It was our pleasure. She's been as good as gold."

"I'm glad," Elizabeth said, glancing around and shivering as the wind whipped over the fields.

"Time for a cuppa?" Annette said. She set off for the house without waiting for a reply. "Let's get in and warmed up."

Tilly slipped inside as soon as Annette opened the front door.

"I hope you've not been spoiling her," Elizabeth said. "She seems to have made herself at home."

"That was Max. He's been giving her special attention. Treating her like a VIP guest!"

A strange feeling came over Elizabeth. It was crazy – she was jealous of a dog. She smiled wryly and slipped off her coat as they were enveloped by the heat of the house.

Hannah Ellis

Chapter 47

Elizabeth followed Annette into the sitting room, where a log fire crackled and popped in the hearth. Wendy sat beside it in an armchair, her feet up and a book resting precariously on the arm of the chair.

"Oh, thank goodness," she said, beaming at Elizabeth. "I was hoping you'd come inside. I've been cooped up for weeks and I'm going crazy! Knee replacement," she added, pointing at her swollen leg.

"You poor thing," Elizabeth said, squeezing her hand in greeting.

Wendy waved away the sympathy. "I'll survive," she said. "Take a seat. I thought I was going to miss you again. Last time you were here I only saw you in passing. Then Max said you two had lost touch. You certainly surprised him when you arrived with Tilly." She looked at Elizabeth, curiosity etched on her face.

"It was good to see him again," Elizabeth said cautiously. "And I'm sure he's been a great help to you…"

"He's been a godsend," Annette said. "I don't know how we'd have coped without him."

Elizabeth couldn't help but wonder if he would appear at any moment. His car was outside so he couldn't be far away.

"He went into the village," Annette said. "He was

meeting a friend for lunch."

"I thought he'd have been back by now," Wendy added. "He knew you were coming."

Annette cleared her throat and glared at Wendy. "I'll make a pot of tea."

"How do you and Max know each other?" Wendy asked quietly once Annette was out of the room. "He was a bit coy about it when I asked him."

"Oh," Elizabeth said, fumbling for the right words, "we, um … we met at Hope Cove. He was staying there and I happened to be there at the same time … and we just became friends … briefly. One of those weird things. It's difficult to explain."

She really hadn't explained it well at all, but Wendy smiled nonetheless.

"He's been helping out a lot, has he?" Elizabeth asked.

"Most weekends," Wendy said. "I had a hospital appointment on Friday so he brought his laptop and worked from here. He does that sometimes."

"But he's still living in London?" She shouldn't be so nosey but she wanted to know everything.

"Yes." Wendy frowned. "We've been a bit worried about him, to be honest. He's not been himself recently. It's since the drama with the wedding. You heard about that, I suppose?"

Elizabeth nodded, but it seemed to be a rhetorical question. Wendy barely took a breath.

"I was never a big fan of Jessica. I always thought she was a bit manipulative, but—"

Annette reappeared with a tray of drinks and biscuits. "You're not gossiping, are you?" she said sternly. "I keep telling you not to involve yourself in other people's business."

"I'm always getting in trouble," Wendy said, beaming.

The conversation moved to neutral topics and Elizabeth was sorry Wendy had been interrupted. She shouldn't be interested in the state of Max's marriage, but she couldn't help herself. She wanted to know. Especially if there were problems. Did that make her a horrible person?

Elizabeth stayed longer than she'd intended with Annette and Wendy. They were an entertaining pair, bickering and bantering good-naturedly. Wendy had a wicked sense of humour and had Elizabeth in fits of giggles several times. Every time Elizabeth talked about leaving, Wendy started another anecdote or asked another question. They talked about books and TV, education and travel: conversations that sucked Elizabeth in so that whenever she glanced at her watch she found time had jumped on again.

"Okay," Elizabeth said, as another tale of Wendy's youth came to an end, "I really have to go now!"

If she was honest, she'd lingered in the hope that Max might put in an appearance, but it didn't seem like that was going to happen. He knew she'd be coming to collect Tilly. If he'd wanted to see her, he would have made sure he was there. He'd probably deliberately gone out to avoid seeing her. That made more sense. She was an idiot, she thought as she stood, shaking her head at the offer of another drink, or to stay for dinner. "I've had such a lovely afternoon, but I need to get home. It'll be getting dark soon."

"Max will be sorry he missed you," Wendy said. "You should give him a call sometime."

"Oh, no," Elizabeth said. "I don't think so. Just tell him I said hello. Besides, I don't have his number." She cursed herself. Why had she said that?

Wendy glared at Annette. "Write Max's number down for Lizzie…"

"No, it's fine," Elizabeth protested.

"Go on," Wendy said to Annette. Reluctantly, she wrote his number down and passed the paper to Elizabeth. "I hope you'll be back with Tilly sometime too. We enjoyed having her around."

Tilly was reluctant to move from her spot in front of the fire but slowly she followed Elizabeth through the house.

"I can walk you to the car," Annette said, picking up the bag of Tilly's things.

"No," Elizabeth said. "It's freezing. Stay inside, where it's warm."

Annette hugged her goodbye and Elizabeth thanked her again for looking after Tilly and for a lovely afternoon.

The air was drier when she stepped outside, and the temperature had plummeted. Frost sparkled on the ground and Elizabeth's breath came out in in hazy puffs as she walked slowly down the drive. She told herself she was taking her time to take in the beautiful scenery of the frosted countryside.

"I'll just wait a few minutes for the car to heat up," she said to Tilly in the car. "Then we'll go home." She was stalling for time, disappointed she hadn't got to see Max again. She glanced at Tilly in the rear view mirror. "I can't believe you spent the whole weekend with him."

Pulling the piece of paper out of her pocket, she studied Max's number. Why had Wendy thought she should call him? She really wasn't a fan of his wife if she happily gave his number out to other women.

She was about to drive away when a knock at the window almost made her jump out of her skin.

It was Max. He looked out of breath. When he opened the door, Elizabeth stepped out of the car.

"I thought I'd missed you," he said.

He was standing too close and it made her uncomfortable.

"I thought you were avoiding me," she said.

"I was."

She wanted to move away, but she was sandwiched between him and the car. And, of course, part of her didn't want to move at all.

"I can't stop thinking about you," he said. "I've tried, but I can't. And seeing you again made it a million times worse."

"Max. I—" She wanted to tell him she felt the same, but he talked over her.

"I made the biggest mistake of my life and I don't know how to fix it. I'm miserable."

She fought for something to say. He was miserable – that filled her with hope. The trouble was, he was still married, even if it was a mistake.

"I'm sorry," he said, taking a step away.

All Elizabeth wanted to do was pull him back to her.

"I probably shouldn't have chosen the pub as a place to hide from you. I drank too much and now I'm acting like an idiot."

"No," she said. "you're not. I think about you too—"

"Do you?" he asked earnestly.

"Yes, but—" He moved quickly and her head spun when his lips met hers. What was he doing? She should stop him. He was married, and he was drunk. For a brief moment she didn't care. It felt so good. She didn't want to think about anything; she just wanted to kiss him.

"Stop," she said, finally pushing him away. "I can't do this."

"I'm sorry," he said. "I'm the world's biggest idiot. This is why I wanted to stay away. Every time I see you I want to kiss you."

"You don't need to apologise," she said.

"Of course I do. I just kissed you. I can't believe I did that."

"It's okay," she said, wanting to reassure him. He looked distraught.

His features creased in confusion as he backed away. "Of course it's not okay."

She watched him go and when he disappeared from sight, she climbed into the car and rested her head on the steering wheel. How on earth would she ever get over him?

Chapter 48

Seeing Max again left Elizabeth feeling unbalanced. She'd spent so long convincing herself that she was happy without him, but their encounter had undone all of that. He'd left her an emotional wreck once again. She called Josie on Sunday evening and had a long conversation about him. It got her nowhere, of course. She just talked in circles. It was time to stop thinking about him, but how often had she told herself that over the past six months?

Thankfully, she had editing projects to keep her occupied for the week, and she got stuck into work.

The slip of paper with Max's number hung on the fridge, teasing her every time she passed it. She was never going to use it, of course. What would she do, call and ask him to leave his wife for her? No. If he wanted to be with Elizabeth he needed to end his marriage first, without any interference from her. She should just throw the scrap of paper away. She really should.

On Thursday morning, she pulled her coat on and headed to Dotty's house with Tilly by her side. She enjoyed dropping in to the knitting club now and again, and she was glad of it today – she was in desperate need of company.

The grey-haired old lady, Penny, sat in her usual

spot in the corner of Dotty's living room and barely looked up from her knitting. Tammy the friendly postwoman was there too. She greeted Elizabeth warmly, as always.

"How was your weekend?" Dotty asked. She handed Elizabeth a coffee, then sat and picked up her knitting. Tilly lay quietly at Elizabeth's feet.

"It was good," she said. "I went up to visit my sister in Oxford."

"Lovely," Tammy said. "It's nice to get away sometimes. What did you get up to?"

Elizabeth gave them a quick rundown of the weekend, and then happened to mention that she'd left Tilly at Oakbrook.

"Oh, it's a gorgeous place," Dotty said. "Annette and Wendy are lovely. Annette is Rob Anderson's sister. He and his wife, Charlotte, used to own your cottage."

"Yes, I know," Elizabeth said. She wasn't sure why she was surprised that Dotty knew. Dotty seemed to know everything about Hope Cove, but it hadn't occurred to Elizabeth that her knowledge reached as far as Oakbrook. "I bumped into Max Anderson, actually – the son of the old owners."

"Those Anderson boys," Tammy said. "They always caused a stir with the teenage girls when they stayed for the summers."

"Oh yes," Dotty agreed. "Tammy used to follow James and Dan around like a little lost lamb."

"I did not!" she protested.

"You did! I'd see you in the village, popping your bubble gum and twirling your hair, laughing like a hyena at everything Dan said."

Tammy blushed. "They were gorgeous," she said. "And for a teenage girl growing up in a village, they were like rock stars! James was always a bit above himself but Dan was lovely. I had a crush on him for about three summers!"

Elizabeth hadn't realised the family had been so well known in the village and it was fun hearing about them, and watching Tammy relive the memories.

"Who's Dan?" she asked.

"The middle brother," Tammy said. "James, Dan and Max – though Max was quite a bit younger. I never knew him very well."

"I thought there were just two brothers?"

"Three," Dotty said firmly. "Poor Charlotte had her hands full. They still seem to cause trouble now, even when they're grown up. Although I think Charlotte has a tendency to involve herself in their lives too much." She turned to Tammy. "I told you about the drama with Dan's wedding?"

"Yes," Tammy said with a pout. "I know I'm happily married with kids, but my heart still broke a little when he got married. You never truly get over those teenage crushes."

"What happened with his wedding?" Elizabeth asked.

"They changed the date," Dotty told her. "Apparently the venue they wanted had been booked up but had a last-minute cancellation. So they organised this huge wedding in three weeks. Poor Charlotte was appalled: a lot of her friends couldn't make the new date at such short notice."

Elizabeth's conversation with Charlotte played slowly back in her mind, and then her recent chat with

Max. She couldn't quite get things straight in her head. It was *Max* who'd changed his wedding date. Dotty must be getting confused.

"Wasn't that Max?" Elizabeth said, trying to sound casual. "I'm sure it was Max who changed the date of his wedding."

"Definitely Dan," Tammy said. "Unfortunately." She caught herself and smiled. "I am happily married, I promise!"

"I must be confused," Elizabeth said, her mind whirring. "Max is getting married this year, then?" she asked. "July, is it?" She hoped she sounded as casual as she intended. Max wasn't married yet after all? And if he wasn't, what did that mean for her? She could call him, tell her how she felt about him. It wasn't too late.

"No, no," Dotty said, her knitting needles clicking as she worked. "That was another little drama. He called the wedding off unexpectedly. Honestly, Charlotte has had such a time of it: one son cancels a wedding and another changes the date, within a couple of weeks."

Elizabeth set her coffee down, worried her hands would shake. Her mouth felt like sandpaper and she swallowed hard. "Max is single?" she asked.

"The last Anderson bachelor," Tammy said, chuckling. "Get in there quick if you're interested!"

There was a pause. The click of knitting needles filled the room.

"I *am* interested," Elizabeth said, her voice a frantic whisper. "Oh my God. I thought he was already married."

Dotty stopped knitting. Everyone looked at

Elizabeth.

"I think you need to tell us more," Tammy said.

"I need to go," Elizabeth said, standing. "I need to call him."

"Don't leave us in suspense!" Tammy said as she and Dotty followed Elizabeth into the hallway.

"He's the reason I moved here," Elizabeth told them as she put her shoes on hurriedly. "I met him last summer when I was on holiday here for a week. I was engaged and so was he, so nothing could happen. We went back to our lives. I really have to go and call him."

"No!" Tammy said. "Finish the story!"

"I couldn't stop thinking about him," Elizabeth said, grabbing her coat but not bothering to put it on. "I knew I had to change my life, so I quit my job and left my fiancé. But when I went to see Charlotte, she told me about the wedding. His brother's wedding, I guess. I thought she meant Max. I thought I'd missed my chance."

"But didn't you say you saw him at the weekend?" Tammy said, confused.

"I did. And he kissed me! I told him I wasn't interested, but that was only because I thought he was married." She paused on the doorstep. "I'm not even sure if he knows I called off my wedding too. I need to call him."

"Yes," Dotty said. "Go!"

"Call him," Tammy said excitedly. "And let us know what happens," she shouted after Elizabeth.

Hannah Ellis

Chapter 49

Why wasn't he answering his phone? Elizabeth was a nervous wreck. Flopping onto the couch, she tried calling Josie but her phone went to voicemail. She didn't bother leaving Josie a message. She hadn't left Max a message either. Maybe she should call again and leave one, or send him a text. Staring at her phone screen, she wondered what to write. It was hard to believe he was really single, and that maybe there was some hope for them after all. She had to speak to him.

She decided she'd leave him a message, then felt shaky as she listened to his phone ring and wondered whether he'd answer. When the voicemail beeped, she panicked and pressed end. What should she say? She didn't know where to start.

She should tell him she thought he was already married – that was probably the main point. And that she was single! But it was such a weird message to leave.

At the sound of a car engine, she looked outside. It was Josie. Elizabeth had no idea why her sister was visiting, but she couldn't have arrived at a better time. Someone to talk it all over with was exactly what she needed.

When she opened the front door, Josie was in floods of tears.

"What's wrong?" Elizabeth asked, ushering her inside.

"Everything seems to be going wrong," Josie spluttered. "I needed to get away so I got in the car and came straight here."

"What's happened?" Elizabeth asked, directing her to the couch.

"Jack broke up with me. He said we were getting too serious too fast and he needed some space."

"I'm so sorry," Elizabeth said, squeezing Josie's hand and wishing she was more surprised by the news.

"And this morning I found out that the TV show isn't going ahead. The bosses didn't like the pilot. So now I don't have a job. Everything is going wrong."

"I'm sorry," Elizabeth said again, hugging Josie. "It'll all be okay, though. You'll find another job. And Jack obviously wasn't right for you."

"He's an idiot," Josie said angrily, then more tears came to her eyes. "But I love him."

Elizabeth hugged Josie tightly. She hated to see her so upset.

When Josie calmed down, Elizabeth suggested they get some fresh air, and they set off to walk Tilly.

"I'm glad you work from home," Josie said as they stepped outside. "It's so nice to be able to visit at any time."

"Yeah," Elizabeth said, chuckling. "I will need to do some work later, though. That's if I can concentrate long enough…"

"Why?" Josie asked. "What's going on with you?"

"There's a bit of a story, actually." She proceeded

to fill Josie in on her morning, and she was touched by how excited Josie was for her, despite her own problems.

"So we're just waiting for him to call back?" Josie asked.

"Yes!"

"Is your phone on loud?" Josie asked. "You don't want to miss him."

"It's on the loudest setting." Elizabeth pulled out her phone to check it again. "I feel sick. What if he doesn't call?"

"Of course he'll call. Did you leave him a message?"

"No," Elizabeth said. "I tried, but I got stuck for words."

"You need to leave him a message and explain everything. Don't just leave a load of missed calls."

"Two!" Elizabeth said. "Just two missed calls."

"So far…"

"You're right," she said. "I should leave him a message. When we get back to the house."

"If you don't, I will," Josie teased.

"I'll do it. I just hope I'm not getting my hopes up for nothing. What if things still don't work out? I still only spent a week with him. Maybe I'll see him again and find we're just not right for each other."

"Oh my God!" Josie said dramatically. "Don't be so unromantic. Once you've explained everything he'll call you straight back and ask you out on a date – I'm sure of it. Then you'll fall in love and live happily ever after."

A smile crept over Elizabeth's face.

"What's so funny?" Josie asked.

"I never thought about dating him," Elizabeth said. "Every time I thought about him, I skipped to the happy-ever-after. I overlooked the dating phase."

Josie beamed. "That's the sort of thing I do! You're supposed to be the sensible one. Just remember the dating stage when you speak to him. Don't go proposing marriage or anything. Don't scare him off after all this."

"Good advice," Elizabeth said, glancing at her phone again. "Let's head home. I want to get this call over and done with."

It turned out to be easier than she'd thought. She sat in the back garden to call him. As soon as she started talking, she relaxed and explained everything to his voicemail as though he was sitting in front of her. There was a lot to fill him in on, but she kept it as succinct as possible. Fingers crossed, there'd be time to explain properly later. She paused when she finished speaking, and told him how much she'd missed him, and how much she wanted to see him again. There were tears in her eyes when she ended the call. She walked inside to find Josie.

"I did it," she said. "Now all I have to do is wait."

"Oh, God, this is torture," Josie said.

"Yes," Elizabeth agreed. "It is. And what if he doesn't call? I feel like a teenager all over again!"

"He'll call," Josie said positively. "Now, I'm going to go upstairs and watch a film on my laptop while you get some work done. And then I'll fetch us fish and chips for dinner." She paused. "Unless he calls and wants to take you out. In which case I'll have fish and chips alone."

"Don't say that," Elizabeth said. "You're putting ideas in my head." There was no way she'd see him that day. But the possibility of it was so exciting that she couldn't help but hope. "Anyway, you're right. I need to do some work. Are you okay?" she asked, realising they'd been concentrating on Elizabeth's love life and not mentioning Josie's breakup.

"I'll be okay," Josie said, smiling sadly. "I'm probably gonna watch some romantic film that'll make me cry, but that's fine!"

"Don't do that," Elizabeth said.

"I'm kidding," she said. "I thought I might call him later and see if we can work things out. Maybe if I suggest we can cool things off a bit—"

"Josie," Elizabeth said, shaking her head, "I don't think that's a good idea. You should be with someone who really wants to be with you, and who doesn't mess you around like this."

"Yeah, I know," she said wearily. "But I love him. I can't give up on him."

Elizabeth closed her eyes for a moment, trying not to say something insensitive. There was a lot she wanted to say on the matter, but probably nothing Josie wanted to hear. "Okay," she said. "But don't get your hopes up too much."

Surprisingly, Elizabeth managed to get some work done that afternoon. She was working on a project for one of Emily's writer friends. A paid job this time. It was pleasant work, too: a historical romance that was enjoyable and well written. Only occasionally did she look over and check her annoyingly silent phone.

She didn't have much appetite that evening, but

picked at the fish and chips Josie fetched for them. They settled in front of the fire and Elizabeth gazed intensely into the flames.

"Are you okay?" Josie asked.

"I just keep going over everything in my head," she replied. "I was thinking about when I saw him again at Oakbrook and things were so strange. He *must* think I'm engaged. It explains everything. Why he was avoiding me, and why he was so apologetic when he kissed me. I thought it was because he was married."

"It also explains why he was angry about you buying the house – he must think you bought it with Phil."

"Oh, my God! Of course." She sighed. "Just one mystery left then: why isn't he returning my call?"

"He will," Josie said. "Don't worry. Everything will work out perfectly."

Elizabeth hoped so, but so far it really seemed like the universe didn't want them to be together. "This is all your fault," Elizabeth said grumpily.

"My fault?" Josie asked in surprise.

"Yes! You changed my Facebook. I bet that's why he thinks I'm still with Phil."

"Oh, come on," Josie said. "You can take some responsibility here. You shouldn't have had your account set up so the whole world can see everything about you!"

Elizabeth tried to interrupt, but Josie continued. "And when you left Max, didn't you tell him you were going back to your fiancé? Maybe that has something to do with it!"

Elizabeth sank miserably into the couch. Why

wasn't he calling her?

"You'll have to call him again tomorrow," Josie said. "All this waiting for him to call is horrible. I can't take it any more."

"*You* can't take it?" Elizabeth said. "How do you think I feel?"

They spent the rest of the evening watching TV, not that Elizabeth could concentrate on anything. She glanced at her phone constantly. But he didn't call, and at ten she decided to put herself out of her misery and go to bed.

It took hours for her to fall asleep. Her phone lay on the bedside table and she kept willing it to ring. She would definitely call him again tomorrow, she decided, or just go and track him down. There was no way she could cope with another day of waiting.

Hannah Ellis

Chapter 50

The first thing Elizabeth did when she woke was check her phone. No missed calls, no messages. Was he just not interested? Why was he ignoring her? She'd worked so hard to make a new life and feel good about her choices, and now everything felt so unsettled again. She'd been happy a week ago, but suddenly felt like her heart was about to be broken all over again.

She was surprised to hear Josie moving around so early. When Elizabeth called out a good morning, Josie appeared at her bedroom doorway.

"Jack messaged me," Josie said, beaming. "He's apologised. He says he made a big mistake and was an idiot. He wants to see me."

It made Elizabeth want to make vomiting noises. He was clearly a player. Josie could do so much better.

"I knew he'd change his mind," Josie said.

"Are you sure he isn't just an idiot?" Elizabeth said with a pained expression. "Maybe he doesn't deserve a second chance…"

"Don't say that. He's great. It was a stupid mistake. I'll go and see him and we'll sort it all out."

"Okay," Elizabeth agreed without enthusiasm.

"Will you be all right, though? I hate leaving you

when there's all this stuff with Max. You've still not heard from him?"

"Nope," she said with a sigh. "But don't feel that you've got to hang around and look after me. I've got work to be getting on with."

"Okay. If you're sure. I'm going to have a shower and I'll leave after breakfast."

"I'm going to take Tilly for a quick walk," Elizabeth said. "Do you want to come?"

"No thanks. I think I'll just get organised."

"Okay. I won't be long."

Elizabeth made herself a coffee and wandered down the garden with Tilly at her side. She'd have to get out and do some gardening now the weather was getting better, she thought.

The sun was only just rising when she stepped through the hedge onto the path, and she was surprised to see someone sitting on the beach. She squinted through the half-light at the lone figure.

She stopped dead.

Her body seemed to forget all about the importance of breathing and pumping blood in a regular rhythm.

It was Max.

For a moment she stood watching him, then moved slowly towards him. Tilly barked and headed straight for him, bouncing around him and licking him. He laughed and made a big fuss of her.

"You stole my sunrise spot," Elizabeth said, surprised by how calm she sounded.

His gaze travelled slowly up to her. "I was just going to call you about the coffee situation," he said, showing her the phone in his hand.

"Really?" she asked suspiciously. "I was starting to think you were never going to return my call."

"I'm sorry," he said, with a pained expression. "I was up at Oakbrook and the phone signal is terrible. Your message only came through this morning. I was going to call you straight back but decided I'd rather talk to you in person."

She sat beside him and took a sip of coffee before passing him the mug. Adrenalin pumped through her body. She was so excited but, unlike Tilly, she kept it bottled up inside, remembering Josie's advice about not rushing things and scaring him away.

They'd only spent a week together. She shouldn't get carried away.

All she wanted to do was kiss him, but instead she looked out at the hazy sun emerging over the horizon, and tried to gather her thoughts.

"You're really not married?" she asked, after getting Tilly to settle down. She lay happily on the beach in front of them.

"No," he said. "Of course not."

"I thought it was you with the last-minute wedding," she said.

"No. That would be Dan."

"I didn't know you had two brothers..." She shook her head sadly. "And you thought I was still with Phil?"

"Yes. I can't believe you were looking for me." Idly, he stroked Tilly's back as he spoke. "I tried to find you too. As soon as you left, I went and called everything off with Jessica. Then I got in touch with the owners of Seaview Cottage and begged them to give me your details..." He chuckled at the memory.

"When they threatened to call the police on me I gave up on them. In the end I found you on Facebook."

"I'm gonna kill Josie! She messed with my profile and put the stuff about Phil. You saw that?"

"It definitely seemed like you were still engaged," he said. "And you looked so happy with your fiancé. I remembered how adamant you were that it was just a holiday romance between us and nothing more."

Her shoulders sagged as she sighed. "I'm never on Facebook. I didn't even know everyone could see my page. I wish you'd got in touch."

"Me too."

"I tried getting in touch with Annette and Wendy," she said, "but at the time, the phone wasn't working and there was no one there when I visited."

"That must have been when Wendy was in hospital," Max said. "Annette closed the kennels for a while, and when she got annoyed with people ringing to make bookings, she unplugged the phone."

"Everything was against us, wasn't it?"

Max smiled. "I thought you'd bought the house with your fiancé." His brow furrowed. "Which seemed like a really weird thing to do!"

"I've had my crazy moments over the last six months, but thankfully nothing that bad."

"So, just to make sure I've got this right…" He reached for her hand. "Since last summer, you've split up with your fiancé, moved here and got a dog?"

"I also quit my job and joined a knitting club," she said proudly as she laced her fingers with his. "It's been an eventful six months!"

"It sounds like it." He paused, then gazed at her intensely. "I couldn't believe it when I saw you at

Oakbrook. I thought I was finally getting over you and then there you were – ruining my life again!" He smiled. "And why did you freak out when I kissed you?"

"I thought you were married," she said defensively. "And it was you who freaked out!"

"I thought you were engaged!"

She laughed at how ridiculous it was, then dipped her eyebrows quizzically. "What did you mean when you said you'd made a huge mistake? I thought you were talking about your marriage."

"I was talking about letting you go," he said, moving closer to her. "I should've fought harder for you. I should've convinced you that we should be together."

"I'm convinced now," she said quietly.

He cupped her face as he kissed her, and her whole body tingled. It felt amazing.

"What happens now?" he asked when they broke apart.

"I think we're supposed to go on a date or something."

"Really? After all this I get a measly date?"

"You don't want to?"

"Not really," he said, smirking. "Dating sounds so casual. Usually people date to see if they want to be in a relationship … and I'm already in love with you."

She felt the heat in her cheeks and grinned like an idiot. "Really?"

"Yes!"

"But we only spent a week together."

He pushed her hair from her face. "It took me a lot less than a week to fall in love with you."

When he kissed her again she pulled away abruptly. "What will we do, though? You live in London and I live here."

"I've been considering spending more time at the coast…"

Her smile was starting to make her face ache. "Really?"

"I know that we should probably take things slowly, but I don't want to waste any more time. What do you think?"

"I think I love you too! I don't want to waste any time either." Now that he was finally there with her, she hated the thought of him leaving. "How about you stay for the weekend and we take it from there?"

"I like the sound of that."

His lips brushed hers once more, then he drew back. "So we're not dating?"

"No," she said, beaming as she pulled him closer, "we're definitely not dating."

THE END

Coming summer 2018

Escape To Oakbrook Farm

Josie Beaumont is a free spirit. She changes jobs about as often as she changes her relationship status. Frequently! The only constant in her life is the pair of comfy old shoes that she refuses to part with.

When unemployment looms again, she's intrigued by a job opportunity at a dog kennels in rural Devon. As someone who thrives on change, a move to the sticks doesn't faze her at all. She's expecting life in the country to be quiet and uneventful.

What she's not expecting is Sam.

The charming sensitive neighbour makes life much more interesting. In fact, when she gets involved in the local community, things really aren't as dull as she anticipated. But just when she finally feels settled, she's offered the job of her dreams back in London. It's time to move on.

Or is it?

Being part of a small community has stirred something in Josie and she begins to question what she really wants. Can she turn her back on her new life and say goodbye to Sam? Or is she ready to hang up her running shoes and stay put? Maybe she's finally found something worth sticking around for...

Other books by Hannah Ellis

Escape to Oakbrook Farm (Coming summer 2018)
Always With You
Friends Like These
Christmas with Friends (Friends Like These book 2)
My Kind of Perfect (Friends Like These book 3)
Beyond the Lens (Lucy Mitchell Book 1)
Beneath These Stars (Lucy Mitchell Book 2)

Acknowledgements

As always I have many people to thank for helping me get this book finished.

My husband, Mario, is top of the list. I really couldn't do this without your unwavering support. Love you!

Next are the wonderful people who read and gave me feedback at the various stages. A huge thank you to: Anthea Kirk, Stephen Ellis, Sarah-Jane Fraser, Meghan Driscoll, Dua Roberts, Fay Sallaba, Emma Smith, Sarah Walker, Kathy Robinson, Sue Oxley, Hazel Baxter, Ki Anglesea, Nikkita Blake, Michele Morgan Salls, Chantal Bérubé and Annie Jagger.

Thanks so much Aimee Coveney for yet another fantastic cover. I love it!

Many thanks to my editor Jane Hammett.

And to all my amazing readers. You guys are the best!

Printed in Great Britain
by Amazon